THE
BOOK
OF
KANE
AND
MARGARET

THE
BOOK
OF
KANE
AND
MARGARET

KIIK ARAKI-KAWAGUCHI

ILLUSTRATIONS BY GAUTAM RANGAN

TUSCALOOSA

FC2 is an imprint of The University of Alabama Press

Inquiries about reproducing material from this work should be addressed to
the University of Alabama Press

Book Design: Publications Unit, Department of English, Illinois State
University; Director: Steve Halle, Production Interns: Gabrielle Brown
and Katelyn Kern
Cover Design: Matthew Revert
Interior Illustrations: Gautam Rangan, by permission of the artist, all rights
reserved
Typeface: Baskerville

Library of Congress Cataloging-in-Publication Data
Names: Araki-Kawaguchi, Kiik, 1983- author.
Title: The Book of Kane and Margaret : a novel / kiik araki-kawaguchi.
Description: Tuscaloosa : FC2, [2020] | Summary: "More like a tapestry than
a traditional novel, *The Book of Kane and Margaret* by Kiik Araki-Kawaguchi
blends magical elements with stories based on the oral narratives of the
author's grandparents and their experiences during the 1940s at the
Tulare Assembly Center and the Gila River War Relocation Center,
two WWII relocation camps in Arizona. The author's technique gives
the novel the effect of working through accretion, collecting one-breath
fictions and conversations with recurring names, voices, and themes that
explore a carceral setting"—Provided by publisher.
Identifiers: LCCN 2019038784 (print) | LCCN 2019038785 (ebook) | ISBN
9781573661843 (paperback) | ISBN 9781573668866 (ebook)
Subjects: LCSH: Japanese Americans—Evacuation and relocation, 1942–
1945—Fiction. | GSAFD: Historical fiction
Classification: LCC PS3601.R3447 B66 2020 (print) | LCC PS3601.R3447
(ebook) | DDC 813/.6—dc23
LC record available at https://lccn.loc.gov/2019038784
LC ebook record available at https://lccn.loc.gov/2019038785

For my grandparents,
Peggy and Kane Araki

And for my parents,
Corinne and
Michael Araki-Kawaguchi

contents

The difference between the scyborg and other orgs in the machine is that the scyborg grasps hir decolonial possibilities. S-he knows hir broomstick can't carry hir beyond colonization, but with it, s-he might rake together a decolonizing golem. Maybe you could be a scyborg, and so I'm writing to maybe you. If so, cite me not, and ghost-ride this book.

A Third University Is Possible
la paperson

THE
BOOK
OF
KANE
AND
MARGARET

evening song

Yoshikane Araki did all he could to temper his desire for the tower guard, but the evening song of the guard would not be interrupted by earplugs of clay or beeswax, by tissue or cotton packing, and continued to pierce Kane's dreams, once inside surging like the ghost-pollen of creosote poppies, and in the morning he awoke mouthing those bewildering words, tongue slack with ghost-breath, a rawness, soreness, the vague belief the sentry's mouth had been all night pinned over his own.

a small fortune

At the age of sixteen, Margaret Morri traded away a small fortune for a West Coast conch of unrivaled size and brilliance, a spire wound tightly enough to pierce flesh, shell top the color of whipped milk, a massive lip brimming with remnants of sea dander, calcium foam, wet sand, salt bath, and for the evenings that followed, Margaret could be observed lingering among the gardens of the southeast barracks, whispering into its mouth, sharpening its spurs, and on one occasion, washing and polishing the conch clean with her hair. Sixty years later, Aiko Morri was cleaning her mother's mantle when the conch fell to the floor and burst, revealing a ringlet of hair and a tightly folded letter from Margaret's teenage lover, Elena Okubo, and although the surface of the conch had bleached, its hull worn fragile over the years, it had preserved the ink of every word in the letter, and though the years had stolen all of Margaret's hair, the strands of Elena's hair were still richly black and smelled fresh as the blossoms of whitethorn acacia.

a marriage

Yoshikane Araki was the tiniest man Margaret Morri had ever seen, at just under eight inches tall, weighing two pounds, six ounces fully clothed, and she loved him passionately, devotedly, from the moment he first parted hair from her face and kissed her, until their final kiss thirty-eight years later, Kane's tears and saliva amounting to a mask of glistening snail movements across her cheek, Margaret asleep, dreaming of Kane's parted lips, then drifting free from the body captured by her illness, slipping from Kane's small, strong fingers, his retreating cheekbones, his flat Greek nose, his blue-black beard.

Margaret's mother, Naoko, had always been a harsh critic of the union. The evening Margaret and Kane married at the Gila River Methodist Chapel, Naoko stood in the doorway of the Morri family barrack for six straight hours, staring in its

4

direction, arms folded, brow puckered. Naoko said she had met plenty of men like Kane before.

"Of course these eight- or nine-inch men are beautiful," she told her daughter. "But their hearts are restless. Mercurial. You will never find a way to hold this man true to you."

This more or less was the content of every conversation Margaret entertained with her mother for thirty years.

Following Margaret's death, Kane attended to Naoko through her senility and until her death eighteen years later. He cooked her meals, washed her laundry, drove her to medical appointments, and accompanied her to the funerals of family and acquaintances. In those eighteen years, Naoko never found a way to verbalize an apology to Kane. She came close some days, the days she could feel him pause while washing her hair or while looking over her hands, her face, and she knew he was looking for a sign from Margaret. She was cared for, she knew, because Kane searched for her daughter through his kindness and suffering. Naoko did dream of her apology some evenings, how the words would lather in her mouth, Kane standing in the palm of her hand, her eyes crowded with tears, her coarse, white hair falling at his feet.

whiskey over barbed wire

The doctor told Yoshikane Araki it happened that sometimes in extreme circumstances of weather or diet a Japanese man or woman might spontaneously sprout a set of wings. He had heard of three or four cases from his colleagues in the East. A woman from west Osaka had saved her village from drought when she'd seeded, by hand, the clouds with silver iodide and pellets of dry carbon dioxide. A man from Kumamoto who had eaten nothing but sweet potatoes for five years awoke with wings and began supplementing his diet with tall-hanging fruit and the eggs of jungle crows. Research was being gathered, but with the war frivolous projects like these were being shelved for greater concerns. The doctor was uncertain what could have triggered such a large, severe pair of wings amidst an Arizona desert. An allergic reaction?

Had Kane been eating a lot of tree nuts lately? Too many undercooked radishes?

No matter the cause the doctor told Kane not to worry. He would contact a surgeon the next day and would arrange to have the wings removed in the following months. It would be costly to fly an anesthesiologist to camp during wartime. But reserve funding existed precisely for these situations. In the meantime it was important for Kane to push hot, clear fluids. To pick his plumes clean of burs and mites. And to take an aspirin at night to dull any discomfort. The doctor handed Kane a tiny glass bottle of tablets and gave his wings a little pat.

Although they were mostly a hot, dusty inconvenience, Kane found his new appendages did afford him one unique opportunity. Because his feathers were raven's black, flight after dusk was nearly undetectable. When the wind favored him he was over the fence and into the nearest Arizona Chinatown in under an hour. There he could walk freely through the streets, in restaurants, in shops selling garments and fragrant herbs. He was indistinguishable to the police who couldn't comprehend the differences between local foul chicken-coop Chinamen and the sinister yellow-menace Japs being battled abroad. On the occasion he'd been stopped by police for jaywalking, he'd eluded capture by speaking in a disoriented Chinese gibberish. In Chinatown he could buy whiskey and cigarettes to share back at camp. Kane, who had never garnered much consideration, was every day meeting new friends who stuffed bills and whiskey orders into his shirt pockets. Pretty girls who had once ignored him now covered him with their sweetness and pity. Some stroked his ugly wings tenderly and promised to knit them a decorative covering.

In a matter of weeks Kane was hauling fifteen or twenty quarts of whiskey over the barbed wire each night. The bottles were swaddled in newspaper and held together in a burlap sack that he slung like an unconscious companion across his shoulders. The generous blackness of desert nights was a blessing, since he was diving in lower, wearier each trip. Parties now resumed on the inside. Legitimate parties with whiskey punch and couples mated over dreamy, affectionate dancing. In no time Kane found himself engaged to a lovely girl called Margaret Morri, and plans were drawn for acquiring her a wedding dress.

Kane was content to pay for an extravagant dress. He'd come into plenty of money performing whiskey and cigarette exchanges. Now his savings had found their purpose. Margaret devoted her afternoons to preening Kane's wings while their eyes moved over the pages of a Sears catalog. Eventually Margaret settled on a dress that was priced at just over one hundred dollars. The snipped photograph along with her measurements were delivered to a local dressmaker who promised he could have the couple's order ready in ten days.

A complication arose when a sentry, a man by the name of Fhilpott, paid a visit to Kane at his family's barrack just days before he was to retrieve Margaret's dress. The tower guards were no dummies, Fhilpott told Kane. They'd known all along whiskey was finding its way into camp. A popular guy like Kane Araki, a popular guy who had found himself with a slick pair of flyers, he was obviously going to find himself at the head of their list of suspects.

Still, the guards didn't have any desire to be hard-asses about it. No need to punish anybody retroactively. Among these circumstances who could blame them? Fhilpott would've done the same if it had been his own kind imprisoned in the Godforsaken desert. But while a bottle every so often was clean American fun—twenty or thirty quarts of whiskey each night, sold at a profit, was called bootlegging. An official report could make Fhilpott and some of his fellow officers look foolish. And he wasn't going to be made a fool before a Jap or two got his knuckles rapped upon. Fhilpott said he'd cut a deal. He'd been informed Kane's surgery was scheduled for the following month. As long as he kept those wings holstered until then he didn't see a further need for investigations.

Kane didn't have reason to disrespect the guard's warning. He had found it civil for Fhilpott to approach him the way he had. He announced that the flight to retrieve Margaret's wedding dress would be his last. He was tired anyhow of buying everyone's liquor while taking all the risk. Relatives, friends of his parents, neighbors pressed him to reconsider.

"Think about your wedding," they insisted. "Don't you want champagne and whiskey for your wedding party? Remember all of the money you're making. A man who is starting a family must be pretty pigheaded not to have to consider it."

But Kane did not waver in his decision. People shook their heads as they handed him their final whiskey and cigarette orders. Demands poured in. Most everyone asked for twice the usual amount. Kane figured he would have to carry everything in three, maybe four sacks. One could be tied to his back. One cradled to his chest. And another he'd have to tie to his legs? Or hang its drawstrings from his neck? The thought of all this labor made him thankful it would be his final excursion.

There are several versions of what happened to Kane as he returned from that last trip. One version says the bag holding Margaret's dress tore from the weight of too many whiskey bottles. And when the guards caught sight of the ghostly fabric hovering over the fence, they fired upon it. In another version Kane attempted to maneuver in over the fence too low. And as he did the sacks caught and split against the barbs. Their cargo rattled the metal wires and alerted the guards who fired upon him. But in the most popular version of the story, Fhilpott had demanded Kane's wings be painted white. And though he'd piloted his way out from camp disguised under a black cloak, there was a divine wind that disrobed him upon his return. That was when Fhilpott and the other guards spotted and fired upon him.

Kane Araki wasn't killed that evening, however. He suffered wounds to his hands, shoulders, groin, knees, and calves. An emergency operation was performed that resulted in the removal of his wings. He awoke nine days later to find his right arm had also been amputated. After the war Kane returned to his family's home in California. It was there he heard Margaret had become engaged to someone else. Someone called Shimmy or Jack or Lawson.

dissolving newspaper, fermenting leaves

To persuade her cricket to eat, Margaret Morri cooked every recipe she had learned as a teenager when working for her family's restaurant. As the rest of the Morri family barrack slept, Margaret slipped into the camp's mess hall and raided its pantries. She minced pork, garlic, ginger, green onion. She arranged dumplings in a pan and ladled hot oil over them until the dough of their skins became tan and chewy. She boiled fistfuls of buckwheat noodles, plunged them into icy baths, and spun the strands into shallow cups. She caramelized sweet onions and doused meatballs of beef tongue in rice wine and vinegar. She uncloaked the pits of umeboshi plums and rolled the sweet, puckered flesh into sheets of salted and dried seaweed.

Everything she held out to her cricket and begged him

to eat. But he stared at her dishes impassively, stroked the ends of his antennae, and turned his face away from hers in disappointment. On the mornings Margaret did not have time to be artful with the presentation of her meals, her cricket was known to wiggle his mandibles in disgust or to emit a sharp, pompous click from the toothcomb tucked beneath his wings.

At the camp library there was a single text containing a passage about the lives of crickets. That text was entitled *World of Insects: Grasshoppers and Katydids* and was written by the famed Japanese orthopterologist, Yoshikane Araki. And if any Gila River resident had cared to check its record, they would've seen it had been signed out by an *M. Morri* a total of twenty-eight times. Based upon her research, Margaret assembled wood crates of dissolving newspaper, fermenting leaves, ripe pods of fungi and delivered them to the burrow of her cricket. Her cricket approached a decomposing leaf, sniffed at it, bristled, and leapt away. From her oldest uncle, Margaret learned that it was common practice for crickets to cannibalize the wounded. On one occasion she tore the hind legs from a desert locust, roasted them over a hot coal, and presented them to her cricket, who instantly recoiled, let loose a series of heated chirps, and would not appear to her for several days afterward.

Though her arms became branded by inadvertent flares of hot grease and steam, though her olfactory nerves grew tired and raw, though her eyes clouded from lack of sleep, Margaret continued to dribble hot oil onto chicken skin until it curled into a sail of sweetened fat. Margaret steamed custards of tofu, ponzu, green onion, and whipped eggs in teacups. Her hands clapped pots of white rice into steaming wedges and garnished their peaks with tart strips of shoga. And if her rice balls were finished before the sun had risen, she transferred them to an open fire, toasted them, lowered them into a ceramic bowl, and splashed over them a broth made from kombu and flakes of bonito dashi.

Still, Margaret Morri's cricket would not eat.

"You must eat," she insisted.

But her cricket merely balked his wings at her, pronounced a fierce, staccato snort.

"If you will not eat what I cook for you, then what will you eat?" she asked.

Her cricket said, "There is just one thing I can eat."

"Yes, anything," Margaret pleaded. "I will make whatever you wish."

Her cricket said, "When you lie down to sleep tonight, place me beside your left ear. We will find each other in your dreams, and I will be able to find a meal there."

That night when Margaret went down upon her bedroll, she did as her cricket had instructed. She placed her cricket in a little nest of hair beside her left ear and was quickly overtaken by the blackness of sleep. During the first months inside the fences of the Gila Relocation Center, Margaret's dreams would transport her back to her family's home in Venice, California. But in the past two years, all Margaret's dreams had been pulled as though by a tether back to Gila. On that occasion, when she came into awareness, she found herself sitting in the darkness of the Morri family barracks. Then she saw her cricket had assumed the form of a man. She was positive this man was her cricket because his voice had grown louder but had not altered. He was vaguely humming a song and cleaning his teeth with a wooden splinter. As a man, her cricket was slightly reminiscent of the local minister from the Venice Methodist Church, the Reverend Jun Shozaburo. He was lean and immaculate, clothing unblemished, hair and fingers well manicured, and something of his smile seemed slightly misaligned, as though his mouth was overly crowded with teeth.

"Now that you are here, I will cook you any food you desire," Margaret told him. "We aren't bound to what I can steal from the canteen and the mess hall anymore. I can find you the most expensive, most marbled cuts of meat. Matsutake mushrooms. Magnificent quail eggs. Or perhaps you are thirsty. Here you can drink a dozen foaming beers."

Her cricket-man said, "I have not come here to eat anything you can cook. The only thing I will eat is your mother."

"My mother!" Margaret exclaimed.

"Do not be frightened, Margaret," her cricket-man said. "No harm will come to your actual mother. I only want to eat the mother of this world. The mother of this dream. That is all I want."

"But my mother! I do not think I could allow such a desecration of my family. Even if it is only a dream."

"Margaret, since pledging myself to you, there has only been starvation. Many times I thought surely today will be the morning I die from hunger. But I always reserved faith that one day you would find a way to feed me the thing I needed."

Margaret began to wonder if she was behaving ridiculously. She looked down at her dream-mother. Who was this woman actually? What was this woman but a wisp of imagination? What was the value of this shadow passing through the darkness of her nights?

"Well I suppose if I don't have to watch, it could be alright," Margaret said. "I suppose she doesn't have actual feelings. She isn't my flesh-and-blood mother after all."

"I knew you would be the one to save me," her cricket-man said. "I knew I could count on you to understand."

Then he scooped Margaret's dream-mother up in a blanket and carried her behind one of the barrack's partitions. Margaret could hear the two of them struggling. She had the urge to go to them, to mediate the horror of this attack in some way, but her legs felt stricken with paralysis.

"Margaret!" she could hear her mother screaming. "I can't get him off of me! Stop him!"

The next morning, eating breakfast shoulder to shoulder with the members of her family, Margaret felt tormented with guilt. She feigned sickness and went back to their barrack to lie down. It went on in this way for weeks. Every evening Margaret would place her cricket beside her left ear, and every night her cricket would transform into a man and ask to devour another member of the Morri family. On the morning that followed, Margaret would be overtaken by guilt and avoid meals, chores, conversation with her family.

It wasn't only guilt and exhaustion that worried her. Margaret was having additional troubles during her waking hours. She found she sometimes had difficulty recalling the names of her cousins and siblings. She found herself having to relearn their habits, sensitivities, alliances, when they preferred to rise and sleep, which jokes might hurt them and which might make them laugh, which friends they loved or despised in secret. On her worst days, she had difficulty recognizing her family, as though their faces, gestures, voices had metamorphosed into something foreign during the night. As this became a regular occurrence, Margaret felt compelled to confront her cricket.

"Count all the members of your family," the cricket told her. "And strike me dead if even one of them is missing from Gila River."

"Of course they haven't gone," Margaret said. "But it's not the point. I'm having trouble remembering them. Yesterday I tried to call out to Tetsuo, but I'd forgotten what to call him. I'd forgotten my own brother's name!"

"Your brother is a rotten brat anyway," the cricket said. "I ate him mostly out of sympathy. In truth, his flesh tasted of ash and rat shit."

Margaret was shocked.

"Save your sympathy then," she told her cricket-man. "I'll never let you touch another person in my family again."

"If you no longer want me to eat your dream-family, then perhaps you will let me nibble on your toes."

"I cannot let you do that," Margaret said.

"Margaret, you are being ridiculous. They are only your dream-toes. I will count them beside you when you awaken every morning. They will be right where you left them."

It was soon after that Margaret found she had trouble walking. When family members noticed her limp, she had to make up an excuse about tripping off the steps of the canteen's loading dock and spraining her ankle. Margaret had always been expert in needlepoint but discovered her hands needed to be re-taught every elementary rhythm and motion. In the mornings she counted all her digits and toes beside the cricket. Everything was accounted for, but it was as though no blood or oxygen had reached them during the night. Those parts of her she dreamed he'd feasted upon were all shot through with tingles and dull aches.

"You haven't been eating my dreams at all," she said to the cricket one evening.

"Never once have I deceived you, Margaret Morri," he said. "Tally all your fingers, toes, and limbs. Count all the members of your family. Everything remains here in this room."

"This is not the room you have been stealing from," Margaret said.

"When you first came to me," the cricket said, "I told you there would be consequences for our friendship. The union between a woman and her cricket is not one that can be sustained through the typical channels."

"I knew something of my life would change," Margaret said. "I asked for you to change it. But I did not say I was surrendering my family or my body."

"Never have I asked you to betray your blood family, Margaret. Never have I asked for one ounce of physical flesh or blood."

"Just because what you take cannot be tied to a specific weight does not mean you've taken nothing. It does not mean you have permission to measure its value to me."

The cricket screamed back at her.

"What I need to survive you create every night in abundance! What would you have me do? Would you have me starve, Margaret?"

"I would have the both of us try to survive another way," she said.

The cricket grew very still.

"Yes," he said. "What you say is right, Margaret. You are right and you've always treated me with sweetness and understanding. Tonight will be the last night I visit your dreams. I will not eat from your dream-body, nor will I eat from your dream-family. But allow me to visit you one world over, so that I might say goodbye to you as a man."

That night, when the cricket-man came to her, he said, "Margaret, you have fed me all I have asked for. And you have suffered incalculable losses because of it. There can be no small repayment for a gift as that."

The cricket-man ran his fingers down the surface of the wall. When he opened his hand he was shaking out a fist of sawdust.

"Tonight," he said, "I will eat this barrack that imprisons you. I will chew back its planks of wood. I will chew back the fences of barbed wire. I will eat the rifles and the shells of the tower guards. I will eat the sand and the heat and the miles between here and the Western coast."

Margaret said to the cricket-man, "I won't pretend a thing more with you. This is just the dream of one woman. The same world will be rebuilt the moment I awaken."

"No, Margaret," the cricket-man said. "Not for you. Not this time. When you awaken, Gila River will be gone. And you will be back in California. Back in your Venice home, with the dank, sweet sea air. And the wet thud of your family's plum tree dropping its black sugar in the night."

Margaret tried to rise but found in her dream that she had no feet or legs. She looked up at her cricket-man from the freezing barrack floor.

"Margaret," the cricket-man said, "you knew at the moment of friendship between a beautiful woman and a cricket, there is always a firm possibility for magic."

And then the cricket-man rose, gripped the rafters, and began to tear down the planks of the Morri family barrack.

our beans grow fat upon the storm

In Gila River, a marriage of stifling heat, roaring winds, cheap windows, loose barrack planks, and the formidable pollens of desert flowers kept the population of newborn babies thoroughly miserable.

In the years after 1945, epidemiologist Shoko Hisaishi recorded several cases of a condition he called "infant paracusia" or "infant paranoia" or "crybaby ears." In his records, Hisaishi noted that Gila River internees had been so beleaguered by the sounds of wailing infants that after camp life, even in solitude, their minds would produce an imaginary baby and its torments: whining, sniveling, blubbering. For some, the auditory hallucinations were subtle, the whimpers emerging faintly as if from behind a thin wall. For others, those counterfeit mewls were clear and emphatic, its sufferers given to throwing up their arms in exasperation or kicking chairs across the room. Furthermore, crybaby ears practically went arm in arm with other undesirable symptoms: weight loss, weight gain, insomnia, perturbation, compulsive thoughts of self-ear mutilation.

During the war, the siblings of Gila newborns could steal a few hours' sleep at school or in church. But mothers of newborns were in a less fortunate position. The unrelenting shrieking and bawling transformed them into phantoms. It was said a Gila mother's hair became uneven and tangled. Their eyes blackened. Their skin paled and looked warty. Their arms grew thin and sinewy. Their teeth grew pointed like a jackal's teeth. All meals were eaten with ferocity. Gila mothers hunched over their food, heads swiveling from side to side, as though their cutlet or drumstick might spring back to life or be spirited away.

There was little remedy for a crabby baby in the desert. Parents who had their hands on whiskey or port or sherry claimed that a capful for the little one before bedtime or naptime was perfect medicine. But liquor was a rare and expensive commodity in camp. The more affordable and renewable solution was the music of Yoshikane Araki. It was said that the lullabies written by Kane, though he was a young, relatively inexperienced musician of seventeen, had the power to anesthetize the most difficult of babes. When Kane performed the lullaby himself, he could topple a rotund baby with a single verse. It was told that even if Kane's performance did not strike the Gila baby unconscious on the spot, the music bewildered the babe into silence. Fathers became misty-eyed feeling their wailing infants turn to slumbering sacks of yams in their arms. Mothers who watched the portly heads of their toddlers dip beneath the currents of sleep sometimes threw their arms around Kane or kissed him.

"I am sorry, Kane!" they would exclaim embarrassedly. "It is just that my son has clawed my face the past three weeks with every attempt to place him down!"

Parents who recreated Kane's verses in their own mouths found the lullabies held their power over three or four weeks. These lullabies produced naps of up to two hours, which were so potent a parent could smack a mosquito from a baby's forehead without waking them. And Kane's lullabies cost only a dime. Arrangements were made through Kane's mother, Kashi Araki, and Kane would arrive at a barrack door holding a guitar case and a little scroll of lyrics. Twenty or thirty minutes were spent instructing parents in the particularities of their melody, at which time of day it was appropriate to sing, which words to take a breath after, which words to say firmly, loudly, which gently, which to swish in the mouth prior to uttering.

"This word as a command," Kane would say, "as though you are ordering an animal to leave the room."

"Now this word at the end of exhalation," Kane would say, "as though the bones of its syllables can hardly muster the strength to extinguish a candle."

"Emphasize this word only in the morning," Kane would say. "Saying this word will produce flavor like a ripened bulb of fruit in their mouth."

Afterward, Kane packed his guitar away into its shell, collected payment, and delicately pulled the barrack door behind him.

If parents could afford Kane's daily service, it cost them a nickel per performance. After his studies, Kane walked from barrack to barrack, singing to red-faced infants and sedating them. Over time, Gila mothers themselves grew appetites for his music. It wasn't uncommon for Kane's lullaby to leave mother and child napping together in the midday heat, to leave mother with her head tipped back and her jaw plopped open for the snoring to thunder forth. The pleasure of a little beauty sleep erased any embarrassments. These mothers said their snores were sweet as honey and lavender upon their tongues.

However Kane's music benefited the recoveries and moods of the women and children in Gila, it pricked at the anxieties of new fathers. In California, Kane had been a short, meaty adolescent with a feminine haircut. Around his neighborhood, his nickname was "Sister," because upon hearing the treble in his voice, people would ask, "And just where is your brother, Kane?" Peers pinched his cheeks, flicked his earlobes, and set barking dogs on him. Even the nice ones tripped him a little and stole his cardboard inserts from his shoes. His music teachers thumped him on the back of the head if they supposed he had not been practicing.

But in Gila River, Kane was surfacing from his teenage years peering six inches over the brows of contemporaries and teachers, with shoulder and jugular muscles like a horse, fearsome hands rumored to be able to hold red-black coals without suffering burns, and a voice dropping as thick and sonorous as a December cloud.

The men of Butte and Canal were highly suspicious of this seventeen-year-old boy who appeared at the barrack door holding a guitar or ukulele. Whose presence set off the man's entire family, rising and bowing and tearing up with gratitude. Whose name aroused lip-smacking and moans of delight among young girls. Whose lyrics echoed in the mouths of recent brides. Whose music echoed in the roof beams and dark dreams above all their heads.

Of Kane, a few spiteful rumors began to circulate throughout camp. One strand of hearsay suggested Kane was a devious seducer of women.

Amongst the din of the mess hall, it was familiar to hear a husband cry out, "Do not let him into your barrack! He uses his music to anesthetize your baby while he has his way with your wife!"

Another thread of rumors suggested Kane hid a jar of ether in his guitar case and used it to drug newborn babies.

"Can you believe we pay him a nickel a day to dope our babies and turn them to drooling morons?" was a common husband-cry.

"Kane is becoming rich from our desperation. I mean, just how expensive is a little ether and a rag?"

These were the rumors of men, wildly emotional and unsubstantiated, and which therefore gathered fire and velocity as they traveled from mouth to outraged mouth. Anguished letters were sometimes posted to the Araki barrack door. These were always anonymous and cowardly, threatening that Kane would be publicly belted or caned if he was discovered making a cuckold of camp men. Occasionally, a drunken husband would wander into the Araki barrack to harass or intimidate Kane in person, the husband poking his finger into Kane's chest or vomiting at the foot of his cot. But these encounters were typically followed by weeping apologies and compensations, a man's entire family appearing before the Araki barrack to acknowledge the failures of the husband and entreating Kane to return to his services.

In a recreation barrack, in the southeast corner of Butte Camp, a men's movement aimed at countering Kane Araki's lullabies was shepherded by the Reverend Jun Miyoshi. Reverend Miyoshi was a short, proud man with a teenaged wife and a daughter who was becoming a camp toddler. Miyoshi was a gifted speaker, scholar, and writer. He and his wife, Viola, were both trained pianists. He purchased space within the *Gila News-Courier* and self-published several of his sermons in order to improve upon the virtues of the internees in surrounding barracks. Miyoshi held strong opinions about parenting and believed children required self-control and discipline above all other qualities.

"Your babies simply want their father's attention," Miyoshi said to a gathering of Butte men in their recreation barracks. "Wailing is their only leverage. It is their sole method for communicating that desire. So when you hear them cry, you must turn your backs to them until they stop. Do not look them in the eyes. Turn on your radio or hum to yourself. Or leave the room. In this way they will learn sour behaviors bring them nothing. Give them your attention only when you want."

In regards to anxieties circulating around Kane Araki, Miyoshi advised that new fathers in Gila form a collective where they could write, rehearse, and trade from their own archive of lullabies. A string of articles penned by Reverend Miyoshi began to appear in the *Courier* on the theory of lullabies. A selection from his first treatise read:

Lullabies should be succinct, repetitive, and plain in their message. There should be animals in lullabies. Those animals should have jobs. The animals should be diligent workers, either producing milk or plowing a field of potatoes or disposing of tin cans and table scraps. They should be creatures of faith. They should respect their animal-fathers, mothers, Gods and forests. Their forest should be kept tidy. Lullabies should reaffirm the power of God and the security of the family. Lullabies should motivate the child to be clean, kind, polite, well-spoken, and respectful of their elders.

Miyoshi held a series of lullaby-writing workshops in recreation barracks throughout Canal and Butte Camp. At first he said he would not charge, but in later sessions he passed the church's collection plate. At first these workshops were spirited and well-attended. To fathers, Miyoshi promised the weight of more dimes and nickels in their pockets and the satisfaction of greater authority in their homes. He promised the lips of their wives and children would soon forget the name of Kane Araki.

But within a month, new fathers lost their enthusiasm. Miyoshi not only ran his workshops like a grade-school classroom, but he had the tendency to evangelize with his instruction. He openly criticized fathers he had not seen in attendance of his Sunday service. He condescended to those who did not pick up on his biblical references. When he wasn't attempting to convert Buddhist fathers, he was separating them from Methodist fathers and tasking them with cleaning the barrack where they gathered.

Few fathers had experience with songwriting or performance. Rather than encourage fathers to devise original melodies, Miyoshi suggested taking popular hymns and inserting personal lyrics. Rather than consider their own lullaby narratives, Miyoshi encouraged fathers to use lambs and angels as characters and to think of plots where children received severe punishments for stealing or fibbing.

"Perhaps there is a child who likes stealing blackberries from his neighbor's yard," Miyoshi would say, "and then he trips and falls into the brambles and gets his eyes gouged."

"Perhaps you sing of a child who lies to an angel about saying his nightly prayers," Miyoshi would say, "and the angel responds by stealing the child's tongue. Or perhaps the angel poaches their remaining baby teeth!"

Most deflating of all, the collective archive of amateur lullabies did little to soothe the infants and toddlers of Gila River. Kane's back catalog sustained some families for a period, but when his visits lessened, spells of hot weather sucked the calm like moisture from all the mouths of babes. Grief blubbered out into the Gila nights. Grief echoed through alleyways between barracks. Mothers again began to lose their hair and their nerve. Whatever hair disappeared from their heads sprouted from peculiar crevices in their bodies. The tiny trumpets of their ears. The creases of their palms. Whatever object was nearest—chewing tobacco, a candy bar, candles, Dixie Peach Pomade, mouthwash—was hurled toward a husband's head along with the edict to visit the barrack of Kashi Araki and arrange for Kane's visits to resume. In due course, Kane was called upon to replace the reverend at the lullaby-writing workshops, and he accepted, despite the notion that any teaching success would run counter to his business. Kane charged a nickel to be paid at the completion of a husband's first lullaby. Even Miyoshi attended as a participant.

"I have only one rule for what I show you," Kane said. "Before giving your lullaby to your child, you first should offer it to your wife. Or deliver a single verse to your eldest child and watch how they fare under its sway. Lullabies can be powerful medicine."

"The secret to my lullabies," Kane said, "is I extend my audience a melody so simple, so repeatable, they can carry it with them into their dreams. This way, even after you have set your children down in their cribs, or beside you in your beds, the lullaby sustains itself in their ear, in the ear of their dream even, and it soothes them."

And then he sang, "Baby go down in the desert, o baby go down in the desert. Baby go down in the desert. Baby follow desert to their dream to their ocean."

"Do you know the origin of the first lullaby?" Kane asked. "It was contained in the mind of a stone dreaming of the river moving overhead."

And then Kane sang, "Poor as you are, my heart, o poor as you are, my heart. Poor as you are, my heart, don't grieve here on earth. Don't grieve here on earth. Too much love. Too much joy. Don't grieve here on earth."

For the husbands who claimed they possessed minds wholly uncreative, wholly unmusical, wholly incapable of constructing original melodies, Kane instructed them to walk in circles around the Butte Camp baseball diamond and hum to themselves until boredom struck them.

"Boredom is your ally," Kane said. "Hum a song you enjoy. Hum a song you know in your bones. Hum until the boredom changes the flavor of the melody in your mouth. Hum while it contorts itself, teaches itself new tricks to excite you. Keep humming. After an evening or two you will be humming a thing that is entirely new. When it happens, hold your child in your mind. As the new melody develops, imagine your child sleeping heavily. Imagine your mouth is a loom and you are wrapping them like a cocoon in your yarn. Imagine their child-mouth is a mirror to your mouth. A baby imitates every song that passes from your lips. Place your melody on the lips of the baby in your imagination."

"The lyrical content is of little consequence," Kane said. "You can sing about a donkey or a grandmother who lost her shoe. But if you have placed yourself and your daughter or son in the lullaby at the moment of its inception, if the lullaby grew flesh and sense and feeling in response to your imaginings, the real work is complete."

The troubles began almost immediately after Gila husbands completed and performed their first lullabies. In his eagerness to measure his first composition, Eddie Honda sang for an hour while rocking his daughter and tranquilized the baby for a period of three days. After the first evening, Jean Honda flew at him in a panic and nearly beat him senseless with a hairbrush.

"The baby snores but she will not eat!" she exclaimed. "She will not open her eyes. What have you done?!"

In an attempt to refine the potency of his first lullaby, Kingo Furukawa sang to himself for two hours and lulled himself unconscious in the center of the Butte baseball diamond.

Because he had been walking at midday, Furukawa sustained severe sunburns and had to be rubbed down in the medical barracks with lidocaine and antibiotic ointments.

Harry Masatani, Henri Shimomi, and Jerry Kashiwagi all attempted to conceive of lullabies that would produce mild amnesia in their new Gila babies so they might forget how to cry. But what occurred instead was the three new fathers appeared to lose a cerebral constellation of words and concepts. What were their babies' names again? What was the purpose of a nipple? Why were fathers also endowed with smaller, ineffective nipples? What was the folding pattern for a diaper? Was a diaper for a baby? Or did it serve some other purpose? Was it a sort of hat?

Uproar was arising from every faction. Mothers complained of strange maladies subduing their babies. Masako Kunishige claimed that at the sound of her husband's lullaby, her son's posture sometimes froze, spread-eagled, as though he was snagged by an invisible spider's web. Joyce Ota claimed her husband's lullaby had caused her daughter's cries to drop so far in pitch that her babbling voice resembled that of her grandfather's.

Terue Yoshihara, the block manager who oversaw the Araki clan, paid multiple visits to Kashi Araki to complain that Gila fathers were running amok with lullaby magic passed on through her son. Yoshihara threatened the Arakis with expulsion from their barrack in central Canal Camp to a barrack on the southeastern fringe.

"And the ticks, scorpions, and rattlesnakes are abundant there," Yoshihara said. "Let us see how Kane manages to soothe them with his lullabies."

Reverend Jun Miyoshi continued to be Kane's fiercest critic. He paced the center of the Methodist Church, slapping the wooden pews and working his parishioners into a frenzy.

"This was Kane's plan all along!" Miyoshi exclaimed. "I should have known he was teaching us a dark magic. And now it has infiltrated our homes! It has infected our children! He has your children possessed!"

In response to the hysteria, Kane announced he wanted to hold one final workshop. He stated that all the parents who had witnessed extreme phenomena as the result of a lullaby should attend since he would be presenting them with every lullaby remedy he knew. He would stay as long as there were questions or concerns. Kashi promised a full spread of nuts, dried fruit, and beverages. The workshop was also free of charge. Word spread quickly and Kashi even took out a column inch in the *Courier* to publicize its time and whereabouts.

On the day of Kane's final workshop, over a hundred fathers from Canal and Butte were in attendance. Jun Miyoshi was there along with Terue Yoshihara, Eddie Honda, the blistered Kingo Furukawa. The Masatani, Shimomi, and Kashiwagi families. The Otas and the Kunishiges. Husbands piled into the recreation barracks from the back and took seats near a makeshift stage where Kane sat with his guitar.

"I will give the boy five minutes," Kingo Furukawa said. "After that his hide will be made an example for all camp troublemakers."

"All the Arakis should be made to pay," Eddie Honda said. "They let a devil walk among us!"

"Come closer," Kane said to the crowd that had gathered. "Can everyone hear me? If you cannot hear me, you will need to move closer."

Men packed in so tightly that a listener could feel the heat and smell the breath of his neighbor beside him.

And then Kane said, "The first remedy is the song for fathers."

And then Kane sang, "A goodnight to fathers. A thousand fathers beneath the wild water. A thousand hands grip the January milkweed. A thousand fleas devour the oxblood. Our beans grow fat upon the storm. A goodnight to fathers. A thousand fathers. A star grows its beard of fire."

Kane's pronunciation of the word "storm" struck many as peculiar. The word seemed to shake in his teeth and reverberate. Many fathers looked up into the rafters of the recreation barrack or ran their knuckles down their cheeks. Though they understood the impossibility, it'd felt to many like drops of icy water had struck the sides of their faces. At the end of the word "storm," the fathers of Gila River closed their eyes in unison. It was as if clouds overhead were filling their heads with water and, growing unmanageably heavy, those heads had to be rested upon the dusty barrack floorboards. And by the time the "fire" passed through Kane's throat, all the grown men in attendance had slumped against one another or upon the ground and fallen into a dreamless asleep.

During those hours the men slept, Kane and the Gila mothers and grandmothers gathered every guitar and ukulele from every barrack in camp, including Kane's, and smashed them upon the rock-hard earth. The shattered wood was gathered into a mountain at the center of Butte Camp, splashed with gasoline, and set ablaze.

And then in the light of the fire, Kane said to the Gila mothers and grandmothers, "Your husbands will awaken soon. When they do, they will be unable to speak. They will remember their lives clearly. They will dress and eat and work and love their families unperturbed. But the part of them that builds words is stunned. You can sing to your husbands, and they will be able to repeat what you sing. If you speak to them, they may repeat what you say. But moments later, all their words will elude them. Their words will seem to them like memories just out of reach."

And then Kane said, "When the war is finished and we can leave camp, this spell will fade. But while we live here in Gila, these men will wield no more power through their voices or songs. It was wrong of me to try and teach them."

"But what of my husband?" Viola Miyoshi asked of Reverend Jun. "Without his voice, he won't be able to write or sermonize any longer. What will become of our Methodist Church?"

"It is time for a mother or a grandmother to be our reverend," Kane said. "When God sees fit, your husband's language will be restored. In the meantime, read to Reverend Jun from his journals and articles. Read him his work so that he will be comforted. Sing to him from his hymnal so that he will be fulfilled."

It was said that even in the decade after the war, Reverend Miyoshi did not regain fluent use of his tongue. It was not until his sixties that he was able to return to his ministry. But in the years between 1942 and 1945, the language of Jun's daughter,

Rina Miyoshi, swelled like an unmapped ocean. There were dozens of utterances that Rina used to ask for bread or cereal. Dozens more for cheese or milk or salt or rice porridge. For apple or for melon or a finger dipped in molasses. For a globe of fried mochi glazed in butter, shoyu, and sugar. Rina found a thousand words that meant she was cold or hungry or upset or delighted. In the Miyoshi family barrack, Reverend Jun could be observed for hours sitting upon the floor with his daughter, echoing, reclaiming language. And then moments later, only the ghost-heat of any word remained in his mouth. Only the most recent posture of his tongue.

It was through Rina that Jun realized the ocean of human language began as something vast and rapidly evolving. And later it would be supplanted by a second ocean, an ocean that was narrow and static by comparison. Every utterance he repeated back to her. If he could have communicated to his wife to record them somehow, he would have. If Rina's primordial language could've been rendered to paper, as music or as text, he would have tried.

He repeated the dozens of baby words that meant love but were all a slightly different version of love. They were versions of love that were made a little bit new. Some of these versions he sang to her. Just moments after he sang them, he could not recall their pronunciations. For years, this was the condition of Jun's voice. It was as if he could see a phrase drawn into a shoreline, and then moments later, a surge of white water dragged its impression away.

He tried to keep the feeling of the words in his cheeks, his throat, his lungs, his blood, his marrow, for he knew of no other place he might later recover them. All the excited versions of love, daughter and father spoke together those years in their small, hot barrack. He planted them in his skin and in his hair. He attempted to bend one behind his ear. This one tucked into his arm. This one clutched in the wax paper of his sandwich. This one beneath the paperweight on his desk.

"Where can I keep this one?" he thought to himself. "Is there a place in this barrack to save this one? Where will this one survive?"

By 1945, Jun understood that daily, Rina was shedding her language. And there would be a morning his daughter would say the English or Japanese word and then everything, a forgotten ocean of language, would be lost. He tried without success to keep the dozens of her words that stood for different iterations of joy, wonder, spirit, love. All the pronunciations that his daughter would leave behind along her way.

a cluster of cactus wrens

According to the recorded history of retired minister and amateur meteorologist Yoshikane Araki, the hottest day inside the Gila River camp occurred in August of 1944, when an outdoor thermometer he'd constructed from wood, glass, alcohol, and acetic acid hovered at 122 degrees Fahrenheit.

It was the same afternoon Ginger Koyamatsu, the teenage pageant winner of Gardena, California, took three steps outside her family's barrack, heard a popping sound from above, and as she raised a hand to gather her hair, her sleek victory rolls shot sparks and went tumbling over her shoulders in crests of red-black fire.

Kazuo Taka, Gila's resident winemaker, whose shelves groaned beneath immense condiment vats, vats that'd been scrubbed and swaddled in aluminum in order to manage the fermentation of crushed grapes, raisins, and honey water, was pressing and hanging his shirts when he caught sight of a red mist rising and then a terrible wail as the vats gurgled and erupted, black wine spurting over him, scalding his outstretched hands and imprinting all his clothes with unfiltered grit, pulp, seed, and stem.

Yuriko Morri was delivering a loose tower of the *Gila News-Courier* to her neighborhood block when the top issues ignited and, to save herself, was forced to fling them into the sky. Passersby who witnessed the event swore it was not a stack of hovering newspapers at all that were burning, but a cluster of Arizona cactus wrens whose wings looked as though they had clipped the sun and were being incinerated in a mournful flash of eye stripes, flurry of ashen wings.

In August of 1944, the Butte and Canal infirmaries encountered so many instances of burning hair and epidermal tissue, scorched clothing, heatstroke, heat exhaustion, unremitting sweating, fainting, and fever that calls were placed to local laboratories and universities to inquire whether or not Arizona citizens spontaneously catching fire was a regular occurrence.

A reply to Butte infirmary's query was printed in a late-August issue of the *Courier*.

Because a person of Japanese descent, or any persons resembling a person of Japanese descent, is not equipped with the complexion to contend with a sustained period of harsh desert sunlight, it is not uncommon to witness the spontaneous combustion of those persons' skin, hair, jewelry, attire, or personal belongings. Similar cases have been documented in New Mexico, Idaho, Colorado, Wyoming, and Utah. Our principal recommendation, based on observation, is for Gila River residents, of Japanese descent or predilection, to dig trenches beneath their raised barracks and wait out the hottest portions of the day in the cooling shade of those trenches.

This announcement caused something of a stir, and within days, half of Butte Camp, about 3,000 internees, had moved the contents of their living rooms into dusty burrows below.

In September at a Butte community gathering, Yoshikane Araki took the stage and announced he'd been gathering his own research. He proclaimed that in order to survive, residents in the hottest neighborhoods of Butte should submerge their shirts and pants in apple cider vinegar.

"And when the weather becomes more extreme," Kane said, "you will need to fill your socks with crushed garlic and egg whites before slipping them on."

And though most of the internees at Butte considered Yoshikane Araki as something of an elderly crackpot, his announcement caused an immediate shortage and tight rationing of chicken eggs in Gila River. In October, Tetsuo Aratani, a member of Butte's unarmed camp police, was found tied up and unconscious at the entrance of a mess hall pantry. All of the eggs and garlic had been spirited away, and for weeks the air surrounding Butte camp stung in everyone's noses like sulfur.

soapberry wasp, thundercloud plums

Margaret Morri met the devil in person just once. It was in a stand-alone barrack, partially hidden beside an oddly lush and vibrant copse of trees, and the ground was blanketed in leaves that were ovate, serrated, blackened by age. And though the trees bore ripe fruit—enormous thundercloud plums, their skins fissuring and gurgling thickly with honey—the crows and ants of Gila River wanted no part of them. The red plums swelled; their sugar broke free and ran down, darkening the sand.

This outlying barrack and copse stood at the very edge of the northwest block, the furthest point from a guard tower, and was where Margaret went to collect petrified leaves, bones, pebbles, berries, seedpods, the scooped-out carapaces of beetles. Anything that could work as decoration in a flower arrangement. Margaret's grandmother had been a celebrated master of ikebana, and during their internment in Arizona, she passed the practice on to Margaret.

He was standing out in front of his barrack, picking his teeth with a metallic splinter that glinted as it pivoted between his fingers. Though the temperature was ninety degrees and rising, he wore a three-piece suit, dark umber, sharkskin jacket buttoned, with a fine, lilywhite handkerchief swelling from his pocket like foam climbing out of agitated champagne. He actually did not look much like a devil to Margaret. The person he resembled most was the Reverend Kenichi Toguri from the Methodist Church back in Venice Beach. He was muscular and vaguely handsome, his eyes wide and light gray, flecks of charcoal in his irises.

"I've gathered a few boughs with plum blossoms over there for you," he said to Margaret. He gestured to a basket laden with wiry branches and a pyramid of dark, bulging fruit.

"I think you recognize me, don't you?" he asked.

Margaret nodded.

"Good lord you look much younger in person, Margie. How old are you? Are you just eleven? Twelve?"

Margaret stared at him but gave no response.

"You recognize me," he said. "The dreams you've been having."

Margaret nodded.

"And you remember what I told you."

Margaret nodded again.

"That's good," he said. "You have a fabulous memory, Margie. If you remember the thing I told you, then I suppose you're carrying them now. Can you let me see them?"

From her pocket, Margaret retrieved three human teeth. They were flat and heavy and embedded with gold fillings. She held them out and let them fall one at a time into his outstretched hand.

"Thank you very much, Margie," he said. "The person whom these belonged to will be very happy to see them again."

"Because you've brought me this gift," he said, "I will let you have a gift of your choosing. What would you like your gift to be?"

Margaret coughed into her fist and tested her voice. She had been wondering if he would ask her this question. He had promised her favors in the nights before, and she'd fantasized about them since. But never while she was awake, never while she was so close she could smell the cologne rising off his skin.

"What sort of a gift is allowed?" Margaret asked.

"Well," he said, "I think you know I have many fingers, Margie. Many fingers in many pies. What sort of a pie matches your appetite?"

"If it can be any gift," Margaret said, "there is a guard who sits in the southern tower."

"Oh? The tower guard of the south patrol. Strong. Handsome."

"I'd like it if he had an accident," Margaret said.

"An accident," he said.

"I'd like it if when he goes into his tower tonight and he reaches for a cigarette and he pulls back the lid of the container, there is a scorpion that crawls onto his hand. And he becomes so frightened he tumbles out of the tower."

"It would be a very long tumble," he said.

"A long tumble," Margaret said.

Abruptly, his face turned melancholy. He closed his eyes and shook his head.

"You surprise me, Margie," he said. "You disappoint me."

"Did I say the wrong thing?"

"This sort of favor. People think it is what I want. But it doesn't give me the sort of pleasure you'd expect."

"There are other things I want," Margaret said. "This is just the first thing."

"I'm afraid the gift is simply too expensive for you, Margie. And I'm afraid the sentries in these towers are protected by power beyond you and me."

"But I think I have something you will quite like," he said. "Please hold out your hand. And don't be startled by what you see."

He reached into his vest pocket and produced an enormous blue-black wasp with bright, angular wings. He set the wasp in the center of Margaret's palm.

"Have you ever seen a tarantula hawk before?" he asked.

In response, Margaret raised the wasp to her eyes.

"They've very intelligent," he said. "And intensely loyal. This one has been my companion for many years now."

"He eats raw meat and drinks the nectar from soapberries," he said. "Sometimes when the berries are fermented, he'll even become quite drunk and talkative. But when a young woman like yourself feeds him, and sings to him, he can continue to grow forever. And he will protect you at night from bad dreams. And in a few years, after he matures to adulthood, he will be able to trade his life for the life of any man. He is absolutely willing to sacrifice himself for you in that way. But by then, you might find yourself very attached to him. I know I have found that."

"Come to think of it," he said, "if I don't see you again for ten years, he will be large as a puppy."

A metallic click rose from the jaws of the wasp. Margaret gently squeezed it by the abdomen and set it upon her left ear.

"God, you're a curious creature," he said. "But it isn't a terrible spot for him to roost."

"One day," he said, "when they're striking the stone of your statue, they'll remember to depict you with a wasp beside your ear. They'll say he ate the false voices. Any poisoned words to keep from repeating."

He lifted the basket of blossoming branches and fruit and placed its wicker handle in the crook of Margaret's elbow.

"There now, Margie," he said. "Take those home. Your grandmother will know the right sort of arrangement for them."

And then he patted his vest pocket, and it clinked with the teeth Margaret had given him. And he turned away and disappeared down the narrow blackness of his barrack.

a white man

Yoshikane Araki was the Gila internee most commonly mistaken for a white man. It was not that Kane had any sort of skin condition. He wasn't freakishly tall nor was his face exceptionally thin or pointed. But there was something contained within his posture, his broad, consummate musculature. He represented something more capable, self-aware, more distinguished than the average Japanese-American occupant. At least, those were the common descriptors. The way military police and other interned white men of Gila River explained away their overestimation of him. Upon learning he was of full-blooded Japanese descent, these men would slap a palm to their forehead or place one over their slack mouth in apology for their astonishment.

"It's only you don't look like the other Japanese men

we've met," they would say. "And you seem so confident and sophisticated, Kane. And your eyes—they seem just so big!"

Newly stationed MPs in Gila River customarily pulled Kane aside to have him point out the gorgeous Japanese woman who had convinced him to live inside this lonely, neglected, dusty wasteland. And how utterly amazing was she in the sack? And how many sisters did she have?

"Oh, but I'm single," Kane would be forced to tell them.

"Jesus friend," they would say. "You mean to say she brought you here to live with her and now she's left you?"

"Not exactly," Kane would say. "Are you speaking about my mother?"

"Your mother," they would say. "We're talking about your Goddamn wife, buddy! Traded a nice guy like you for what? One of these little, yellow-dick Tojos! And now you're sticking around here trying to win her back?"

"Win her back?" Kane asked. "There's nobody here."

"So she's with him right now, Goddamn! Probably getting her to do disgusting things too. I've heard stories that would keep you up at night. You sure you would take it back? After he got his slime up in there?"

"I don't think I would want to see anybody's slime."

"I hear you, buddy. If I see him, believe that I'm going to give him hell."

"I don't see a reason for that. I still don't know who we're talking about."

"Look, I feel for you. But Jesus, man. Get your free train ticket back to California. There's other fish in the ocean. There's fish, squid. There's whales. A penguin. Whatever you like. Who knows how long we're keeping these Japs in the desert. It's no place for a man like you to live."

"I don't think you understand," Kane would say to them. "I'm not in Gila by choice."

"Jesus, boy," they'd say. "She did a number on you. She has you thinking you belong here. She really must be a freaking tiger in the sack!"

Though these encounters were to Kane mostly embarrassing or frustrating, he quickly found the confusion surrounding his heritage afforded him one irresistible luxury. He could climb into the cab of any vegetable truck without explanation and leave camp. In the neighboring Arizona towns where the trucks stopped to load, he could pat the driver on the arm, tell him he'd be returning in one hour, and walk to the nearest drugstore to buy whiskey and cigarettes. Leaving or returning to camp, not a single sentry ever asked to check his papers.

"Do you need to check my identification?" Kane once offered a sentry.

The man laughed and slapped him on the shoulder.

"Sure, buddy," the sentry said. "And pretty soon I'll be checking papers for the radishes, potatoes, and cabbages you're hauling as well. Maybe I'll ask the loaves of bread if they're carrying any contraband! Get out of here, you crazy sonofabitch. I'll see your stupid-ass tomorrow."

Though Kane preferred to drink and smoke alone, it was because of him that parties began to emerge in Gila River. Kane became known as the resident hakujin who could get you cigarettes and booze. He would write down the orders of a few young women and men, hop into the cab of an outgoing loading truck, buy a crate of whiskey in Casa Grande, and be back to distribute the bottles in a matter of hours. His only conflicts arose when fellow internees became suspicious of him. At what sort of markup was he procuring these goods for them? Why would he risk his neck for a neighborhood party he wasn't even attending? And most baffling, just what was this white man doing roaming around camp without a Japanese wife?

"I'm not white," Kane would have to tell them. "My parents are Tomiye and Yoshi Araki. My brothers are Dennis and Shimmy Araki. My sisters are Ruthie and Zee Araki. We all live together in the southeast barracks."

"I know," they would say. "But where were you born?"

"I was born in Santa Maria, California," Kane would tell them.

"Well that doesn't sound like Japan to me," they'd say.

"There aren't more than a few hundred people here who have seen Japan in the flesh. Goddammit your whole family is from Los Angeles!"

"I know but my ancestors were from Kumamoto."

"Precisely. So were my grandparents. They probably knew each other. They probably farmed sweet potatoes side by Goddamn side."

"Alright so maybe that landed you here. But tell us, just where and when did you get adopted?"

The most traumatic incident for Kane occurred on an afternoon when Tomiye Araki mistook her son for a white military officer who had broken into their family's barrack. Kane's ritual preparation for a whiskey run involved starching and dressing in his only suit and tie. Then he would slick his hair back with Wildroot Cream Oil. A measure that seemed to him enhanced the disguise of his whiteness.

"Rape!" Tomiye cried out upon seeing him. "There's a hakujin in here trying to rape me!"

The incident drew the attention of all the Araki neighbors, many of whom felt it necessary to beat Kane with sticks and wrestle him to the ground. It took nearly an hour of explaining before interveners felt convinced first that Kane was not there to rape his own mother and second that he was not in fact a white man.

"I am not a rapist!" Kane had to cry out. "Mom, it's me!"

"Kane, is that you? Jesus, what are you doing disguised like that? You must be trying to give me a Goddamn heart attack!"

Kane Araki lived and worked, more or less as a bootlegger, in Gila River until 1945 when most of its occupants left for cities like Seattle, Chicago, and Detroit. It would be several decades before he ever discussed his experiences living as a suspect hakujin in camp. It was in the late eighties, back in California, that Kane found himself talking to his neighbors about what he, his wife, and his parents were planning to spend their reparations on. Perhaps on flights to Japan, as none of them had ever gone and had never paid respects to their great-grandparents' burial sites.

"Jesus," his neighbors said, shaking their heads in disbelief. "So the President even plans to spend our tax dollars paying reparations to the white people who lived in the internment camps voluntarily? Kane, it sounds like you came up with a pretty slick deal on that one."

yellow creosote blossoms, piss-stained gaillardia

Of the fourteen thousand internees at the Gila River Relocation Center only one was briefly given the privilege of a private outhouse. Her name was Ruthie Araki, and although every garment, every curve and gesture, every second of laughter emerging from her lips gave the impression of womanhood, she had been born Yoshikane Araki, eldest son to Yoshi and Kashi Araki, and into her adulthood was accursed with twin hair-covered nuts and an eight-inch cock.

It was commonly agreed that camp latrines were the most degrading aspect of the years in Gila River. Men and women alike defecated through wooden planks. The planks punched down the line with anywhere from six to a dozen ass-sized ovals. The planks balanced over trenches cut three- to five-feet deep and reinforced from cave-ins by concrete. The trenches were cut at a slant so it would take very little water to evacuate feces and urine from the peak of any trench out toward the septic tank. Only the person who sat at the highest point of the trench had the benefit of flushing their waste when finished. It was a greatly vied-for seat because when water did rush down, inhabitants down the row were regaled with raucous wastewater spitting up at their asses. If you were unlucky enough to be the last on the plank during a flush, it was typical for you to feel the cold thud of a foreign, bobbing turd.

Though some of the women's latrines were outfitted with partitions, the men pissed and shat shoulder to shoulder. While unpleasant for all, for Ruthie it was the most abject, anxiety-ridden set of circumstances she had ever been forced to endure. Her friends assumed it was thrilling for Ruthie to watch the young men strip down to nothing but their wiry curtains of pubic hair, their long, crinkled penises. But the truth was that most of the naked men she saw, especially those her age, frightened or disgusted her. Ruthie wanted to fall in love far more than she wanted sex. And even when she did feel horny, it became impossible to prefigure a lover once she'd sat nearby while he fidgeted and grunted and farted and spurted.

Ruthie attempted to save any unpleasant bodily functions until the dead of night when the latrines would likely be empty. But at that hour scorpions were difficult to avoid. She quickly became the most frequent visitor of Butte Camp's infirmary. Some evenings Ruthie ventured over to the women's latrine, but because of her unpleasantly large cock, women of the older generation objected to her company. It later became a proposition of her neighborhood's community board that led to the design for a private pit toilet.

As the military police would not recognize Ruthie's dilemma, the pooling of materials, the building, and the maintenance of her toilet fell upon the internees circling her surrounding barracks. Supplies were credited and shipped in by friends and relatives on the outside. The construction passed quickly as there were a number of local experts in architecture, engineering, and waste management. Ruthie's beauty had always made her something of a celebrity and it was relatively easy to assemble volunteers who dug the eight-foot catch and poured the concrete. In a week the ventilation pipes were raised, the fly screens bolted. The walls were nailed together, painted. An anonymous admirer even placed a bouquet of desert wildflowers at its entrance: yellow creosote blossoms, the wine-colored spurs of snapdragons.

The problems began just a month after the pit toilet's christening. Ruthie relished the privacy it afforded but admitted it was unfair that she solely be given rights to a structure that so many had joined together to build. So she declared the pit toilet public for anyone who wanted an opportunity to relieve themselves in solitude. Though she did ask that all help her by contributing sawdust, ash, or lime to keep the room fresh and sanitary. Before long, lines of neighbors formed to use Ruthie's outhouse. And soon thereafter the lines swelled with internees coming from all corners of Butte Camp. Some walked from blocks a mile away and might still wait an hour for the chance to void with calm and dignity. A photograph of Ruthie's pit toilet was taken for the *Courier*, an evenly spaced row of seven or eight

Butte internees standing nearby in wait, holding magazines to their faces. Designs were exchanged. Modifications discussed. And plans were drawn up for more pit toilets to be reproduced all over camp.

It was after a scuffle broke out that the military police were alerted to this private-toilet situation. The scuffle was of no concern. Just an older man struck down and kicked once or twice in the neck for cutting the line. An arrest was promised but hardly necessitated an official report. Still the MPs did not like the idea of additional structures being erected by Jap internees. It was troubling enough that some families had been given their own private barracks where collusion was likely. But it would be nothing for one of these outhouse chambers to contain a secret installation for radio broadcast. Then all manner of scenarios became feasible. The Japs could be flying overhead the way of Pearl Harbor, gunning guards down, leaving the watchtowers in a wake of fire, black smoke. And who could imagine what might be staged in the desert? Once the American Japs considered themselves obligated to these foreign Japs, post-rescue, who knew what brothers of a common grudge might wage against a nearby city?

After mere weeks into its operation, the camp MPs ordered Ruthie's outhouse be burned down. Ruthie filed a complaint, more or less read only by Ruthie and her neighborhood board that held no authority with the military. The fire happened on a cloudy morning, when a miraculous desert rain almost saved the structure from igniting. But MPs arrived to splash the walls with gasoline. Gasoline down the throat of the toilet and into the ventilation pipes. And then an inferno. Combined with the methane that had stored underground, Ruthie's pit toilet blistered and hacked rank smoke into the night. The stench of smoldering shit lasted for weeks. And Ruthie's block became infested with vultures, attracted by what they assumed was the smell of corpses.

palo verde, prairie broomweed

Yoshikane Araki was the name Margaret Morri gave to her pet mouse, a creature of shocked white fur and thin cloak of gray, and she made his home in a discarded hatbox, furnishing it with alluvial soil, the crowns of palo verde, the slinky blooms of prickly poppy, and she fed him, groomed him, and exchanged daily troubles with him until the age of nine, when she introduced Yoshikane Araki to her boyfriend, Jack Maeda, who exclaimed that her ugly mouse was just some string and burlap and buttons, nothing better than an old, busted doll.

Following that incident, Yoshikane Araki remained sealed up in Margaret's hatbox for over sixty years and was transported from Gila to Chicago to Detroit and finally to California, when one evening Margaret's granddaughter, Sumi Maeda, knocked the hatbox from a shelf and Yoshikane Araki tumbled out.

"Who is that?" Sumi asked Margaret.

"Why, that is Yoshikane Araki of course. He is my pet mouse."

"What does he like to eat?"

And though it had been sixty years since Margaret had fed Kane, she knew instantly, absolutely his favorite things to eat were the seeds of mesquite, creosote bush, and prairie broomweed, precisely the plants that were growing wild in her yard.

the glorious chizuko

When he was twelve, Kane Araki came to be owner of the most sought-after image in Gila River, Arizona—a detailed illustration by Hawaiian artist Eve Shimabukuro rendered upon card stock four inches high, six inches long, sixteen-thousandths of an inch thickness, referred to as *The Glorious Chizuko*, a depiction of Gardena, California, beauty queen Chizuko Miyamoto stretched beside an apparition of diaphanous foam upon a California shoreline, wringing a ringlet of luminous hair into the puckered mouth of a sea anemone, skin bronzed and wet, half-nude, half-clad in a laurel-green slip, at the tender age of fifteen, this depiction mythologized to endow its witnesses with startling strength, an astonishing tolerance for pain, an immunity to earthly maladies, a lycanthropic sprouting of beard, pubic and chest hairs, a momentary glimpse rumored to have given the Reverend Hisako Kido near-fatal heart palpitations, its hour-long incarceration rumored to have shocked the coal-black strands of Sister Nami Nadoka's hair as white as Mojave buckwheat, and from the years 1942 to 1945, daily it was stolen from Kane's possession, sometimes by Shyogo Ishimoto, the hulking teenager friends called The Lion, or by Masumi Iriyama, most devoted judoka of Butte's recreation barracks, or by decorated linebacker Misao Kanda or even by sweet Masao Oyabu, Kane's closest, most incorruptible friend, becoming another in the pack of cannibals crazed for radiant flesh, all whom Kane was forced to battle back, Kane more often than not becoming recipient of the severest of ass whoopings, endless fistfuls of hot sand cast into his face, merciless Kesagiri chops and slaps, eye gouges and rakings, neck knucklings and ears boxed, hair grasped and yanked like a fur hat from his scalp, joint locks and chokes, headbutts and bootings and forearm smashes, elbow drops and leaping clotheslines, genital clawings and knee strikes, dirty flicks and baps to his deflated nutsack, still every dogfight ending with Kane hightailing it, customarily in the fashion of a sort of half-hop, half-limp, in the direction of his family's Butte Camp barrack, leaking a trail of triumphant snot and tears, *The Glorious Chizuko* gripped within his swollen purple-black mitts.

Kane Araki's final duel and subsequent defeat was after three wondrous years of combat. This defeat came at the hands of Chizuko Miyamoto. By 1945, Chizuko was in her thirties, fit from her work as a taiko instructor, president of the Gila River Fencing Society, and attacking midfielder for

Butte Camp's most savage club soccer team, The Furious Cuckoo Bees, and Chizuko was able to reclaim the postcard-sized image of herself after repeated forearm clubs upon Kane's neck and abdomen, various high-flying Enzuigiri kicks, and the apocalyptic combination fireman's carry into body toss that delivered Kane into a patch of Arizona organ-pipe cactus. Following her internment in Gila River, her years through Chicago, Minneapolis, and Detroit, and her return to California, Chizuko kept Eve Shimabukuro's illustration hidden at the bottom of a locked chest, concealed beneath her diaries and family albums. She never let a single lover, not even Yasujiro Imamura, the husband loyal to her for forty years, lay eyes on that portrayal. Although she did permit herself to glance at it every few years, to be reminded of the full, wild sublimity of her youth. Before Chizuko passed away in her late nineties, she made certain it was erased by flames. The entirety of the locked chest rising from its pyre into a mammoth ghost of white smoke, riding into the sun.

an ocean

Yoshikane Araki was conceived in 1943 near the southeast barracks atop a frayed blanket spread over scorpion molt and scalding desert stones, and as Youko Araki carried him through those torrid months, she spoke to him through her belly of her family's home beside the coastline, the aroma of the sea strong as an arrangement of sour flowers held to her face, the monstrous blacklip abalone clinging within rocky crevasses, the feral dogs who burrowed in saltmud and tore through sand crabs, all she could remember, every gull song and whale song, every sea succulent and blossom, and on the day of Kane's birth, when Youko opened her legs to deliver, an entire ocean rushed forth and submerged the Gila Relocation, the hospital, the mess hall, the chapel, the barracks overrun by whelk and toxic jelly and sardine, so that it took her three days' search by rowboat to recover the infant Kane, found swaddled in kelp and froth and fish spittle, suckling the coil of a limpet as though it was his mother's nipple.

doorway of blossoms

Margaret Morri was a rugrat when she carried to Gila River a single clingstone, pried from a yellow Tulare peach, stone she held like an amulet in her sleep, stone to be activated in the center of her fist, in her dreams Margaret watched the stone grow flesh, flesh that orbited her skull, flesh that crawled through the skull's electricity and caught fire, bubbled over with sugar, hissed sweetness from its nearby flowers, a whiskered peel becoming flush in the desert sun, Margaret waking one morning to discover the stone lodged in the barrack floorboards beside her, fractured hull giving way to radicle and plumule, shoot splitting from axil, sapling spreading into new fluttering leaves, and upon a subsequent morning, a yellow Tulare peach pumping like a heart in Margaret's palm, hot to the touch, ambrosial, and over the next three years in camp, the Morri family barrack gradually inhabited by the marriage of stone and dream, Margaret's parents, Masahiro and Mariko Morri, having to step over or kick away clumps of flocculent roots, having to stoop to the nearly snapping branches descending from the barrack's roof beams, and though relatives warned of tiger beetles and red harvester ants, though Margaret's brothers complained of the yellow peach tree's debris littering their hair, the tree sap staining their shirts, the Morris never allowed so much as a penknife to be raised in the direction of the spreading branches and every night continued to be drawn into campaigns of flicking earwigs out of the doorway of blossoms.

six notes of cicada songs

During the second half of the war, Margaret Morri famously became regarded as the singer in possession of the most inspiring, most thunderous voice in either of the Canal or Butte Camp divisions. She was the prized green-black cicada of a teenager named Mieko Morri, daughter to Yohiji Morri and Brownie Onitsuka. Prior to relocation, the Morri and Onitsuka families had made their livings in the orchards of the Stanislaus Valley carrying picking crates beneath branches bearing white and yellow peaches. In Gila River, the Morris maintained one of Canal Camp's vegetable gardens, and they packed Mason jars of chopped cucumbers, carrots, cabbages, and turnips in a pickling broth of sugar, vinegar, and hot pepper to be sold at their neighborhood canteen. After the war, Mieko would own and operate the Morri and Onitsuka Farms Tsukemono Stand, all its labels bearing the insignia of a small group of trees and a luminous green-black cicada sailing over them.

When it is Mieko who tells the story of how she and Margaret came together, it begins in 1942, just after nightfall in the Tulare Assembly Center, on a dirt pathway between the racetrack and the Morri family barrack. In the absence of overhead lighting, Mieko could not fully make out Margaret's form. But there was the intermittent flash of cicada wings as they appeared to catch and retain moonlight in short bursts. She knew instantly she was in the presence of a rare cicada, because the songs resonating behind those wings were not in the key of any standard belligerent chirp. They were instead songs comprised of sustained and mournful notes. Mieko had studied music since girlhood, and friends referred to her as the "Thief of Lips," because if set before a piano, she could reproduce thousands of melodies she had heard hummed on a single occasion. Mieko followed the cicada song for what felt twice the regular distance of the path leading her into the light of her doorway. It was there Mieko found Margaret Morri perched atop the barrack's wooden handrail.

She was the most enormous cicada Mieko had ever seen. Too much animal to fit comfortably in just one of her hands and armored with mesothoracic plates that resembled hide shields constructed for warfare, painted in a manner to be equal parts mesmerizing and terrifying. When it is Mieko who tells the story, it is typically concluded with this wonderment. Mieko describing the way she fell into sleep that night with Margaret Morri whirring in the blackness above her cot and to this day never approaching sleep without hearing that sound.

On the morning following their union, Mieko discovered that during the course of the night, three people had been attacked by scorpions, all along the same dirt road leading away from the racetrack. The two who had been most severely envenomed were a married couple from Santa Maria, Mitt and Columbus Okawa. The other recovering patient was Kunio Itami, the barber from Turlock who monthly cut her father's hair. Mieko arranged three sets of flowers—California jewelflower, Kern mallow, and larkspur—tied them in abandoned sheets of newsprint, and delivered them to Tulare Center's hospital barracks. During her visit, Mitt, Columbus, and Kunio advised Mieko to treat her bond with Margaret Morri with the utmost respect.

"It is very peculiar for female cicadas to sing or to become attached to young people," Kunio said. "It is usually the business of males. This can only be the most unique of circumstances. There is the strong possibility you and Margaret are members of the same bloodline. Did you have an uncle or aunt recently pass? It is possible a spirit has returned to protect you."

Mieko named her cicada Margaret Morri after Margaret Morri, her only sibling, who had died in infancy following severe fever. Despite Brownie's efforts, Margaret Morri's headstone in the Turlock cemetery had always become overgrown with woodsorrel, and though the sourgrass was less common in Tulare, Mieko twice observed her cicada carrying a stem of it between her jaws. In August of 1942, Mieko transported Margaret Morri in a hatbox lined with fresh white sage, chamise blossoms, and her father's silk handkerchiefs on the train from the Tulare Assembly Center to the Gila River

Relocation Camp. The journey lasted four stifling days and four restless nights. There was no chance for bathing, and passengers filled blouses, trousers, and dress coats with their daily sweat. An earthy musk, a scent like sour flowers thickened the air. In cars that held newborns and the infirm were the acrid smells of urine and infection. Military police ordered every window blinded. There was fear that if locals observed a procession of trains transporting Japs, some would fetch rifles and fire upon the cars. Mieko occupied her time by whispering songs into the hatbox and replenishing Margaret Morri's bottlecap of cool water from her canteen.

In the Canal division where the Morris were relocated, Margaret lived atop a small, richly embroidered throw pillow on a dresser beside Mieko's cot. At night, Mieko transported the pillow to a desk beneath a barrack window so that Margaret was allowed to fly out, feast on tree sap, or flex the full power of her tymbals. The branches of the pinyon pine near their window became inhabited by an inordinate population of non-singing cicadas, and Mieko often wondered how many evenings Margaret Morri slipped out to seduce a mate.

Though the properties of a cicada's song were common knowledge amongst the older generations, it was months before Mieko Morri learned of them. This took place in the camp library, where Mieko asked Yoshikane Araki, Canal Camp's assistant librarian, for a text that would help her care for Margaret Morri. Kane delivered her a single, yellow-paged volume titled *World of Insects: Katydids and Grasshoppers*, which among chapters on crickets, mantid lacewings, and phasmids, also explained the six notes at the disposal of the cicada.

The section written by the famed hemipterologist Alice Josephine Sherman explained that the first note of the cicada was said to be low and sustained, similar to a stroke of sandpaper moving across a long plank of wood. The first note would always be repeated, like a twin voice being squeezed back and forth from the bellows of an accordion.

The second note would be fibrous and staccato, not unlike when a vegetable-fiber brush is taken rigorously to a sink crowded with mussels. And the third was a shattering sound, like that of the mussels being emptied into a high, metal stockpot.

The fourth note was said to be the loudest of the cicada's rattles, stirring and escalating its energy, before releasing into a fit of tiny hacks, the same as a broom full of grit being knocked against the floor planks.

Following the fourth note, the corrugated tymbals of the cicada were said to have buckled and relaxed, the song relocated to the abdomen where the cicada could produce its most complex notes. This was the home of the fifth and penultimate note, which most resembled the high-pitched wail of warm-blooded creatures. The song becoming battered against the inner walls of the abdomen, trilling, shivering. Spitting the breath past the cicada's churning pool of acid, its tears and tree sap.

The sixth note of the cicada was the most highly debated among entomologists. It was said to occur when the song reached the last chamber of the tracheae. Hemipterologists and some orthopterists referred to the last chamber as its "terminating chamber." But scholars of myth called it "the ghost chamber," because while all cicadas bore it structurally, very few possessed the size, health, and strength to open it and produce the final note. The book explained human ears could not detect the sixth note consciously. But conscious or not, it was the sixth note that could produce inexplicable behaviors in people and other creatures including blindness, fever, amnesia, and madness. Songs utilizing the sixth note were also reputed to be able to cure minor ailments and ward off bad dreams.

At the end of their first winter in Gila River, Mieko began to become inundated with offers to buy or trade for Margaret Morri. Rumors circulated Canal Camp that the songs of the Morri cicada were endowed with powerful healing abilities. May Joyce Okada, a chronic insomniac, claimed that the nights she heard Margaret sing, she slept and dreamt easily. Canal's eldest couple, Takashi and Shiori Oda, claimed when listening to Margaret Morri's nightsongs, the arthritis in their wrists, hands, and knees disappeared. A neighbor, Ren Horibe, admitted to Yohiji Morri that due to an accident, he occasionally suffered from impotence. But on nights Margaret Morri's song drifted between the barrack partition, his erections were firm, sensitive, and abiding.

The visitations of Canal residents were a daily affair for the Morris. Hulking billfolds of cash, jewelry, seashells, watches, clocks, dresses, hats, watercolors, and musical instruments were offered in exchange for Margaret Morri. Those without money or valuables offered to trade labor or tutelage. Keiko Hattori, the acclaimed ikebana artist from Kumamoto, was prepared to mentor Mieko in arrangements of petrified leaves, bones, pebbles, berries, seed pods, and the scooped-out carapaces of beetles. Tadanobu Gennosuke, the most skilled carpenter from

Turlock, claimed he could construct a multi-level basement beneath the Morri barrack where, even during the harshest months, temperatures wouldn't rise above seventy degrees. Yuki Funatsu offered to make Mieko her only student and recipient to over sixty years of koto expertise. Minoru Fukami promised he would cast Mieko and her family members in any Gila River Kabuki production they wished. Manju, dried figs, cactus pears, and smuggled whiskey appeared on the Morri doorstep along with notes requesting an hour or two with the most famous songstress in camp.

When the offers to purchase Margaret Morri became more insistent, more confrontational, and Mieko began turning visitors away, the voices around Canal Camp turned hostile.

"Why is it only the Morris who enjoy the company of the cicada?" their neighbors asked. "Isn't a creature like this a gift from God? Was Margaret Morri not delivered to this desert for all of us?"

"You are monopolizing the time and energy of your cicada," Mieko's aunts complained. "You are a healthy, teenage girl. There are sick and aging people in camp who deserve her attention. Let us manage the cicada's time for you. We promise there will be some profit in it for your parents."

Mieko's uncle, a man called Glenn L. Morri, claimed he could purchase homes and farmland for the Morri families in several Midwestern or Eastern cities should he be allowed to barter the services of the wondrous cicada.

"I know a wealthy hakujin whose son is deathly sick," Glenn Morri said. "This man is willing to pay any amount for a cure. Should Margaret Morri's songs provide even the slightest improvements to this boy's condition, we may yield a reward of unimaginable size."

"If you are in communication with the man," Mieko responded, "you can tell him to bring his son to camp. It might be the will of the Gods that he is cured for nothing. But I will never choose to part with Margaret Morri. My life is indebted to her and so must serve her until she releases me from our partnership."

"You mannerless, idiot girl!" Glenn Morri exclaimed. "You do not suggest a man of this esteem visits these desert barracks! The cicada must be taken to him directly for a demonstration."

Yohiji had to strike Glenn Morri several times across the face in order to force him out of their barrack. And it took an intervention by Canal Camp's police to stop his hammering upon their barrack door.

"The creature upon your daughter's embroidered pillow is holding an opportunity to transform our family's prospects for generations!" he called out. "And you are pissing it all away!"

Stories attempting to disparage Mieko Morri also began to surface. In the mess hall, Mieko was shocked when she heard people she had never met vilifying her. The name Mieko lathering thickly upon their tongues with poison and enmity.

"There is a snotty teenager called Mieko Morri who keeps a rare cicada tied up and in a cage," she overheard someone say. "When she wants the cicada to sing, she threatens it with fire and dismemberment. And only after the song does she allow it to eat some thin broth and stale, tasteless crumbs."

Mieko endeavored not to let these rumors intimidate her. Any offers that came her way she responded to by saying Margaret Morri did not belong to her. Margaret spent her days on a pillow by an open window. And if she ever wished to live with another person, she would make no attempt to prevent it. Near dusk, Canal internees came with folding chairs and beach blankets to sit and listen to the cicada songs emanating from Mieko's window. A small party of pregnant women was invited to sit within Mieko's nook of the family barrack, share handfuls of dried fruit and nuts, voice concerns over oblivious husbands, and rub their expanding bellies. These women kept eyes upon Margaret Morri's pillow and claimed the music of this cicada was a cure-all for the discomforts of pregnancy, including leg cramps, backaches, pelvic pain, morning sickness, swelling, and heartburn.

In spring of 1943, Mieko began to hold concerts of sorts for Margaret Morri. From the hours between dinner and nightfall, Mieko transported Margaret's throw pillow to a makeshift stage in one of Canal's recreation barracks. People set down mats at the foot of the stage where they shared caramels and other sweets while they listened. On some occasions it seemed Margaret did not produce any music at all. But those became her most renowned performances, as attendees claimed those were the occasions when songs of the sixth note were played. Canal's longing for Margaret Morri was evident. Some evenings when she fluttered in later than expected, her audience erupted into applause.

In place of monetary gifts, attendees placed popular records into Mieko's hands. These included albums by The Mills

Brothers, Billie Holiday, The Song Spinners, The Ink Spots, Ella Fitzgerald. Some evenings Mieko played the records before Margaret Morri appeared, and those present sang together or danced. By the end of their second year in Gila River, the concerts of Margaret Morri were drawing crowds of hundreds of Canal and Butte residents. Despite the frequent gatherings, medical barracks in both camps were reporting significantly lower rates of communicable diseases as well as asthma, pneumonia, insomnia, rashes, chronic dehydration, and dysentery.

It was in the autumn of 1944 that Glenn Morri plotted to kidnap and sell Margaret Morri. Not everything is known about the confrontation that occurred between Glenn and Mieko. When interviewed by camp police about the incident, Mieko stated her uncle approached her beside her family's garden just after nightfall and asked that she and Margaret Morri accompany him back toward Canal's recreation barrack. As she walked past him, she was struck at the back of the skull by something broad and solid, perhaps a rock.

Mieko was unable to raise her hands to brace her fall. Her face cracked against the dirt before her, and for a moment she lost consciousness. When Mieko opened her eyes, she was flat against the dirt. She could sense something hot and metallic in her mouth and saw her front teeth lying amongst the stones before her. She saw her uncle had cast a mesh netting over Margaret Morri and was attempting to stuff her into a gunnysack. Mieko rose and threw herself, shoulder-first, against him. He struck her twice more in the face. When her uncle leaned in to grasp Mieko by the hair, she took the opportunity to stab him twice in the groin and once in the foot with her penknife. The two of them fell back together, but she was first to her knees. She grasped a flat stone nearby and with all her weight, came down with it upon his hand, smashing all his fingers. While her uncle screamed nearby, Mieko untangled Margaret Morri.

Mieko's claims following the moment after Margaret's liberation appear on no official record. They surfaced later, in the personal journals of camp authorities who copied down her story. Mieko claimed that as her uncle rose to charge her again, the air grew heavy and crowded with vibrations. And then came the overwhelming sound of thrashing rattles, and the space between them swarmed with cicadas. The air so thick with noise and motion her uncle fell to his knees and began screaming. Mieko claimed there must have been ten thousand cicadas that interrupted their confrontation. Mieko ran into a neighbor's barrack where camp police were alerted.

A more rigorous military investigation was never commissioned. Glenn L. Morri was discovered the morning after the incident at an offsite medical facility where he was being treated for various ailments. These included self-inflicted scratches, ruptured eardrums, disorientation. The official determination of his death was suffocation. From his autopsy report, it was noted that Glenn L. Morri had gone to sleep looking much improved than when first admitted. But when the first morning shift arrived to examine him, his mouth and throat were found packed with no less than two dozen live cicadas. Margaret Morri herself was the deepest embedded of them all. The records imply that considerable mutilation of Glenn Morri's chest and throat was required to extract the colossal cicada still moving within him.

an hour

Of the failed inventions of Margaret Morri and Kane Araki, Gila River's most ingenious aviation pioneers, the most catastrophic trial belonged to a frail basket of coiled animal hair, dry grasses, and blackberry briars the two called *The Tear of Kumamoto*. The craft was adorned with steel rings all along its perimeter and was to be hoisted by the power of ten thousand birds.

It had taken Kane and Margaret six months to capture their birds, followed by another six months merely to fashion and fasten tethers of varying materials, weights, and thicknesses to the thighs of every gnatcatcher, wagtail, nightjar, grosbeak, thrush, finch, warbler, sparrow, jay, and wren indigenous to Gila River.

The morning before their maiden flight, Henri Kamitaki, a writer and editor from the *Gila News-Courier*, was sent over to interview Margaret and Kane on the details of their preparations. If all went as intended, there were special dispensations being prepared for the couple to leave camp and demonstrate an ascent of *The Tear* in Chicago, Detroit, Madison, Minneapolis, Milwaukee, Pittsburgh. Kenneth Yano, the *Courier*'s most coveted photographer, had planned on accompanying Henri to the interview. But at the last minute, Henri had requested to go on alone when meeting the pair in the removed silo where *The Tear* and its birds were being housed.

The sight of the contraption was a shock. From desert floor to the removable section of roofing, the room was outfitted with shelves and racks where thousands of birds roosted. An incomprehensible web of nylon twine connected every body in the room to the craft at its center. It was a city populated by rope and steel and flesh and persistent movement.

"How can you live every day in the overwhelming sound and smell of this place?" Henri asked. "Doesn't a normal person go deaf?"

"We wear earplugs made of wax," Margaret said. "Wax and cotton. The smell is only overpowering for the first few minutes. By the time you leave here, you won't smell a thing."

"What do military police think about all of your aeronautical experiments?" Henri asked them. "Isn't anyone concerned you two will cause a disturbance in Butte or Canal? Or in Casa Grande?"

"We have a written agreement that *The Tear* won't move outside the boundaries of Gila River," Margaret said. "Military police have been out on several occasions to inspect our vessel and have confirmed it poses little threat of violence or terror."

"I've heard they are giving you the clearance of a starter pistol and a single bullet to provoke the birds into flight."

"That plan has been slightly altered," Margaret said. "We will be coordinating with a tower guard. We will leave it to him to fire the instigating shot."

"After you take *The Tear* up, how can you be sure your birds won't tangle?"

"The tethers vary in length. Schools of birds have been trained to fly together. Every school will fly at different altitudes."

"There are ten thousand birds here, of unequal speed and size," he said. "How can you expect to unify them?"

"We've spent a lot of time with our local team of ornithologists, physicists, engineers," Margaret said. "The strength, health, flight patterns of our birds have been assiduously documented. All has been accounted for. I expect the precise math would go beyond the constraints of your story."

"My readers won't understand the math," Henri grumbled. "That is a perfectly good explanation."

"A document of several hundred pages exists on *The Tear*'s construction," Margaret said. "But I know that journalists work in inches."

"And how will you steer your little wicker basket?" Henri asked.

"Steel pipes that exceed the length of the tethers," she said. "Well, perhaps you can think of them as extraordinarily long flutes. The vents at the ends of them are wadded with honey, millet, safflower, suet. Our birds are incentivized to fly toward what is unreachable."

"All of your science still sounds much like a carrot waggled in the face of a donkey," Henri said.

"That is a perfectly good analogy," she said. "Ten thousand plumed and flapping donkeys."

"Perhaps that should be the name painted along the side of your ship," Henri suggested.

"We've already chosen a name," Margaret said. "But you are welcome to use it for the title of your article."

"How will you descend?" Henri asked.

"We plan to stay airborne for at least an hour. Then we will begin reining in the lowest birds and sacrificing them. Eventually we'll descend low enough to drop a series of anchors."

"You're going to murder your birds," Henri said. "Would it not be just as easy to cut their tethers?"

"We aren't trying to be cruel," Margaret said. "But you have to understand the tethers are made of materials that make them relatively expensive."

"Relatively," Henri said. "Relative to the birds."

"That's right. The birds of Arizona are free and plentiful."

"I doubt the birds think of it that way."

"We're hoping to keep as much of the craft intact as possible," Margaret said. "We've had a fair bit of interest in the purchase of our project."

"Military interest?" Henri asked.

"Oh good lord no," Margaret said. "But some artists and art collectors have expressed interest."

"No bird collectors though," Henri said. "Otherwise you would have to keep them alive."

"That's right," Margaret said. "We have every intention of donating what we can. We're in communication with some universities and taxidermists."

"Why is there no cushioning of any kind in your craft?" Henri asked. "What will happen to you if it crashes?"

"There won't be a crash, Henri," Margaret said. "We wouldn't fly if we thought crashing was a possibility."

"You're floating a basket in the air. I'd say that about creates possibility."

"If it crashes," Margaret said, "what do you think would happen to us?"

"Is that a joke? I'm pretty certain you and Kane would get spread like about two hundred eggs all over camp."

"*The Tear* was designed to be as durable as it is lightweight," Margaret said.

"Sounds very reassuring," Henri said.

"Projects like these carry an intentional risk, Henri," she said. "That is part of what makes air travel worthy of admiration. We aren't afraid."

"People in Butte want to read this story, so I plan to write it," Henri said. "But I still see little purpose for this sort of a project. You're risking Kane's life and your own to test the most impractical machine ever used in transportation."

"Tomorrow when you see us in the sky," Margaret said, "you might understand we are attempting to stretch the boundaries of this camp. But we agree that it is a very quiet revolution."

Later, after Margaret had gone for a meeting with Gila River's military police, Henri seized Kane by the shoulder, guided him out, and pushed him up against the back wall of the silo.

"You've really decided this is the most productive way to spend your time?" Henri asked.

"This was my work before Gila River," Kane said. "I won't wait to see if I outlive this camp to work again."

"No one in Butte is fooled by your marriage to Margaret," Henri said. "She is pompous and boring. And she's Goddamn plain. If you would've married someone more youthful and symmetrical you might've convinced me."

"It's fortunate then the goal of my marriage wasn't to convince you of its legitimacy," Kane said.

Henri's hands were shaking. He'd been carrying a satchel with his journals from the *Courier* and now he threw it to the ground. His journals spilled out and their pages flapped in the dry air.

"Jesus you sound like her, you know that? You sound like you're Goddamn brainwashed! You married her because she's too old to have children. So no one would become suspicious of you."

"Thank you for your friendship and generosity, Henri. When you're done accusing me and my marriage of being a hoax, I have ten thousand birds to feed."

"For you, hoax will always be a better word than what I am. And who you are."

"I don't believe I've ever suggested the time we had together was not meaningful to me. When I told you I wanted you, I meant it. It was not a hoax to me then or now. But I'm someone else's husband and collaborator. It isn't to hurt you that Margaret is a woman."

"It is," Henri said. "You like punishing the both of us."

"I think you've said all you came here to say," Kane said. "I love Margaret better because I knew you. For that I'm thankful. There's no other gratitude I owe you."

"You might die with her tomorrow," Henri cried. "Have you considered that? You could die, and the only person nearby will be someone you can't love."

"No one is going to die," Kane said.

"And you aren't doing her any favors," Henri said. "She could die with a person incapable of loving her."

"You are the most selfish person I can imagine," Kane said. "You really don't give a Goddamn about me. You feel sorry for yourself because you're pitiful and lonely."

Kane picked Henri's bag up, brushed the grit from it, and handed it to him.

"In the most important ways, we are nothing alike," he said.

The next afternoon, Henri Kamitaki watched the maiden flight of *The Tear of Kumamoto* beneath the overhang of the *Courier*'s barrack. Margaret and Kane reached an altitude of sixty feet. The two hovered in the air for just over twenty minutes when a cloud of locusts moved through Canal Camp, and over half *The Tear*'s birds dashed for them.

After *The Tear of Kumamoto* tore in two, the half containing Margaret crashed into the Aoki family barrack. As the Aokis were outside watching the flight, they remained unharmed, though many of their family heirlooms were badly damaged. Margaret fractured a great number of bones in her feet and legs, and hundreds of the birds attached to her were maimed or killed.

Kane wasn't nearly so lucky. Though Kane broke no bones in his fall, his half of *The Tear* landed atop a watchtower, collapsing it and crushing the tower guard beneath. He spent the remainder of the war in an underground cell of a detention facility in the Santa Catalina Mountains.

saguaro flower, desert apricot mallow

In Canal Camp of Gila River, Margaret Morri was known as a practitioner who would make house calls for ailments of a small or embarrassing nature.

For excessive or unendurable flatulence, she claimed a dark spirit inhabited the gut. The infirm was given a tonic made from crushed fennel seed, pulverized ginger, mint leaves, all whisked together into one part rice vinegar, two parts rice-rinse water. And then Margaret would hunch over the stomach of the infirm and direct a cycle of burning threats down into what she identified as the face of the dark spirit.

"Spirit!" Margaret would scream into the night. "Do you think I care one inch about this half-witted teenage girl? Spirit! I carry a sword! If you do not appear to me, I will slice open this belly, pull it over my head, and drag you out by my teeth!"

Roughly tapping the flat side of a butter knife against the waist of the infirm, Margaret would say, "I am sawing into this bitch now! Spirit! Prepare to have your skin made into a blanket for my horse and to have your sniveling pecker thrown into my fire!"

"My mother says you really did look after horses in California," the infirm would say.

"Quiet now," Margaret would whisper. "These demons are easily provoked by mention of animals hoofed or magnificent. They are jealous creatures."

Then Margaret would erupt into a throaty laugh and say, "I can feel that skin blanket now. Riding up my ass while I guide over my pony to piss and horseshit into your mother's uncovered grave!"

For unbearably smelly feet she recommended a footbath of rock salt, dry sage leaves, and the bruised blossoms from the governess bush. This was to accompany a friend or relative whacking a sheaf of living sage upon the calves, knees, thighs of the infirm while Margaret, ever antagonist, yelled profanity into every blister, boot sore, wart, corn, bunion, and blackened rim of toe jam.

For a rash upon the male genitals she recommended the infirm bake a kabocha pumpkin, carve a medium opening, and with the cavity still huffing steam, penetrate it employing the swollen or stingy flesh. This was paired with round-the-clock screaming at the rash. Either from behind, the rash assumedly receiving Margaret's earsplitting insults via the chamber of the anus, or piercing the wall of pumpkin rind, which she claimed stored and condensed the healing powers of her aggression.

Margaret's credentials were unknown. Her business operated on the hearsay she had lived amongst communities of healers in Kumamoto and in California. Nearly all Margaret's remedies involved an element of severe embarrassment or yelling. The remedies were rigorous, time-consuming, and expensive. But it was difficult for the infirm to criticize her methods. This was not at all because her patients made the fullest or speediest of recoveries. Few had any urge to insult or confront Margaret out of fear she would discuss their ailments publicly.

Still, remarkably, Margaret remained very well liked. She was tireless and she flew into diagnosis and treatment with conviction. She responded as promptly in the dead of night as at first light. After a client's conditions subsided, her visits continued as maintenance to their good health. She was the first to furnish a newlywed with an envelope of crisply ironed currency. She was the first to extend koden wherein her bills were of an appropriately sad and disheveled nature. And she was never late in her attendance for any shower, baptism, or recital in Gila River.

In the late fall of 1944, Margaret Morri stunned all the residents of Canal Camp when she herself became profoundly ill. Her granddaughter, Sumiko Alexandra Morri, was sent to her barrack to care for her. From the crown of her head to the heels of her feet, Margaret was covered in painful sores. She ceased making house calls. Then she stopped taking her meals in the mess hall. Sumi Morri shuttled back and forth carrying rice porridges and thin kelp broths. Previous patients invited themselves over daily and delivered her small gifts.

"Are they the dark spirits attacking you, Margaret?" her visitors would ask. "Do you think they have come back for retribution? For all the exorcisms and banishing you have performed?"

"Oh it's the spirits alright," Margaret would say. "Pretty unfair, don't you think? That they return to torment me and not you? It's always the dang healer. Never the host. It's a God-forsaken peach of an arrangement."

"But you're such a strong and resilient woman," her visitors would say. "Does it really hurt very much?"

"You know when your body is dipped in fire?" Margaret would ask. "When your body is dipped in fire and then molten iron is poured over you? And your skin melts and becomes the iron, so you are paralyzed in a burning cast of your own dissolving body?"

"We cannot even imagine that!" they would gasp.

"Well," Margaret would say. "It's ten times worse than that."

"But what can we do to help?" her visitors would ask. "Isn't this partly our fault? Our responsibility? What can be done to ease your suffering?"

"There is only one treatment that can cure me," Margaret would say. "But it would be an impossibility here in Gila. No, I think I'll just lie here and shrivel up and die in misery."

"Tell us what it is!" her visitors would exclaim. "We can arrange the money!"

"It is not only a matter of cost," Margaret would say. "It would defy a number of wartime laws. The only treatment for my condition is to be given a bath of ocean water straight out of the Pacific. It's the only way to cleanse myself of these dark and powerful spirits."

Over two weeks' time, potential solutions were drawn up and discussed. Could Margaret somehow be smuggled back into California? Could she be hidden within a train? In a closet or bathroom stall or in a crate with breathing holes? In the bed of a truck? Could she be covered with a blanket and traded off in the trunks of cars? What was the risk if she was discovered? Could it be considered a form of espionage? Of treason? No one in Gila River, or in any other war camp they knew of, had attempted anything like it. Given Margaret's age and immobility it did not seem feasible she would be able to make the long and uncomfortable journey.

It ultimately took the work of over a dozen people for Margaret Morri to receive her bath of Pacific Ocean water. Michi and Tadashi Aoki had friends in Guadalupe willing to scoop and bottle a hundred Mason jars of green-blue water straight out of the surf. Chiye Kamo had friends who could ride with the crate of jars on a train as far south as Santa Barbara. From there it was Elsie Iwamoto's friends who drove the crate to Los Angeles. It was not until the crate came into the possession of Chiyo Koga's friends that the crate began moving east. The crate changed hands through Palm Desert, again below the Salton Sea, in El Centro, Yuma, and Mohawk before it was delivered on the backs of three donkeys to the Casa Grande post office. Then it was loaded secretly into a bread truck and driven past the sentries, past the barbed wire, and into Canal Camp.

When the Mason jars arrived, their Pacific Ocean still jostling with sea grit and foam, many worried it was too late for Margaret Morri. Though her skin appeared to be fighting back the sores, Margaret scarcely spoke or moved. Sumi Morri poured lemon water into Margaret's mouth three times a day and massaged her throat. Besides that, Margaret would accept no food. Friends and relatives took turns at her bedside, gently patting Margaret's hand. Her patients arrived with bouquets of saguaro flowers, desert sage, globemallows, ironwood, and netleaf hackberry branches. And they thwacked Margaret across the face and body the way they remembered her performing healing on them. When the jars of seawater were delivered into her barrack, poured into a large metal basin, and Margaret was laid inside, she opened her eyes and asked all of her visitors to return to their homes.

"If these spirits leave my body, they will be on the prowl for new hosts," Margaret told them.

"But who will help care for you in your vulnerable state?" they asked. "At least a few of us should stay."

"You've all done me an impossible kindness already," Margaret said. "Plus eventually I'll need to get naked. I can't soak in this tub in my pajamas all night."

"Well if you're sure you're alright," her visitors said, already to her doorway. "We're glad you have your cure!"

The next morning, Sumi Morri entered Margaret's barrack to a terrifying sight. Her grandmother was nowhere to be found. But swimming in the metal basin of ocean water was a long, black eel.

"My God!" Sumi exclaimed. "The spirits have transformed her into an eel!"

Upon hearing Sumi's weeping, Margaret appeared from behind her changing curtain, chewing a hardened bread roll. Though her complexion remained slightly red and pockmarked, she had regained more mobility and lucidity than she'd had in weeks.

"Oh you're here early," she said. "I thought it was one of my patients trying to sneak up on me soaking in my birthday suit."

"I thought you had been transformed into this eel!" Sumi cried.

"Don't be ridiculous. People can't be turned into eels."

"But then where did this eel come from? Is he a dark spirit you've trapped in an eel fish body?"

"Don't get yourself worked up. This is just my eel. I've had him for some time. This is a good home for him."

"But where have you been keeping him," Sumi asked.

"The only place that I could," Margaret said. "I've been keeping him in your father's dreams."

"You have?"

"For over a year, hasn't your father complained of dark dreams? As though every figure in them was inhabited by a second shadow? Doesn't he complain of waking in a sweat as though being misted all night by a salt breeze?"

"And he has been complaining of headaches!"

"Right. Naturally from fattening up this fatty eel. The weight of him sloshing heavily through his dreams."

"My gosh," Sumi said.

"My God, you gullible idiot girl," Margaret said. "Your mother raised a fool. I'm only joking. This eel has been over in that soup pot in the corner. Now it has gotten too cramped. You read too many fantasies."

"So he wasn't in my father's dreams?"

"Why would I put an eel in my own son's dreams? If that was even possible I'd have hidden him down the block. In the head of Masami Kamiya. He's got a head the size of a birdcage. And a brain the size of birdseed."

"But why would you smuggle and raise an eel here in the desert? It must've taken so much planning and work."

"There is so much a woman like me can do with an eel," Margaret said. "Are you aware of the healing properties of a black eel? The opportunity for magic? Swallowing the raw flesh of an electric black eel will impart the capacity to channel fire within your bare hands."

"Really? No one has ever told me."

"Probably because only young and stupid people rely on magic to account for what is inexplicable in this life."

Margaret tossed the rest of her bread roll to the eel.

"This year is my first anniversary without your grandfather. That man really loved a good eel."

"As a pet?"

"As a pet," Margaret said. "For a while, as a pet. Then usually butterflied and grilled over coals. The meat plucked directly from the metal grate and dunked into mirin, shoyu, ginger, honey, spring onions. Or if he had spring allergies, he would prepare a kelp broth with honewort and slices of yuzu. Or a sweet stew with mountain yam, carrots, burdock. Over a bed of steaming rice. We'd set aside the spines and bones. Some evenings I swear I am still listening to them. Sizzling in the hot oil, being fried into bone crackers."

an egg

Yoshi K. Araki had only one great love during his lifetime. Her name was Margie Morri, and though she was one of the most beautiful creatures in Gila River, it was her eating rituals he fell in love with and memorized fluently as the Scout Promise.

For breakfast she prepared a slice of hot white toast, a wisp of melting butter, and two large spoonfuls of Arizona desert honey. The crusts were trimmed into four tan stripes, lowered into the butter and honey and gobbled up. The remaining square she folded in half and tilted into her open mouth, never letting a bead of honey escape.

At lunch she ordered a hamburger bun with sesame seeds, and on it she assembled fried cuts of bacon, ice-cold slices of tomato, pickles, chopped cabbage, thin rings of raw zucchini or yellow squash, and Italian salad dressing. The sandwich was cleaved down the center and eaten from corner to corner in slow, contemplative bites.

At dinner she ordered soup, ladled into a shallow bowl she brought with her, a cup of white rice, and one uncooked egg. The egg was rapped upon the table's ledge, its contents unbuckling onto steaming rice, and whipped into rich froth, coating every grain. Salt and pepper were shaken like a religious rite over the bowl. And then a nest of warm egg and rice was submerged by tiny wooden ladle into the broth of her soup and bathed there before being raised up to her lips.

Until the war, Yoshi K. had endured a life tortured by a relentless appetite. As a child he could eat five or six bowls of rice with dinner. If he came upon a fruit tree or a bed of mussels, he devoured all there was until he was sick. He had once eaten an entire row of early potatoes, perhaps twelve pounds of them, unpeeled and encrusted with wet soil. His parents often had to beat him from the kitchen table to keep him from poisoning himself with too much vinegar, hot mustard, mayonnaise, ground red pepper.

But when Yoshi K. observed the eating practices of Margie Morri, it made him feel oddly satiated. The day he first observed her was the day he stopped hiding bread rolls in his jacket pockets. He quit slinging rocks at the desert wrens and skewering them over hot coals. And though they never spoke a sentence to each other, Yoshi K. watched nearly every bite that sustained Margie over their three-year relocation to Gila. He craved the routine of her meals as much as his own. On days he could not watch her, his hunger returned and was so overwhelming he could hardly see or stand straight.

Yoshi K. and Margie had only one day of communication with each other. This happened the morning after Margie injured her arm from a fall off the Morri family's barrack steps. She arrived at the mess hall later than usual, right arm tucked into a sling, left arm carrying a plate of toast. Because her friends had already eaten and gone, she sat directly across from Yoshi K. She did not know his name at the time, but she recognized him as one of the young men whose pastime it was to lift weights, play ukulele, and smoke cigarettes down beside the racetrack. She had wandered by that track often and had fantasized about sending a friend over with an invitation to accompany her on a walk.

Generally Margie would've felt too humiliated being across from a stranger without a way to hide her injury. But the sight of Yoshi K. sitting alone in the near-empty mess hall was somehow exhilarating to her. She was further encouraged when she saw his plate of food was untouched, and he'd have to remain in her company for the duration of his meal.

It was in a hospital bed, on the Central Coast of California, decades later, where Margie would admit to her children and grandchildren that her most enduring memory of camp was the morning Yoshi K. cut the crusts from her toast for her. It happened without a word passing between them. There was something oddly rehearsed about it all. It was as though the two had eaten together the evening previous, and she had instructed him in the manner she wanted to eat in tandem. At the moment she attempted to manipulate her knife with her non-dominant hand, Yoshi K. instinctively took the knife from her and cut the crusts from her toast into four stripes.

When she finished eating them, he folded her toast in half and carefully placed it into her left hand. When he did, it felt as though she were remembering it, as though he'd placed food into her hand a thousand times before. When she was finished eating, he placed her empty plate atop his own and carried them back toward the kitchen.

At lunch Margie found Yoshi K. again. This time he assembled two sandwiches atop sesame buns. Bacon, pickles, cabbage, raw slices of yellow crookneck squash. On one plate he cut the sandwich down the center and slid it across to her. He stared down at his food while they ate. A strange routine formed between them. She didn't ask any questions, and he didn't provide any answers. She felt like a partner in a long, comfortable marriage that weighed its silences as equal with its conversations. At dinner Yoshi K. was waiting for her. In his hand he was polishing the surface of an uncooked egg with his napkin, ready to be cracked over a bowl of rice, whipped, seasoned, and dipped into a cup of broth.

Margie would never have an opportunity to eat with Yoshi K. again. On the evening of their first meal together, a scorpion crawled into Yoshi K.'s mouth as he slept, and its venom suffocated him. Margie didn't learn his name until after he had perished and his obituary appeared in the *Gila News-Courier*.

dolls of the toymaker, yuki shimada

In the matter of finding a toy for one's child in Gila River, it ordinarily meant a correspondence of sending away for catalogs, mailing order forms and then two to four months waiting before one's paper kite or checkerboard or pouch of marbles or wooden figurine appeared at the Butte Camp postal barracks. If it was not the tedium, it was surrendering the exorbitant amount for toys on display on the back counters at the Butte canteen, and even the doctors and lawyers who made between sixteen and nineteen dollars monthly could scarcely afford the canteen's toys for their sons and daughters.

The only other means of procuring a toy was by paying a visit to the toymaker, Yuki Shimada, who maintained a workspace and gallery in a corner of one of Butte's recreation barracks. Shimada was a small, immaculate man from an erudite family. His sister was a surgeon, and in Kumamoto, his parents had been art instructors. He had a little skill in painting murals and in stuffed creatures. But he was most known for carving and assembling beautiful wooden dolls upon which he painted facial features and expressions. He also hardly charged for his labor. Shimada dolls were never more than twenty cents greater than their material costs of wood, glue, sandpaper, paints, brushes, and varnish.

There were three catches to buying from Shimada. The first was the toymaker could not fabricate anything terribly imaginary from wood. He produced figurines based on the Butte internees living in his immediate vicinity. This practice aroused some tensions, since Shimada never asked a relative, acquaintance, or stranger permission before shaping and painting to a person's likeness. And it placed a new onus upon parents to instruct their child not to point out in public the similarities between their dolls and their neighbors.

Secondly, Shimada did not possess a diverse population of wooden dolls. Shimada created in inescapable phases. Though he might construct several dozen figures in a month, they were likely to be close iterations of one another. If Shimada was in the mood for dolls resembling Chizuko Miyamoto, the renowned beauty queen from Gardena, he might paint up to fifty versions of that exquisite face with its dimples and slightly crooked nose. If Shimada was in the mood to carve out the freckled and potbellied teenager Minoru Kamibayashi from wood, there could be a hundred of them before moving on to the next pattern.

The final catch was Shimada did not take requests.

Whatever occupied his shelf was what was for sale. While internees at Butte Camp requested wooden beasts and insects and wolves and princes and spirits, Shimada found his hands could only create from obsession.

"My hands cannot see it," he would sometimes apologize. "It is like a spell has possessed me." It was not that Shimada was resistant to pleasing those around him. A man of only twenty-seven, he was desperate for affirmation. But if commissioned with a task, he would encounter paralysis. He stared into the wood, unsure of where to carve notches. He mixed palette after palette feeling all the emerging colors inappropriate. He became like a crazed songwriter who had lost the ability to tune his instrument. If Shimada did not succumb to the urges of his visions, the first steps toward creation would strike him as hopeless and insurmountable.

Shimada's business remained steady. The price was right, and customers were happy to buy his models and make their own alterations. Children in Butte learned how to fashion paper clothing and develop their own narratives around the figurines of Chizuko Miyamoto or Minoru Kamibayashi or Tokio Onitsuka or Hideki Maeda or Shoko Hisaishi that imbued them with unique personalities.

Shimada's practice was viewed as merely eccentric until the summer of 1943, when his creations began to take on an upsetting nature. Inspired one morning when he witnessed the youngest son of the Fujinami clan, a boy called Tetsuo, soil himself, then flee, sobbing, limbs flailing, through the center of the mess hall, Shimada embarked on a period of nearly a hundred miniatures locals referred to as "Weeping Pee-Pant

Boy." Though parents felt sympathetic to the distress of the Fujinamis, Butte children were ravenous to own them, and they sold widely. It incited protests by the boy's parents who claimed Shimada's dolls would only deepen their son's shame and increase Tetsuo's chances of being ridiculed at school and church.

A month later, Shimada became inspired when a rumor circulated around Butte Camp that Elsie Kashiwagi had nearly perished from the most severe manifestation of desert constipation hospital staff had ever encountered. Though he sold less than a dozen from his Elsie period, Shimada fabricated and placed over three hundred dolls upon his shelves. These bore a face squeezed with effort locals dubbed "Old Woman in Anguish," much to the displeasure of the Kashiwagis.

"You do not have to create every instant you have a compulsion," his family members complained. "Or at least do not display your compulsions in your shop! We worry for all of our reputations if you carry on in this way."

Terue Yoshihara, the block manager who oversaw the Shimada clan in Butte, paid multiple visits to the toymaker's barrack workshop. Yoshihara could not find official grounds to intervene in Shimada's production of impertinent dolls but could not ignore reports of how Shimada's dolls were sparking resentment and discontent.

"What you are doing just isn't right for morale, Yuki," Yoshihara pleaded. "If you go on in this way, I will have to suspend your access to raw materials."

Anonymous letters appeared atop Shimada's worktable that threatened to burn his workshop to its foundation. Some letters held crude portraits of Shimada, depicting him as bald, sickly, pockmarked, and as a bearer of rotting teeth. Some portraits depicted a naked Shimada, genitals undersized, or on one occasion, Shimada crying over his detached genitals, wizened over desert stones. Some envelopes bore warnings and threats.

Teach yourself to wipe your ass with both hands, one letter read, *because I am going to come into your barrack at night and chop off your carving hand.*

Another read, *We are going to stick your carving knife so far up your ass you will be holding it between your teeth.*

And another, *I'm going to carve your ass into my jack o'pumpkin.*

"These letters have a lot of your ass and carving your ass in them," Terue Yoshihara said when Shimada surrendered a stack over to him. "A lot of hostility here. You should take them seriously. I don't want to have to clean up after some carving party of your ass."

But the letters did not impede or alter the toymaker's work. The infatuations of the toymaker were buried somewhere in contradiction between the fear and the thrill of conflict. Shimada desired a life of propriety. But the dolls were his elemental desires to make concrete all his fantasies of breaking with what was respectable, sophisticated, or kind.

The straw that broke his camel, as it turned out, was Shimada's project of rendering defamed Butte Camp beauty Margaret Morri into wood. Margaret Morri was the recent bride of bodybuilder and judoka Kane Araki, and although their union appeared joyful, the birth of their first daughter, a nine-pound baby just seven months after nuptials, generated gossip that theirs had been a shotgun wedding.

Over one thousand impregnated Margaret Morri figurines were designed and intricately painted. The expression of the doll varied, but the version which provoked the severest uproar was described by locals as "Shocked and Wet Morri," the depiction of the doll's mouth agape thought to indicate the exact moment of rupture, the very second the soup of Margaret Morri's birth fluids spurted upon Gila's hot desert sand.

The pummeling of Yuki Shimada by Kane Araki took place in mid-January of 1944 in front of Butte Camp's Christ Methodist Church. Though Shimada was plainly outmatched, the fight lasted several minutes without interruption. As witnesses would describe, Kane was afforded ample time and space to beat the top half of Shimada's face into a raccoon mask and flatten his nose into a saddle. Those who had disapproved of Shimada's work previously, namely the Fujinamis and the Kashiwagis, looked on at the thrashing unsympathetically, stating that the discourteous toymaker had had every opportunity to avoid a violent punishment.

"He had been asking for it for months," Elsie Kashiwagi said and shrugged when she described the incident to Butte Camp's neighborhood police. "It was almost as though the beating gave him pleasure. Like it released him. So why deny him? He will hardly stay a week in the hospital barracks."

As far as the toymaker's tenure in Gila River, the final phase of Yuki Shimada dolls were self-portraiture. "Battered Yuki Shimadas" as referred to by locals, the dolls marked by swollen cheeks, chipped front teeth, and blue-black complexion, sold moderately well. Children were in need of a figurine they could characterize as a villain for their heroines, spirits, and princes to maim and defeat.

It was in the midwinter of 2002, thirteen years after Yuki Shimada's death, when in the modest farming town of Santa Maria, the Japanese History Museum received permission by Shimada's grandchildren to exhibit a collection of hundreds of Yuki Shimada dolls. Though Shimada would have never thought his life's work worthy of display, the curators insisted the likes of "Woman in Anguish" and "Weeping Pee-Pant Boy" and "Battered Yuki Shimada" captured the sorrows and discomforts of the Gila River relocation and internment experience.

a steady diet

Kane Araki's childhood insomnia was once so severe he did not sleep for eight days, and it happened that on the fifth day his dead grandfather, Yoshimi Araki, a consistent inhabitant of Kane's childhood dreams, pushed through the doors of the mess hall, in the flesh, sat down, and asked for a bowl of soup, pickled turnips, and rice, and before the bedlam of Yoshimi's appearance dissipated, the sixth day of Kane's insomnia ushered in low-lying stratus clouds, icy precipitation, and then the battalion of elephant seals, a thousand strong, surging through camp, those monstrous sea Gods that'd for years been an obsession of Kane's, the hulking bulls thundering into one another, black sea flesh rippling like electric current, barking through their probosces, the females blasting through mud, turning the swamped baseball diamond into nursing wallows for their pups, and before a single seal turd had been dealt with, on the seventh day the architecture of Santa Maria began its emergence, the transplanted landscape of Kane's dreams, pharmacies, schools, mortuaries, feed stores, theaters, apartment complexes, butcher shops, department stores, bars, diners ruptured from the desert, claiming their positions between barracks, behind the canteen, rising up beside the patrol towers, so that on the eighth morning the decision was made for military police to investigate, intervene, six men raiding the Araki barrack, knocking past his family members, subduing Kane, feeding a rubber hose past his throat, funneling into him a milk-thick sedation.

It was during Kane's dreamless sleep that Yoshimi vanished. The parade of elephant seals puckered and dissolved. The clouds burned into invisibility. The ghost edifice of Santa Maria crumbled and fell back into the Arizona dust. From that day, Kane was administered a steady diet of barbiturates, and within months of his tenth birthday he was showing severe signs of retrograde amnesia. On the day his mother held his train ticket to leave Gila River, he no longer recalled Yoshimi Araki, his fascination with Californian elephant seals, or any particular storefront of the home city he'd left three years previous.

kidneywood blossom,
groundcherry husk

Shoko Hisaishi was resident epidemiologist in Butte Camp between the years of 1942 to 1945. In that period, he wrote on twelve incidences in which Arizona deer mice urinated into the eyes, nostrils, and mouths of sleeping detainees. In each of these cases, detainees showed recurring bouts of hysteria. He referred to the condition as "rat pee bliss," because amidst an episode, detainees stripped their garments, writhed upon the floor, and groaned as though experiencing climax. Episodes could last anywhere from a few minutes to an hour and could result in a sore throat and dehydration.

In 1943, Hisaishi wrote on a Gila River colony of western bonneted bats whose echolocationary cries, though largely inaudible to detainees, appeared to cause similar fits of madness and sexual excitement. Detainees who encountered the bats overhead or perched in trees outside their windows were overcome with the urge to strip, writhe, and groan. Hisaishi labeled the condition "great bonnet rapture" and recommended Butte canteens stockpile calamine lotion to treat detainees rolling around on hot sand and cough syrup to treat those exhausted from hours of animal moaning and gurgling.

But it was the series of articles penned for the *Gila News-Courier* on the observed effects of the Sonoran shadow-damsel that Hisaishi described the most dramatic Cupidian symptoms he ever witnessed. The Sonoran shadow-damsel, also called "the blue shadow" by locals, was a species of damselfly possessing black-yellow eyes and an immense synthorax the color of lapis. Bred out of the southern dike slicing through the Gila River Indian Reservation, it was the largest damselfly in Arizona, endowed with a wingspan up to eight inches and a body length of nearly six inches.

Hisaishi's articles noted unusual behaviors by the blue shadow. The shadow swarmed in the thousands. Even more peculiar, they swarmed in the evenings. The blue shadow was attracted to young people, especially teenagers, and if granted contact, was shown to practice aggressive, pseudo-mating contortions. Hisaishi provided a few crude figures alongside his descriptions. If a blue shadow was permitted to perch upon the face, it would clasp the rim of the young person's nostril and thrust the base of its abdomen into the nasal cavity. This established a sort of "half-heart position" between the damsel body and the lateral lobe of the nose, a position that allowed shadow-damsel to stare directly into the eye of a person, disorienting or perhaps hypnotizing the young man or woman, while simultaneously thrusting wildly the terminal segments of its abdomen into the nostril. Hisaishi called this behavior "painting," because teens who allowed these actions reported a strange smell, somewhat like the fumes off fresh paint. For this, Hisaishi recommended sufferers hang their heads over a bowl filled with lemon wedges and salt until the odor dissipated.

But it was the symptoms that developed over the twenty-four hours following "painting" that unnerved Butte Camp residents and bewildered Hisaishi. The manifestations differed somewhat, depending upon the gender of the detainee. Within two hours of encountering a blue shadow, a male teenager completely lost his ability to speak. It was not a dysfunction of lungs, throat, or mouth. A detainee was able to moan. He was still able to mimic the tone and rhythm of speech patterns. But genuine language eluded him, and his communication, if forced, emerged shaky and garbled. This stunned most young men into silence. And within six to eight hours, he was running an intense fever. He tore from his clothes, shedding coat, shirt, pants, and briefs behind him like a creature casting aside the fibrous hull of its cocoon. And then he began staggering through the grounds of Butte Camp in a sweaty, speechless stupor.

It was Hisaishi's notion that detainees who had come into intimate contact with the blue shadow were locked in a primeval state of being. It was a state on the far side of inhibition and propriety. Female detainees held onto few fossils of their language. As observed by Hisaishi, a young woman directed her male counterpart to "Lie back" and to "Look at me sexy" and to "Put this belt in your mouth" and to move "There, behind those bushes." Rather than stumbling naked around open streets, young girls hid in the alleys between barracks, behind trash bins, and in the branches of white mulberry trees, stalking their potential mates.

If a young woman caught hold of her man, he was straddled and ridden upon the dust or the pile of leaves until all the muscles of her lower body were spent, until her calves were strained tight as wads of rubber bands, pelvic muscles tender as a marshmallow dipped into fire, until a human broth of saliva and sweat and sex covered them, until young woman's groans lodged like a red pepper in her throat, and the young man's balls spat only tonic water. And then both partners were overtaken by a deep, amnestic slumber.

Shoko Hisaishi's office occupied the southwestern corner of the Butte hospital barracks, and he was afforded generous access to patients of what he called "the blue shadow euphoria." As a high percentage of young couples conceived while in their euphoric state, Hisaishi was keen to monitor this next generation of detainees, and he published his observations with the *Courier*. Though couples worried they would be delivering abominations into camp—infants with immense gossamer wings, children bearing the bulbous heads of damselflies—these fears never came to fruition. Their babies looked and behaved in good health. Hisaishi noted that infants conceived in a euphoric state attracted damselflies, who would perch upon their ears. These babies showed decreased rates of infection, fever, colds, and allergies.

Hisaishi and his colleagues raised many conjectures about the purposes of the Cupidian insect. Perhaps a surge in the

Sonoran shadow-damsel population was intended to stimulate copulation in other desert animals. Had the blue shadows somehow been thrown adrift? Had Butte Camp introduced a novel smell or landmark or magnetic field that was shifting their navigation? Had something evolved in their internal compasses? A contingent of detained ornithologists observed a decrease in the populations of bird species indigenous to Gila River. The numbers on gnatcatchers, wagtails, grosbeaks, thrushes, finches, warblers, sparrows, and jays were diminishing. These were odd circumstances indeed since the birds feasted on damselflies.

A meeting of the odonatologists, hemipterologists, and lepidopterologists in Butte Camp theorized the marriage of the blue shadow and detained teenager might indicate an additional phase in the development of the insect. Could detainee be surrogate for shadow-damsel? Could blue shadow pass its genes through the nose of detainee? Through nose and into blood and human genitalia and, by euphoric copulation, pass into newborn infant? And if they were witnessing a new stage in the hemimetabolism of the insect, if they were witnessing a replacement of the nymph stage, what would the next stage in development look like? Patients of blue shadow euphoria did not exhibit lasting effects. But what of the shadow-damsel was growing in the veins of the next generation in Butte Camp?

The Reverend Jun Shozaburo, detained former minister of the Venice Methodist Church, believed the episodes were trials of God. Was relocation not a test of a person's compassion and temperance? Were these rows of barracks not a test to a person's patience and cooperation? Were these manias not a test of their primordial desires? If detainees behaved as beasts they would exist in the purgatory of beasts. Would their devil always appear as an ignoble reptile? Or might he attempt to fool them by appearing in the form of a lovely, diaphanous damsel? They could not afford to be so easily deceived.

Shozaburo organized a neighborhood watch of Methodist women and men who carried lanterns and switches torn from palo verde trees, manzanita shrubs, and Arizona alders. The Shozaburo Watch stalked through Butte Camp after sundown, looking into barrack windows and through alleyways and in open fields, whacking teenagers whom they observed mid-copulation. Mosquito nets were ordered and disseminated. Slowly the population of the blue shadows lessened in Butte Camp. The number of teenagers who were chased off with a switch striking their naked backside was squeezed to five or six in an evening.

The blue shadow was linked to just a single fatality amid all the reported incidences of euphoria. This occurred in October of 1944, and it involved Butte Camp's eldest detainee, a man of ninety, called Yoshikane Araki. Kane had fallen asleep one afternoon on a beach blanket beside his wife, Margaret Morri, upon a little hill shaded by a copse of small, flowering kidneywood trees. In her interview with Hisaishi, Margaret Morri reported her last sensations before nodding off. She remembered hearing the hum of insect wings in the boughs above her and a handful of dislodged kidneywood blossoms falling upon her cheek.

When Margaret Morri awakened from her nap, she discovered Kane's sleeping body swarmed by thousands of blue shadows. The sight and the noise of it nearly made her faint. It was the outline of her dear husband's body, but every inch of him was covered with motion, the twitching of wings, the flashing of compound eyes, the quivering of blue and black striped abdomens. Margaret Morri swiped at the insects, but she could not rouse her husband. She brushed away what she could, covered Kane with the beach blanket, and hurried to the block manager for help.

Kane was treated at Butte's hospital barracks, but medical staff found few ways to intervene beyond rehydration and cold compresses. He was revived and returned home within a week. Following the incident, Kane sometimes complained of headaches, back pain, and nausea. If scraped, he bled continuously like a poisoned rat. The slightest bump would produce a bruise like a black bloom upon his limbs. Within two weeks of the swarming incident, it seemed Kane's skin had grown thin as the papery husk of groundcherries. Kane also described a persistent hum that sometimes would startle him awake in the night.

"Do you hear it?" he would ask.

"What do you hear?" Margaret Morri would ask.

"It's the song again. Someone is singing that song for children."

"I can't hear anything."

"It's a lullaby. I think it must be parents putting their child to bed. *The damselfly and the dragonfly—they're drunk on sweat and mulberry wine.* You really can't hear? There's more than one person singing it."

"It can't be neighbors. There are hardly any children in this block."

"They sing it over and over. Why don't they rest? At some point a lullaby wakes a child rather than putting him to sleep."

"I can't hear. Your ears must be better than mine. Does a dragonfly really drink a person's sweat?"

"You should have let them devour me," Kane would say.

"Who are you referring to?" Margaret Morri would ask.

"You know who I mean. It would not have been the worst way to go."

"They were never biting you. They were only looking for a place to perch. They probably just thought you were a log or something. Maybe your aftershave attracted them."

"I know what I felt. I could have shooed them when they first landed, but then I thought, maybe they understand this life better than me. Why would I be the one to know when it's time? How would I know?"

"Don't talk like that. I need you to keep me company in this place. I need you to protect me this far from home."

"I'm not leaving you. I'm only becoming the next thing who loves you."

"Don't talk in that way. I need you to keep this thing that loves me. I need you to be my husband."

"There is no husband. Husband is only a suit I tried on once. But there is together. There is no taking that off."

In the last week of October 1944, the Araki-Morri children and grandchildren gathered near Kane and Margaret's barrack to celebrate the birthday of their youngest grandson.

Amidst the celebration, Kane rose from his chair and asked Margaret, "Do you hear the song now?"

"I can't hear it," Margaret Morri said.

"It's close," Kane said. *"The dragonfly and the damselfly— they're drunk on milkwood and turpentine."*

"Come have a glass of cold tea," Margaret Morri said.

"I don't want you to worry," Kane said. "You take it off when you need to take it off."

And then Kane walked out the door of their family barrack, down its steps, and collapsed into the hot desert sand. As his body smashed into the ground, his skin seemed to burst and cover everything in a second blanket of sand. A second sand that was a dark crimson. Witnesses reported that it was like watching a gunnysack of fine confetti cast over the earth. For an instant, the shape of a man, the next moment tumbling through a succession of brief phantoms.

And then ten thousand Sonoran shadow-damsels clambered from what was left of Kane Araki's body and grappled the heavens on red wings. As the damsels took the air, the sun struck the plates and hemolymph of their wings, and for a heartbeat, turned the sky into a flurry of pink light.

a transcription

In the records of the Reverend Kashi Uchihama, it is written that Margaret Morri and Yoshikane Araki were married on September 20, 1943 in Canal Camp at the Gila River Methodist Chapel. Although they had not discussed the matter with her explicitly, Uchihama's notes suggest suspicion she was conducting the Araki-Morri ceremony in secret. The ceremony was held at dusk on a Monday evening, and not a single Araki or Morri family member was in attendance. Teenage friends of the couple, Mary Moriguchi and Pete Yamamoto, served as witnesses.

Before taking their vows, the couple asked if they could read a few words they had prepared for each other. As Moriguchi and Yamamoto drew nearer, Kane explained that their statements would actually only be for Margaret and himself.

They would whisper their first set of vows, their shadow-vows, lips pressed into the pink coral of each other's ears and then take their traditional vows aloud.

The couple seized every opportunity for secrecy, it read in Uchihama's notes.

The couple did not know Kashi Uchihama had been born with ears sensitive and discerning as any who lived. The couple knew little of Uchihama at the time. She had been chosen to perform the service because she was young, because the couple had rightly assumed her services would be cheap, and also she and Margaret had participated in the same bowling league in Santa Maria. But the Uchihama siblings, six sisters and three brothers, claimed Kashi could hear the flight of a wax moth diving toward the candle on her writing desk, so that she would extinguish the candle a second before the moth arrived for immolation, still some of its dust striking the ghost-heat of the flame and flaring into a small plume of mothgold.

Uchihama was therefore able to hear and later transcribe much of what Margaret and Kane shared with each other. What Kane whispered had been unwritten and brief.

"I want us to live happily," he whispered. "I want to take care of you. We will have three children. When I die, they will take care of you."

Margaret's statement had been neatly written upon ruled paper and then folded to resemble a pointed frog. Her fingers shook nervously as she disassembled the crisp, white frog and read into Kane's ear.

Her words were, "My love for you is actually all about death. Or it may be division. Because we say this part of us outlives the rest. It is my way of saying this thing will kill us. It is my way of saying somewhere in the field ahead, I see myself already dead. And in the greater distance still, where there are no such things as possessions, whatever molecules fall upon the distance, I will love you with whatever I call myself then. With all my strange and unknowable hands."

At the end of their ceremony, Kane and Margaret paid Uchihama from a shared coin purse and never again returned to her church.

Not even for a Christmas service, it read in Uchihama's notes. *Not even after the birth of their first daughter.*

Kane Araki was killed in an accident at a dehydration plant just months after leaving Canal Camp. After his death, Margaret Morri relocated from Chicago to Detroit, and eventually back to California. It was there she remarried and had two more daughters.

It was decades later, after the death of Margaret's second husband, as Kashi Uchihama was walking home from the service, that she wondered if she had somehow cursed that first couple when she intercepted the private message between them.

Should I have excused myself? she wrote. *Should I have covered my ears? Should I have forced a competing thought through my mind? Should I have made myself forget? What did I change when I pressed their secrets upon my paper?*

a wig

Margaret Morri lay in a quickly darkening field of silverleaf tomato weed and Arizona creosote poppies. She had plucked one of the hard, yellow nightshade tomatoes and was pressing it like an unfurled rosebud to the end of her nose. Beside her Kenji Hirayama lay, half-asleep, half-expired cigarette riding his bottom lip. Vaguely attempting to adjust his cheap, shag wig. With the exception of the wig, Ken was naked, though the low-hanging smoke seemed fitted to his body as though a white tuxedo. Margaret brushed at her arms, calves, dust that'd caked along with her sweat, reached across Ken's body, picked her blouse up from off the sand, and began buttoning it.

"Tonight I'm going over the southern wires, Margaret," Ken said. "I'm going over the southern wires and into Casa Grande."

"There are four guards securing the southern wires," Margaret said. "Four guards, four rifles. You're asking to get yourself shot."

"Tonight there will be only two guards posted," Ken said. "Two guards and I'm friendly with them both. There's Clarence and there's Gerry something. Or maybe it's Bernard. Clarence and Bernard. Anyhow, they're both alright."

"Alright meaning they speak to you from the other side of the wires. They smoke your cigarettes and tell you which of us they'd like to screw. Tell you how when they're in their towers they can look down their rifles and into our rooms while we're changing into nightgowns."

"I mean it that they hate their jobs and hate Gila River the same as us. And they understand they're part of a problem but don't have any power to change it."

From the petal of a nearby creosote blossom, a tick the width of a fingernail tumbled belly-up onto Margaret's beach towel. She held it down using the last of her burning cigarette.

"Then letting you cross at the southern wires when they can be reported is unlikely," Margaret said. "If they say they're men without power, that's saying they're a link in the power of another man who doesn't believe in being lenient with Japs."

"I'm going over those wires, Margaret," Ken said. "There's a diner in Casa Grande. It has a counter that sells cigarettes and whiskey. I'm going to bring it all back and sell it. People want to have parties again. People want to listen to music and dance and get tanked. I can help them do that, and I can make money."

"What good is your money?" Margaret asked. "If we never make it out of Gila River, there's nothing to own. You want to buy your own barrack from them?"

"We aren't going to die in Gila River," Ken said. "The war will end. We'll go home together. We'll need money to start again. I want to begin in the right way."

"Stay here tonight," Margaret said. "Be with me. Go to Casa Grande next month."

"No," Ken said. "It's tonight. I'm going tonight. And if I come back, if I can make us a lot of money this way, I want you to consider having a baby with me. It's been a year. We don't have to wait until we're back in California to start a family. There are good doctors and a decent hospital here."

Margaret stared hard into Ken. She was dressed now, an unlit cigarette bucked upon her lips. She struck a match and drew it to her face. The tobacco crawled in the fire. A white moth of smoke climbed into the air.

"Stay here tonight," she said. "I want you to be with me. Go to Casa Grande next month."

"I'm not staying," Ken said. He flicked at a spot on his chest, a dark circle he thought was a biting insect. But it was only a small, raised mole.

"You don't remember," she said. "You don't remember what to say next."

"I remember," Ken said. He ground his cigarette into the hot sand and struck up another.

"You remember," she said. "Only you won't say."

"That's right," he said.

"What you say," Margaret began, "what your line is,

is 'Margaret, I'll stay if once we leave Gila, you have three daughters. Three daughters just like you.'"

"It isn't right to say that, Margaret," Ken said. "I'm writing my own lines now."

"You aren't allowed to write your own lines. I've explained this to you before. You say what I've given you, or you have to go. That's all there is."

"I know that isn't true," Ken said. "It's been nearly a year. I know you can get past this. I know there's a way for you to start again."

"I'll stay with you, Margaret," she said. "I'll stay if you promise you'll have my daughters. Three daughters like you."

"That isn't what happened," Ken said. "I'm sorry, but your husband didn't stay. He never promised you he would. He left over the southern wires. He didn't come back to camp alive."

"Not in this version," Margaret said. "In this version, he stays. And I promise to give him three daughters."

"There aren't any Goddamn daughters! You aren't a mother yet, Margaret. Don't act like this!"

Ken removed his wig and threw it into the dirt. Beneath the wig, Ken was nearly bald. What hair remained looked green and dismal in the remaining light. He wiped the sweat from his scalp and flicked it. The nearby rocks darkened with his sweat.

"If I wasn't clear with you, then I apologize," Margaret said. "What all this is about—we aren't ever going to be together. You play a role. If you don't play it, it has to stop."

"I know this isn't the first time you've done this," Ken said. "You think it's a secret what you do? I've heard this before from

121

Jack Shinoda. He told me there were others before him. Men you made wear this wig and Kane's old clothes. And made them say the same Goddamn crazy things."

"You're right about everything, Ken," she said. "It's just the role that's irreplaceable, not the actor."

Margaret picked the wig from off the ground and shook the hot, golden debris from it. She held it out to Ken.

"You're good at playing Kane," she said. "You don't look like him. You're a little small. And you have a small, sad face. But you're kind like him. You can go on if you like."

"No, Margaret," he said. "You know Kane is gone."

Ken reached out for his clothes and began to dress.

"I'm going over the wires tonight," he said.

Margaret wasn't looking at him anymore. She was combing her fingers through the wig as though in search of something.

"Why would you do that?" she asked.

"Because Kane was right. There's good money in it if I come back. People are desperate to feel different. They're drinking wine made from sugar water and raisins. They're drinking vanilla extract. They'll pay three or four times what a bottle of whiskey is worth."

"And what'll you spend your money on? Is it money for chewing gum in the canteen? Money to rot like leaves beneath your mattress? It's as valueless today as it was two years ago."

Margaret set down the wig beside her. A brief current took it for a moment and it rolled once, covering itself in a fine golden dust.

"More people are leaving Gila," he said. "I have family in Detroit and Colorado. I'm going to Detroit in a month, and

I'm staying until they open the coast to us again. You can come with me."

"That won't ever happen, Ken," Margaret said.

Ken was dressed now. He was back in his own clothes. Kane's clothes lay in a folded pile beside the wig.

"The same tower guard patrols the south," Margaret said. "He carries the same rifle."

"I've talked to him about it," Ken said. "He's taken some money as a security. He understands I'm going and coming back."

"You can't count on him for anything."

"I'm not afraid."

"How do you plan to find your way in the desert?"

"I have a light. I'll follow the road."

"You should let him keep your money," Margaret said. "And you should go to Detroit next month."

The sun had fallen and steeped the sky in red. A scorpion shuffled out from a tent of bark and slipped into the crown of Kane's wig.

"This is your chance," Ken said. "I'm afraid for you, Margaret. Your obsession with this unattainable thing. This ghost. If you keep doing this to yourself, I'm afraid of what you will become."

"You don't understand what you're talking about," Margaret said. "When you've been loved so badly by someone who dies, you already live between this place and the world over. That is who the ghost is. She is the one who can't leave."

Margaret folded Kane's clothes and tucked them beneath her arm. Then she walked out of the silverleaf tomato weed, the Arizona creosote poppies, and back toward the southern barracks of Butte Camp.

over the fence and into the desert

Kane Araki saved few pictures of himself from his years in camp. But he had been the subject of a series of portraits by the Hawaiian-Okinawan painter Eve Shimabukuro. It came as no surprise an artist of her proficiency would've wanted to immortalize Kane in top form. He had been a bodybuilding champion two years prior as part of a community-building event at Tulare's assembly center.

Eve's paintings developed over a series of months during which the color of Kane's swim trunks dwindled from robust green to a shucked, moth-eaten yellow. And the muscles in his upper body grew massive and terrifying. Eve asked him to stop the incessant lifting for a few weeks. She likened him to a child who outgrew his slacks the morning after being fitted for them. He was ruining the integrity of her portraits. A dozen times she

125

claimed the canvas upon which she'd been working needed to be made anew. She also did not like it when people dropped in at the recreation barrack to see her work and commented she must be exaggerating, perversely, the size of Yoshikane's desert-burnished pectorals. Likely, some said, because the two were sweet on each other.

When Kane heard this last part he was appalled. He'd engaged in their collaboration because he'd thought any romance between them would be seen as impossible. Eve was an emerging spinster. Eve was squat, rotund. Eve was not pretty and did not wear makeup. She never even attempted to conceal the effects of a grisly oven accident she'd had as a child. A leash of bark-colored scars ran alongside her bare arms and thighs. He'd thought all this would be an opportunity to make him appear tolerant and sensitive, since he'd once been told that girls became more attracted to men who showed affection to beastly women. Now he found he was being insulted behind his back.

Kane immediately took up with a pretty girl called Margaret Morri and stopped spending so much time posing shirtless beside barbed wire. He took to openly mocking Eve among his friends and family. After the Methodist service, he went out of his way to avoid Eve's parents. And his mornings and evenings retreated into a furious exercise regimen so that every vein gripping his chest became frantic and swollen. He also began denouncing Eve's war art as pointless since the people of his generation would never want to be reminded of these years.

Still, Kane was convinced he deserved to see a finished portrait. He had wasted so much time with Eve's nonsense already it only made sense to see it through to completion. And so he continued to succumb to Eve's requests. Making the slow, stifling trek past the mess hall, the chapel, the tracts of scorpion-infested barracks. Carrying her stool and easel for her toward the watchtower. Then stripping down to nothing more than sandals and his dust-colored shorts.

On their last afternoon together, Kane asked if Eve had never thought about finding a husband. She was too old to produce her own children, of course. But Eve's younger sister had two sons. She could help raise them or adopt one or two of her own. He commented Eve might look more approachable if she started wearing a tiny bit of makeup. He went so far as to suggest his own girlfriend might provide her cosmetic supplies and instruction.

"But I have a husband," she told him. "And a stepson."

Kane was astonished he'd never heard this before. Where was her husband? Her son? Why had he never seen or heard of them?

"They're living outside camp," Eve said. "Still in Los Angeles. Venice."

When they finished painting that afternoon, Eve told Kane his company was no longer required for her to finish the piece. She would let him know when it was finished and he could stop by her family's barrack and have a look.

When Kane asked if he could see what she had made presently, she hesitated. But after a moment she shrugged, rotating the canvas in her hands for him to see. To Kane's horror he saw the subject in her painting was headless. The neck terminating into brown gnarls like an upended tree. What could this mean? Was she mocking him? Anger shot through him as though a chill. He began shaking, sputtering. He raised her easel and cast it over the fence and into the desert. Then he stomped away hurt and confused.

It was not until he was in his nineties that Kane saw Eve's painting again. By then her project had expanded to over a thousand iterations. A thousand hulking Kane Arakis testing the resolve of the barbed wire or climbing the rotted planks of a watchtower. Kane lying upon a deposit of scalding rocks. Kane pricking himself, his blood merging into the syrup of a desert pear. A vast exhibition of Evelyn Shimabukuro pieces inhabited the walls of the Japanese-American museum in Los Angeles where Kane padded through on his walker, unable to recognize his prior body. Nor would he acknowledge the resemblances between the artist's photograph and his own wife.

"She looks just like her," Corinne Araki said, touching the plaque that held Evelyn's wide, impassive face. "They're the exact same build even. I don't understand why you don't see it."

"How do you know my wife?" Kane asked. "She's been gone a long time. Were you one of her students?"

"I was her daughter," Corinne said.

"Oh," Kane said. "I thought you were the curator."

Sweetly he took her hand and apologized for not recognizing her.

river thistles, celestial sage,
rosy opuntia pears

It was public knowledge in Butte Camp that Kane Uchihama-Araki, son of the distinguished clay sculptress, Kashi Uchihama, and the Guadalupe shark fisherman, Yoshio Araki, at the delicate age of nineteen, had propositioned six other girls with marriage before meeting the *Gila News-Courier's* beautiful young typist, Margaret Aiko Morri.

The names of the six women before Margaret were Rie Hyosaka, Chiyo Kunishige, Hackey Sugai, Shiori Kawafuchi, Nobuko Funatsu, and Tomiye Moriguchi. These women were accomplished musicians, cooks, athletes, painters, and scholars. But none before Margaret was particularly known for her physical attractiveness. Rie Hyosaka had been bullied as a young girl as the result of bulging eyes and broad-rimmed glasses. Nobuko Funatsu's face was pulled wide and taut as by invisible fingers. And the complexion of Hackey Sugai's skin was closer to green-yellow than a milky white. Margaret was aware of Kane's infatuations with these plain girls, but she took it as a sign his love was for competence and disposition more than worldly beauty or reputation.

Upon her acceptance, Kane explained to Margaret the stipulation that he would not be able to consummate their union until after the war was finished and the two could return home to the Central Coast of California. Kane said it was family lore the children of the Uchihama bloodline could only be born within proximity of a large body of water. To be birthed, or even conceived, in the Arizona desert would spell disaster for their daughter or son. Kane's twin uncles, Kasey and Indian George Uchihama, were rumored to have emerged cursed at birth with webbed toes, added eyelids, and salamander-ish tails because Obaachan Uchihama had gone into labor with them while traveling through a particularly dusty and uninhabitable portion of Bakersfield.

This was the reason why none of Kane's brothers would have children with their wives in camp. It was why none of his sisters were accepting suitors. It was why even at his parents' advanced age of forty-six and forty-seven, Yoshio Araki had sequestered himself in a barrack on the furthest reaches of Canal Camp. And it was why none before Margaret had ever thoroughly considered his proposal.

Margaret Morri agreed to the terms of their marriage because she thought Kane handsome and devout and honest. Before him she had known only selfish and cruel men. Her former boyfriend had been the seductive and infamous Kingo

Kadota. It was said Kadota had even the ability to woo female dolphins with the reverberation of his voice and that local beaches could become strewn with green dolphins who had been convinced to throw themselves upon the shore. It was also said Kadota persuaded Sister Nami Nadoka to skim from her church's collection box and, in a two-year period of clandestine meetings, surrender her flesh to him over and over. It was said Kadota poached the salaries of his lovers and turned every cent of them over at the blackjack tables. Kingo, his neighbors said, would rest alone only if wearing his high school football helmet and athletic cup, because so many of his prior lovers returned to pummel him in his sleep. Margaret did not believe all the rumors, but she had surrendered five or six month's salary over to Kingo. This had been her life in Boyle Heights when Margaret was a teenager, persevering through an almost deliberate naivety. She believed she had matured considerably after finishing school and relocation and that Kane's small addendum to their marriage was no comparison to the complications of the men in her past. The pair was married in Butte's Methodist church by Margaret's father, the Reverend Isaburo Morri, and a humble reception with fruit punch and yellowcake was planned in a recreation barrack.

Margaret did not expect it would be a strain to share Kane's bed while they abstained from lovemaking. After all, into her twenties, how many nights had she slept without a partner beside her? How often had she lamented sharing the awkward sexual routines of young men? Kane's mouth would be too hungry and graceless. His hands uncoordinated in unfastening buttons, unclasping or untying nightgowns.

Kane himself appeared to have little trouble with the arrangement. In their private barrack, he proved to be a gentle and attentive and undemanding husband. Every week Kane bought Margaret a present. A new record or art supplies or a box of something sweet. Outside of their bedroom he was more affectionate than other married men. He held her hand and kissed it publicly. If she needed to walk across camp to her family's barrack, he accompanied her. And on some evenings he did not even bother to kiss her before closing his eyes and departing into a language of unconscious smacking and throat-clearings and snores. Through the silence and darkness of the night, Margaret ached with her lust for Kane. Margaret came into the sense that her skin was becoming new again. It was as if nothing of her had ever been touched, and when any small fragment of her skin brushed against Kane's legs, or if she felt the warmth of his breath against her, she was shocked and embarrassed by the pleasure it gave her. Margaret thought this was what it must be to unreservedly love a person. If she had not been a newlywed, she would've thought she was dying.

During the daylight hours, Margaret did all she could to avoid thinking of sex with her husband. She worked the maximum shifts the *Courier* would allow. If she thought of sex while at work, she clamped and squeezed the skin of her arm until her eyes watered. After work, she filled a bucket with cold water and dunked her face into it. To keep from inhaling Kane's alluring musk, she feigned sniffles and every evening wore a thick mustache of Vicks VapoRub. She stocked up on foods and spices thought to be anti-aphrodisiacs. Dried figs and radishes and pinquito beans. Marjoram and hot peppers. But ultimately the scrotal quality of the figs came to arouse her. And radishes only came to provoke her desire to tear the shirt from Kane's chest and bite hard into one of his ripe nipples. To have him bite down on her. To claw at each other like starving moles in their palaces of dirt, their kingdoms of starchy root vegetables.

In the dead of night, Margaret made clandestine trips to the women's latrine in order to masturbate. In the first weeks of her marriage, she felt shocked by the number of other Butte internees whose masturbating she seemed to interrupt. The noises were unmistakable. A labored breathing. An urgent, animal gurgle. And then as her steps could be heard approaching, ten or even twenty minutes of silence. Then a cough and a resounding flush. There were also nights another woman's footsteps or grunts in a nearby partition disturbed Margaret's activities. She never saw the faces of any of these women but felt in a perpetual competition with them to be last to leave her partition. She wondered, was there no woman in Butte touching herself during the day? Or in the privacy of her own barrack? Eventually any frustrations or insecurities fell away. She could not help but continue her visitations. Her libido was so insistent, she worried by not alleviating herself it could do some injury. She was no doctor. What would be the effect of all this internal fire? Was it ruining her chances for orgasm or for childbirth at a later date?

It was in the first few months of marriage that Margaret began experiencing intense and disturbing sexual dreams. Once or twice she dreamed of knocking Kane upside the head, or smothering him with a pillow, in order to make love to his unconscious body. In another, she saw herself attacking Kane when she discovered him lying naked with another woman. Margaret ended up strangling both Kane and this stranger, and then later, inexplicably, making love to them as well.

In her most recurrent dream, she and Kane were moved back to California and in a dark, foreign room, were making love for the first time. Margaret had pinned Kane to a dirty and unfamiliar mattress and was riding him violently. The bed's iron frame slid upon the floor and rattled against the wall. The box spring huffed with years of dust and neglect and a mist of it rose around them. And then Margaret looked down at Kane's body and saw that his skin was running thick with pulsing veins. The color and texture of his flesh had gone gray and leathery. A collar of white fur encircled his neck. Margaret looked down into the wet black of Kane's upturned snout and understood she had been making love to an enormous bat.

The instant she recognized it, Kane's moans shed all their human qualities and became high-pitched squeals. He spoke to her from a shrill, unworldly voice.

"I need you to help me lay my eggs," Kane said. "It is time for my eggs to find the fire of another body."

"But bats do not lay eggs," Margaret said. "You are no bird."

"Do not tell me what I am," Kane shrieked.

And then he rose from under her. He rose off the bed and hovered above her. And his wings tore gashes into the moonlit walls.

"You're ruining the walls," Margaret said. "You are ruining our home."

"You think I care about this false house?" Kane asked. "My home is where I drag the next body. My walls are the darkness."

Though the dreams horrified her, she was embarrassed to admit they also titillated her. Even the dream in which Kane metamorphosed she awoke feeling slightly damp. And because she felt scared and ashamed, she did not feel comfortable seeking help from a doctor or relative. In the Butte Camp library, she located the anthologies of southwestern magic and medicines and practiced their remedies of lemon balm, valerian drawn from stony soils, and dried leaves of the passionflower. But Margaret did not put much faith in oils, teas, and powders. Her conviction was that any madness would curb if she and Kane could make love. A dozen nights, she broke down and asked Kane if it would be serious betrayal to break their chastity on a single occasion. What about her birthday? On their anniversary? She wanted to honor his family's beliefs. But what if the war did not end during their lifetime? Was it not unnatural for wife and husband to share their bed and never touch or see each other? Never behold each other's naked bodies? Was the glorious condition of these private areas not going to waste? Margaret had been assiduously monitoring her cycles. They could choose a night when their risk of pregnancy was extremely low.

But Kane never faltered.

"I need your help and your trust," he said. "This camp will not see the end of us. This camp will not even see our third anniversary. I need you to have faith in our promise and in our future."

The agony went on for two years. When finally the war ended, Kane and Margaret collected twenty-five dollars each in recompense, packed all of their belongings into one duffel and one suitcase, purchased a loaf of bread, a jar of peanut butter, honey, dried fruit, and chocolate bars from the Butte canteen, and pinned the train tickets for California to their front door. Margaret had also gathered carrots and sweet potatoes from the Butte gardens for the journey. And plucked from the Opus cacti lining the barbed wire fence, Margaret carried a sack brimming with rosy prickly pears.

Over the four-day train ride, Margaret spent most of those hours imagining the first California night in bed with Kane, as she cautiously removed the barbed glochids from the prickly pears, carving the fruit in two, and slurping the delicate innards beside her husband. Luckily her in-laws had decided to travel first to Chicago and Detroit before returning to the West Coast. Temporarily, Kane and Margaret could claim any of the Uchihama properties for themselves.

The Uchihama home Kane selected for them was drafty, and there were pigeons nesting in every imperfection of its roof. Moss or insects governed every corner. There were wooden boards to be pried from its windows. Sheets hung over all the furniture. Moths had devoured the sweaters hanging in the closets. And on their first evening back under California sky, Kane disappointed Margaret when he said it would be their final time sleeping together without the possibility of lovemaking. He explained the first night beside the Santa Maria River afforded newlyweds the potential for Uchihama magic.

"It is family lore that while we are chaste we have an opportunity to become wealthy," Kane said to Margaret. "Tonight, remove all the hair from your head. We will take your hair and bury it beside the river. In the morning, when we uncover the spot of your buried mane, every curl, every strand will have transformed into a fragment of gold. Then we will have a fortune to begin our lives here."

"Your family has many legends and practices," Margaret said. "I am happy to respect them all. But I don't want to wait any longer. I don't care about the money. I would trade it for one more night to love you."

"We will have tens of thousands of those," Kane promised her. "Just be patient one more night. There is a reason why the Uchihamas all owned their homes and farmland before the war."

"But if I cut all my hair I will be hideous!" Margaret exclaimed. "You won't want to look at me for months afterward."

"You will still be a beautiful woman without hair," Kane assured her. "Don't say ridiculous things. I will love you even after time steals both our hair. I will love you when time steals both our bodies even."

That night Margaret did as Kane instructed. Standing in the middle of white bed linens, she cut all the hair from her head. Then Kane held a mirror for her while she used his straight razor to shave all that was fine and remaining. She only nicked herself once, and Kane kissed the tiny pink bloom until it stopped bleeding.

"You have a fair, beautiful head," Kane said to her. "I will watch it every night like another moon."

The couple gathered all of Margaret's hair in the sheet and carried it down to the riverbank. In a remote clearing, they covered it over with riverweeds, the periwinkle blossoms of celestial sage and mud. Returning home, passion did not overwhelm Margaret. Instead the fatigue of their journey struck her, and when she lay down beside Kane, she was whisked away to sleep.

When Margaret awoke in the early light, her husband was nowhere to be found. She called to him and searched the entire property. No note had been left for her. Even the smell of him was absent. The air and dust of the rooms felt still, as though no one had been moving through them for several hours.

Margaret walked down to the Santa Maria riverbank to the clearing and found the area where they had buried her hair. Long before she reached the scene she knew she would find it disturbed. There was no fortune to be uncovered. Kane's pants and shirt lay strewn on the shore. And radiating pleasure in the sun, there sat an enormous gray frog covered in her hair.

"Ten thousand lies," Margaret said. "Ten thousand lies you covered me in."

"I'm sorry, Margaret," Kane's voice emerged from the frog's mouth. "I'm terribly sorry. Your devotion and your hair were the only magic back to my body."

"It was all a mask," Margaret said. "You were never my husband."

"No," Kane said. "Yes. You're right. Never. Thank Jesus. No offense."

Kane jiggled a little, clearing some of Margaret's hair away from his face and mouth.

"In my position I had to ignore the costs," he said.

"They weren't your costs," Margaret said.

"You think I'm evil," Kane said. "Because I did this to leave a human body behind. It must be shocking to you."

"I don't think you're evil," Margaret said. "You are a cold sore. Like so many men are predictably and unapologetically cold sores."

"Call me whatever you like," Kane said. "If it helps you manage the shock, I encourage it. It's just you don't understand what it is to be cursed. I am a deceitful frog. You've earned the right to tell that story. But my children and grandchildren will tell the story of a frog who planned an ingenious rescue for himself."

"I don't care what stories you collect for your filthy babies."

"Margaret, your lack of understanding disappoints me. You want to mourn two years of borrowed hair? I was a prisoner for eight years. Six years to find a maiden who would shear her hair for me. And two more years of waiting in camp before I could bring that maiden's head hair back to this river."

"But why did you ask me to care for you? Why promise me a future? You could have struck a bargain for my hair."

"Don't be naïve. Foul curses require foul remedies to be undone. They require virtuous frogs to be underhanded and innocent women to make crushing sacrifices."

"All those nights I wanted you. You made me feel like it was petty and deviant to feel that way."

"I could not have made love with you even had I wanted. I was already married. I had to stay faithful to my beloved."

"You were married?" Margaret exclaimed.

"She is queen of this river. I return to her this day."

"Of course she is," Margaret said. "God those nights I burned. It was so easy for you."

"Yes, well, the idea of making love with a person is repugnant to a frog. No offense."

"I am grateful I never went through with it."

"Right. So good for you too then."

"Your family knew it. They were there at our wedding. They watched me save my salary in a metal can to pay for a wedding dress. They helped me to fasten it over my body. They complimented my ham-fisted bouquet of desert flowers. They watched my father weep as he pronounced me a wife. They saw the laughter in my face. All along they knew what was waiting for me."

"Try not to judge my family harshly. They kept silent out of love for me. Perhaps we are callous when it comes to deception. The Uchihamas have centuries of curses to bear."

"Even as I watched my hair fall at my feet last night, I never wanted to be rich this morning. I did it to please you."

"There is a little gold in the river," Kane admitted. "I wish I could share. But you cannot really expect frogs to give the riches of their river away. I solemnly promise if you ever visit this bank, I will provide you all the dragonflies you could possibly eat."

"I will never eat a dragonfly. Every word and object that has touched your mouth disgusts me."

"Probably because losing my tongue," Kane said, dipping one leg into the nearby water. "For your language—my losing tongue. Mouth my ear it holds on to none of the words."

Margaret bent down and retrieved a few flat stones resting at her feet. She tested their weight in her fist.

"I will take something small for my troubles though," Margaret said.

"Sorry," Kane said. "English is far away. Now back in frog suit—lungs they forget how to burn with it. Guess now away I go—dissolving into the river?"

"I suppose it was lucky for me," Margaret said. "I suppose it was lucky that before I took the scissors to my hair, before I took every handful of my hair off, I washed it in the juice and pulp of an Indian fig."

When Margaret said this, the frog's frog eyes grew wide.

"The bag of prickly pear," Kane said. "You tricked me."

"Now I know you were losing your words a moment ago," Margaret said. "But I think we understand each other very well."

In the Butte Camp library, within the texts on California magic, it was well documented that a cursed woman, man, or child might transform back into their original body, be it fox or frog or cuckoo bee, if said-cursed creature could cover itself in the shorn hair of a maiden or bachelor who loved them.

But lesser known were the texts on Arizona magic. This perhaps was because those volumes had been so frequently signed out and after the war were never returned. If any Gila River resident had bothered to check the records, they would have seen the bound series on Arizona magic, their translated title *World of the Second Moon: Recipes for New Skin*, written by the famed investigator and practitioner Alex J. Sherman had been signed out by an M. Morri on eight occasions over a two-year span. The last volume in the collection contained a passage on the powers of the fruit of the Opus or Opuntia cactus. And it stated that if a cursed creature used hair that had been laundered with the juice of a prickly pear, their life would forever be in ownership of the bearer of that hair.

"I read that I can stop your heart with a song," Margaret said. "A little death song activates something in your heart. Actually I believe I only have to *think* of the death song for it to work."

"I hadn't read of it," Kane said thickly, his mouth dry.

"It was an exciting passage," Margaret said. "Sometimes I get so excited by what I read, my arms get numb and my chest begins to feel tight. Do you also feel your chest getting tight?"

"Are you going to kill me?" Kane asked quietly.

Margaret rattled the stones lightly in her hand.

"No," Margaret said. "I don't want to kill you. You have a wife waiting for you. I want you to go to her and to live a long life."

"Thank you," Kane said. "You are kind and forgiving and merciful."

"But all of the fortunes of your river kingdom," Margaret started, "all of the gold from your wife's river kingdom, now belongs to me. Every night until the day you die, you will carry a dirty, froggy mouthful of it to the banks of this river. You will carry it to the banks of this clearing where you wallowed in my hair and transformed your skin."

Margaret tossed the flat stones at the frog's feet.

"The size of those stones seems correct," she said. "Gold will be a little heavier. I hope you are a strong swimmer or you will have to work hard not to drown."

"You said everything that came from my mouth disgusted you," Kane said bitterly.

"I did say that," Margaret said. "It is so fortunate there is this kingdom of shining water here for me to rinse it with."

Partly this was the story the Uchihamas told each other to account for the disappearance of Kane following the war. None of them was particularly surprised or upset by his departure. Margaret Morri eventually met and married a kind man called Leo Minami. They were known to be a wealthy couple who purchased much of the land bordering the Santa Maria River. It was said that Margaret's hair never returned and that she wore a wig until her death.

Between a small group of the Morri-Minamis, it was discussed that Kane Uchihama-Araki did not die for another two years after Margaret. And until his last days, Kane continued to bring mouthfuls of gold to the banks of the Santa Maria River. It is rumored there is a small clearing where hundreds of these mouthfuls were abandoned upon the shore.

the thief's body

Kio Joyful was the name claimed by the imaginary creature who haunted Yoshikane Araki's dreams during his Gila River camp years, 1942 to 1945. Kane was six-years-old and unconscious when Joyful's name first emerged from his lips. The cries began as whispers, *Joyful, Kio Joyful, Kio Joyful*, and then intensified into howls. Kane sobbed and his clothes darkened with sweat. Then Kane twisted himself partially awake, *Joyful, Kio Joyful*, his throat inflamed, and the name fell agonizingly like burning sand past his mouth.

Kashi and Yoshi Araki had no remedy for their son's misfortunes. Shaking him out of the trance did not lessen the frequency of Kane's dreams. Tinctures, tonics, cold compresses, massages, and acupuncture provided no discernable impact. The Arakis asked the interned Reverend Kenichi Toguri to perform religious healing and cleansing of their Butte Camp barracks. Toguri spent three days and three nights on his knees, humming, praying, gesturing, spreading his anointing oils, igniting his safflower incense, but Kio Joyful relented for neither man nor God. *Kio Joyful, Kio Joyful.* The words lived like a set of black wings roosting in the planks and rafters of the Araki family barrack.

Kane's dreams of Kio Joyful began in a stifling train car on the Araki family's four-day journey from Tulare Assembly Center to Gila River. With no opportunity for bathing, passengers filled their dress socks, blouses, dress coats, kerchiefs, and pork pie hats with their daily sweat. An earthy musk, a scent like sour flowers thickened the air. In cars that held children and the infirm were the acrid smells of urine and infection. The passengers who succeeded in falling into a shallow, troubled sleep managed just a few hours. Like a shrewd mosquito, Kio appeared the moment Kane nodded off in the heat and his exhaustion.

At the beginning of all his Kio Joyful dreams, Kane walked through his family's avocado orchard on the Central Coast of California. The day was uncomfortably bright, damp, airless. Kane's shirt gripped his skin the way a darkened peel of fruit clings to its too-ripe flesh. In the distance, standing before a green-black copse of trees, Kane saw a uniformed man waving him over. The man was holding a small object that glinted blindingly as it struck sunlight. A pocket watch? A mirror? A ring of keys? By the time Kane approached close enough to make the object out, it was too late for him to turn and flee. Kio Joyful held out a needlepoint knife.

Kio was a dwarfish man, perhaps six inches taller than Kane. He was immaculately dressed in a dark blue tunic and trousers, a flattop cap and horsehide ankle boots. But the spotlessness and formality of his attire only worked to contrast the most monstrous face Kane ever had witnessed. Kio Joyful had the yellow-orange complexion of a marigold. His face was broad, his ears pointed, his nose flattened. His most gruesome features sprung from his mouth. Kio had both a set of buckteeth and a pronounced set of upper canines that resembled fangs. Kio's teeth were so large that he was unable to shut his mouth entirely, and a streak of drool ran down his chin. When he spoke, his lips and mouth hardly moved, and the voice that manifested was low, clear, and eerily calm.

"You have come home early, Kane," he said. "A sweet little boy shouldn't be without supervision. A boy needs to be watched at all times so that he won't be tempted to dip into any naughty or tricky behavior. And so that the naughty and tricky behavior of this world won't be tempted to come down upon his sweet little head."

"I've seen your face before," Kane said. "I've seen it on the walls of the pharmacy. I've seen it at the butcher's shop."

"I am very famous," he said. "If you can recall my name, I will grant you a wish. But if you cannot remember, then you must grant me a wish."

Though Kane was certain he had seen Kio Joyful's face before—certain he had heard and given voice to the name before—in that moment, an icy, sweaty amnesia swept over him, and he could not retrieve the name.

"I don't know how to grant wishes," Kane said.

"Oh no," Kio Joyful said. "That is bad luck. I believe that means I will just have to take my wish whether you like it or not. Where are your parents, Kane?"

"I'm not sure," Kane said. "Why do you need to see my parents?"

"I need to talk with them," he said. "I need to tell them how bad and forgetful and disrespectful you have been. We have met many times before, Kane, and you still don't remember my name. How do you think it makes me feel?"

"I could remember," Kane said. "The thing you are holding in your hand is blinding me. If you put it away, I could remember."

"I will not put anything away," Kio Joyful said. "Especially for a boy so impolite and oblivious. When a person tells you that you have no name—when he tells you he is giving you a new name—when he tells you that your name and your brother's name and your neighbor's name and the butcher's name and the druggist's name and the local thief's name—are now all the same name—do you know why he is offering you that name, Kane?"

"I can't remember," Kane said.

"He is offering you the name in place of your body. He is telling you that your body is allowed to vanish. The butcher's body may vanish. The druggist's body may vanish. The thief's body. Your father's body. But there will always be a new body we call by the old name, don't you think, Kane?"

Then Kio Joyful turned and pointed the needlepoint knife to a neighboring row of avocado trees.

"Oh!" he said. "Oh, there is your father. My wish is already coming true."

And when Kane turned to look, Yoshi Araki's tall, muscular figure, his back turned to them, stood with a padded crate and a netted fruit picker. The large, leathery fruit dropped into Yoshi's net. Before Kane could call out, Kio Joyful bounded over and stuck the needlepoint knife through the back of Yoshi's throat. Kane's father made no cries of distress. No sound of any kind. His body tumbled to the ground. Yoshi's avocadoes thudded and rolled upon the dirt in every direction. And then Yoshi's body half-vanished beneath the loose soil, beneath the black and rotting leaves under the avocado trees.

Kio Joyful retuned to where Kane was standing, wiped Yoshi Araki's blood against his blue trousers, and handed the knife over to Kane.

"That was very good, Kane," he said. "That was precisely what I wanted. You are better at granting wishes than you understood."

Kane looked down at the needlepoint knife in his hands. It was as though his neck muscles would not permit him to see another thing. The light it reflected shot through Kane's vision.

"My name is Joyful," Kane heard. "My name is Kio Joyful. Kio Joyful. Kio Joyful. Kio Joyful. Do you think it's a strange name?"

But Kane had lost his voice. His lungs felt squeezed. There was no air to answer.

"You have been told my name four times," Kio Joyful said. "When I come tomorrow to visit your mother, you will remember it, won't you?"

In response to her grandson's dreams, Yuki Araki took to the Butte Camp library to research the ghosts, beasts, and spirits populating the deserts between California and Arizona. What devil was known to be so cowardly as to exclusively menace such a young boy? Who was the cowardly monster that would not risk showing himself in the flesh? Who preferred the fog and primordial terror of a child's dreams?

Over the Araki family's camp years, Yuki Araki queried every block manager of Butte and Canal Camp. She spoke with every unarmed officer, every minister, every librarian, every mythologist, every schoolteacher, every nurse, and Nisei doctor. No one knew of any man, demon, or spirit who referred to himself as Kio Joyful.

Reverend Kenichi Toguri suggested that Yuki take Kane's shirts—shirts Kane had sweated and cried in—and fabricate a garment from them and then for Yuki to wrap herself in that garment at night. Before nightfall, Kashi and Yoshi were to rub Kane in ethereal oils distilled from cedarwood, wild mint, mountain pepper, lemon balm, and then to disguise him in Yuki's clothes or the clothing of a neighbor.

"We need to divert Kio Joyful from Kane's scent," Toguri said.

For a time, Kane's nightmares subsided. Kane rested soundly and reported no visitations when sleeping in the clothes of Yuki Araki. And Yuki sat up all evening wrapped in the cloak of Kane's shirts. In one hand, Yuki smoked Lucky Strike cigarettes. All night the burning ember traveled back and forth from Yuki's lips to the sardine tin of sand upon her lap. In the other hand, hidden beneath the cloak, Yuki held onto an iron pipe.

"If this devil ends up showing himself," Yuki said, "I plan to smash every tooth in his slavering mouth. I plan to rattle the eyes out of his face. I plan to whack every dirty, thinning patch of hair off his skull."

In 1946, the Araki family was given permission to return to their homes in California. It was back on the Central Coast they discovered their first worldly manifestation of Kio Joyful.

The modest farm home of Kashi and Yoshi had been raided and vandalized. Windows had been smashed through. Furniture was slashed and rain-damaged. A crude, chaotic brush had slathered Joyful's face in white paint along the side of the home.

The features Kane had described were prominent. The painted face was broad, the ears pointed, the nose flattened. The mouth possessed both buckteeth and fangs. A streak of white drool ran from its chin. In addition were the words, *NO JAPS BACK HERE EVER*. Yuki and Kashi Araki assembled buckets of soap and water and washed the caricature and words from the side planks of the house. Reverend Kenichi Toguri delivered cans of fresh paint. The face of Kio Joyful was obscured in the second coat.

absence of an ocean

Prior to the war, Y. Kane Araki was the most accomplished long-distance swimmer living on the Central Coast of California. He was born in Santa Maria and raised by his mother and grandmother, the renowned seamstresses, Hamako and Amaya Araki. But it was said Kane grew no hair upon his arms or his legs because his father was Kingo Koga, the sly, mythic green dolphin who seduced young girls frolicking through the feathery sand crab molt and gritty waters off Guadalupe Beach.

It was told Kane's momentum drawn from a single stroke, cupped at the crown of his head and dragged beneath the length of his body, could propel him through calm waters for an hour. It was also claimed Kane could hold his breath for eight days. Or that underwater, a set of clandestine gills could be observed flapping. That to tear a small gash in his flesh would reveal a coat of luminous, cycloid scales. That he shaved three times a day because otherwise he would grow barbels like a catfish. That he slept curled within a tepid pool in the clawfoot bathtub. That stipe and blade of kelp he gnawed and kept crammed in the pouch of his cheek like chewing tobacco. And that he possessed the thick, prehensile procreant equipment of a baleen whale.

But most evidence of Kane's aquatic accomplishments was lost after 1942. The trophies, plaques, ribbons, and certificates were either stolen or burned. What remained were myths and the trench. The trench was cut five feet deep, four feet wide, and ran a mile through the Canal and Butte camps of Gila, Arizona.

Local celebrities can be loved with more devotion and ferocity than the singers, actresses, or athletes who never walk the aisles of the same hardware store, the same supermarket, never near enough to be called to or touched upon their shoulders. In Santa Maria the locals were infatuated with Kane. The old and the young. The brilliant and hopeless. The lazy and the industrious. Rich and poor. It was common to observe dogs and unattended children following a few paces behind Kane as if attracted by an invisible current. On days Kane had a swim meet, the outdoor bleachers facing the public pool groaned and threatened to implode under the weight of half the city.

In races of short distances, fifty or one hundred yards perhaps, Kane was easily defeated. He appeared to move at only one pace. This somehow was an essential characteristic of his majesty. No coach or teammate dared ask him to sprint.

"Would you ask a dolphin to move any faster?" they would ask any naysayer. "No? So shut up your pie hole and watch him."

It was not Kane's speed that mesmerized his audience. It was true that in events of distance he was unrivaled. But to watch Kane move through the water made you understand he was not racing any person in the lanes beside him. There were his magnificent strokes and, behind, his unvarying, tireless kicks. But those were features of a disguise. Greater than any aspect of his technique, Kane appeared to ride upon the affection of the water. Kane was lifted, carried upon the shoulders of that green-blue Santa Maria public pool water in the same way a crest's diaphanous foam was carried by oceanic wave.

It was said that during his youth, Kane was offered twenty-eight proposals of marriage. The first dozen or so occurred during the years he attended high school and later when he studied aeronautical engineering at the local community college.

An admirer, summoning her courage, might approach him and say, "Kane, last week I watched you buying some cucumbers. I thought you would very much enjoy this fifteen-pound sack of cucumbers I picked this morning."

And Kane would say, "Thank you, Mary."

Or, "Thank you, Emiko."

Or, "Thank you, Rie."

Or, "Hackey, that was so kind of you. Would you like to sit and eat a few of them together?"

"Oh!" she would say, unable to keep the elation spreading like fever across her face. "That would be very, very nice."

And later, while the firm, melon-green flesh broke between their teeth, the tart, glassy seed bodies, and the mild, cucumber-perfumed water sluiced over their lips, she would say, "Yeah, my family is big in this area when it comes to cucumbers. You could visit the farm to pick and take home whatever you like."

And Kane would say, "Gosh, thanks so much, Seiko."

Or, "Gosh, Chiyo."

Or, "It's a kind offer, Evelyn. Though I think I'll likely be alright for cucumbers at least a little while."

"Yup," she would say. "Any person who marries into my family can eat all the cucumbers they can handle. All the pickles they want too."

"Sounds like they would be getting a good deal," Kane would say.

"All the strawberry and cucumber salad. All the mint and cucumber cocktails. All the cucumber and cream cheese sandwiches. Only have to marry into my family. That man would be set for cucumbers for life."

"They would have to marry into your family?" Kane would say, his butt cheeks scooching a bit away from Sugar or Kimi or Betti. "They couldn't just be close friends?"

"Friends are alright," she would say. "Dating, sure. Going steady. But eventually a girl thinks to herself, surely, it seems like this person is getting more than his fair share of cucumbers without ever making a decent commitment."

"Friendship is not a commitment?"

"There's that saying. You can only date the cow so long before you must marry the cow. And then the cow will turn into a princess."

"No one ever told me that version."

And then she would ask, "Do you ever think about getting hitched, Kane?"

"I'm waiting for the right person."

"You know, I'm the same way. Sometimes I think I'm looking for just the right cucumber. Green. But not too much green. It can't be boring with greenish-ness. It has to have a bit of a yellow coat. A small outburst of yellow. Do you understand what I'm saying?"

"I think I'm following."

"Long. But then again, not too long. Not so long it seems it got its long-ness only to be showing off. Plump. But not too much plump either. It can't be some kind of unusual, fatso cucumber. Do you hear what I'm telling you?"

"I didn't realize those traits changed the flavor of a cucumber."

"Sometimes the right cucumber, well, it was staring you in the face the whole time. Staring right into your face, buddy. You just needed to look down and realize you'd already picked it. You had been holding it in your hands."

And that was when one of these Santa Maria girls would reach down and take Kane by the hand.

And then she would say, "So what do you think?"

"Oh, it's great. I'm learning tons about cucumbers today."

"Right. Okay, that's a start. But do you think you've already picked it?"

"Picked what?"

"The one you were looking for?"

"I can't be sure. Didn't you pick these for me?"

And then she would say, "I'd like to do this again, Kane. I'm available. Do you understand what I'm telling you when I say that I'm available?"

"We'll see each other again soon."

"We could see each other every morning. Nighttime too. You wouldn't need to see anyone else."

"I'm going to need a little time to get back to you on that one," Kane would say.

"I feel as though the two of us understand each other on this higher level. We resonate with each other. What do you call them? Up in the bell tower. We match like those. A lot of couples won't get the chance at something like it. When you have a feeling like that, you have to say it out loud. You have to act on it loudly. Don't you think?"

"Do you feel better now that you've said it?"

"I do," she would say. "I feel complete. Chimes! Is that what they call them?"

So it went for the daughters of Central Coast farming families of lettuce, tomatoes, yellow squash, avocadoes, artichokes, pumpkins, grapes, blackberries, huckleberries, strawberries. Kane became expert in pickling and making preserves. In their kitchen, Hamako Araki would help him process the flats of berries, the pillowcases bulging with artichokes. The two of them worked shoulder to shoulder swiping roots and tops off their cutting boards, measuring pectin, pouring sugar, working a wooden spoon through a steaming and ever-thickening pot.

"Seems like you found another admirer," Hamako would say. "Someone trying to plead her case. What did you think? Was she pretty?"

"She really was very pretty," Kane would say, lowering his ear to a pumpkin and rapping upon it with his knuckles.

"Alright. You don't sound really very excited."

"Do you want me to get married soon? How badly do you want me out of your house?"

"How badly do you want to leave?"

"Not at all."

"So stay then. What do I need an extra room for? Look at the free salads we eat."

"You think I should be taking it more seriously."

"That is not my advice. Do you feel like being serious?"

"I can be serious. But no one makes me feel that way."

"Alright. So then why buy the cow? Right?"

"What's that?"

"Well there's the saying about a cow. You don't have to buy her because there's so many other cows in the pasture. And they all basically have the same stupid cow-face and terrible breath. So why worry if any one cow runs away? She probably can't run very fast anyhow."

"I didn't realize the saying maneuvered in that direction."

"Right, well maybe you don't enjoy cows. Maybe you want a donkey. Or some camels."

"Most of the time I'm into people."

"Right, well that's good enough," Hamako would say. "You had still better deliver some jam and cookies back to her family. They'll spread rumors that we're rude if you don't."

It is known there were even bolder girls who attempted to arouse Kane Araki's passions with competition. Heather Osaka, the sixteen-year-old backstroking champion from

Arroyo Grande, publicly challenged Kane to an ocean race of eight miles that would mean weaving between eight buoys in the shark-infested waters off of Avila Beach. The morning of the race, Heather arrived wearing a custom racing suit no heavier than a veil of smoke. And then armed with a straight razor and bar of shaving soap, she knelt beside a rockpool and swept an hour's hair growth from her limbs.

"Kane, when I overtake you in this race, you understand what it means," Heather Osaka said. "You must agree to marry me. Marry me and we'll have three daughters."

"Is that a question?" Kane asked.

"Isn't that the prize of choice for every elite competitor?" Osaka asked.

"Usually you just win a sash or a pie or something," Kane said.

"I would rather win my competitor."

"What will I receive if I am the winner?"

"I promise to bind myself to you for life."

"So you chose both prizes. What do I choose?"

"Fine. If you win I will pull off this swim cap and let you shave my hair off. And you can spit in my face. And you can change my name to something disgusting. Pig girl dog. Or Dog pig."

"Jesus. Why would I want that?"

"Well think of how humiliated I'd be."

"That is not at all the same as letting me choose a prize. I thought some new socks? Sweatpants?"

"I will not put my reputation on the line for sweatpants. You aren't taking me seriously."

"We're swimming out to some buoys. It doesn't have to be a Greek myth where the loser becomes a slave."

"I never used the word slave. I said I want you to marry me and put daughters in me. It doesn't have to be today. It can be in a year or two years. Does that sound like slavery to you?"

"I'm sorry," Kane said. "I'm not trying to hurt your feelings. But it seems like you're hearing what you want to hear."

"So we're agreed," Heather said. "First I'll kick your ass. Then your other girlfriends. I'm going to find all their asses. I'll kick those down too."

Following relocation, first to the Tulare Assembly Center, and later in Gila River, Kane was admired from near and far. Even in the absence of an ocean, without a way of showcasing his talents, his mythos grew in strength and fanaticism. In Gila, lines were cut, seeds ordered and delivered, gardens exploded with leafy suncatchers and globes of earthsugar. And then Hamako and Amaya observed the repopulation of love letters along with jarred preserves, pickled plums, paper sacks of dried fruit, tins of almond shortbread cookies atop the shelves and counters within their barrack.

"It is fine he doesn't consider marriage," Clara Hiramatsu or Hisako Furukawa or Kayo Hyosaka would say to Sachie Kadota or Elsie Koyama. "But then he won't consider dating? Or kissing us even? Are we all such repulsive dogs to him?"

"He gives us all the same stock story," Yukio Moriguchi would complain to Annie Katsuda or Nobuko Kunishige. "He is still searching. He can't take marriage seriously now. He works too many hours at the Canal mess hall. He is learning to play the ukulele. He is training for a weightlifting competition."

"Maybe he is only being kind," Michi Furuya would say to Shiori Fujinami or Yumiko Ikeda or Sharon Kamo. "He doesn't want to damage our feelings."

It was early in 1944 that Alfie Ota, a nineteen-year-old farm boy from Venice, California, single-handedly began to cut a trench near the foot of the Araki-family barrack. Alfie was mammoth, broad in every direction, a dark mane that rode upon his shoulders and with hands the size of a catcher's glove. In the sour haze of sweat and the packed earth exploding beneath his pick mattock, his skin appeared awash in gold and deep brown. By the end of his first week, the trench was cut four feet across and three feet deep and moving in the direction of Butte Camp.

"He'll break somebody's neck with that hole," Kane said to Hamako and Amaya from their barrack window. "A person walking after dark will do a header into it. Probably it's going to be me."

"I don't think it's called a hole," Amaya said.

"What do you call it?" Kane asked.

"I think he calls it a lane," Amaya said. "It's a single lane. It's made for a single swimmer."

"It's a safety hazard is what it is."

"You could walk out there and ask him about it," Hamako said. "Tell him to hammer in a little sign. About not falling in there face-first."

"You think I should feed his craziness with attention?"

"Just looking at a dry pool makes me thirsty as hell,"

Amaya said. "Go and take him some water."

Outside, under the dogged sun, Kane rested a hand atop one of Alfie's mountainous shoulders. Alfie's skin was damp, hot to the touch, and emitted the vague fragrance of blooming evening primrose.

"Alright," Kane said to him. "It's very nice work here. Shall I get you a cup of water?"

Alfie wiped his face with the back of his hand, his eyes emerging between a pale stripe among the red-gold dust.

"I want you to know this is not a pool," Alfie said.

"That's alright," Kane said.

"I mean it is a pool, of course," Alfie said. "It will be. But it isn't *your* pool. It isn't a pool for you to swim in. If you came outside to make fun of me, don't waste your breath."

"It isn't why I came."

"I know some people go to desperate lengths to get the attention of Kane Araki. That isn't what this is about."

"What have you heard?"

"That a hundred men and women have pretended to drown themselves so that you would rescue them."

"I've seen swimmers get calf cramps. If that's what you mean."

"You don't really know me. Maybe I'm about to swim in it myself."

"Okay, so will you want that cup of water? For drinking of it?"

"I have an entire pail sitting there."

"The one you're using to moisten the sand?"

"That's right."

"It's been sitting in the sun."

"All we drink here is lukewarm."

"I have a few glass bottles I keep under our house. They pass for cold if you use some imagination."

At that, Alfie attempted to stare past Kane. The expression on his face was one of befuddlement. It was as though Alfie had been reading lines off a script, but now his view of it was being obscured.

"Fine," Alfie said. "Only don't distract me for long. I have a lot of work to get done."

A month of Alfie's determined and punishing work passed. At Amaya Morri's request, Kane planted a rim of aloe vera along the side of the Ota family barrack.

"You can snap the leaves and harvest their jelly," Kane said.

"I don't use that gunk," Alfie said. "I never sunburn."

"I suppose your face is only red from embarrassments then."

"It's none of your business. I probably ate something spicy earlier."

On another late afternoon, when the trench had expanded to twenty-five yards in length, Kane said, "I understand this pool is not for me to swim in. But hypothetically if a person wanted to get my attention, then digging a pool is going overboard. Someone could just ask me to go for a walk."

"Are you talking to me?" Alfie asked.

"I'm a little blind," Kane said. "Is anyone else out here?"

"The pool is not for you. I haven't even seen you swim. Why would I care about digging you a pool?"

"I'm not saying you would," Kane said. "Alfie, look: I want to be friends. Would you care to be friends?"

"I never said I did."

"Fine. I'll screw off then."

"I'm open to it," Alfie said. "I just hadn't thought of that myself."

"Okay. Right now, I am not occupied with another person, hypothetical or fleshy, who is desperate for my attention. You could use a rest, excavating the pool that is not for me but is in front of my house. So maybe the two of us should take a walk and get some fresh air."

"You want to walk around the track."

"It's not difficult as it sounds. If you remember how to ride a bike. Except you are more upright and your feet slowly pedal that sand in front of you."

"Okay," Alfie said. "Sounds okay. Come back in a couple of hours. I'll be finished with what I need by then."

When Kane returned it was twilight, and he found Alfie stretched out and snoring at the bottom of the trench. This was the first occurrence of a ritual for them. At first light, Alfie took to the trench like a warrior, half-nude, warpaint of sweatmud running across his face, hurling shovel or pick mattock or grub hoe or fork into the dirt, pushing back its wall by inches. The sheerest gown of sweat he swiped from his body and cast into the wall to moisten it. The thinnest gown of saliva his tongue lathered and spat as a target to strike metal into. An hour or two after returning from his work at the mess hall, Kane walked to the day's edge of the trench and, with considerable effort, retrieved Alfie's massive, dozing body, pulled it over his shoulders, and carried it to the Otas' doorstep. To support Alfie even half a block would cover Kane with sweat, and upon completing the task, he would collapse beside Alfie on the desert sand, panting like an asthmatic.

"You're all wet," Alfie would sometimes complain, if jarred into a half-wakefulness. "Is it raining?"

"It's my sweat," Kane would say.

"Oh. Well that's yucky."

"I was carrying a gorilla."

"You say weird things," Alfie would say. "Is this a dream?"

It is rumored that Alfie broke two-dozen shovels in his mission to finish the trench. It is said he wore the length of the tines of a forged digging fork down to the tines of a salad fork. On some afternoons he could be observed digging with his hands.

Discussion of his project resonated throughout all of Canal. In the recreation barracks, Kane's admirers gathered and pined.

"Just kill me!" Sherilyn Oishi moaned. "Alfie Ota completely stole my idea! I was going to be the first to build Kane Araki a swimming pool."

"It's true," Akiko Makimoto said. "We discussed it months ago. Could Alfie have heard the two of us talking?"

"Do you see all the attention Alfie is getting? I want to die!"

"Why didn't you dig it then?" Yasuko Okamura asked.

"I was getting around to it. Now I can't! Someone would call me a copycat!"

It took Alfie Ota eighteen months to soak and spike and claw apart the pool bed nearly a mile long, four feet wide, and five feet deep. At the end nearest the Araki barrack the trench plunged into a slope eight feet in depth to accommodate diving. When Alfie came to a stop in January of 1945, he'd lost more than eighty pounds. His hands were gnarled, permanently fists, permanently squeezing the shaft of an invisible digging tool. His back curled. A brief history of flying rocks was scattered in tiny scars across his chest and sides. Much of his skin was darkened with burns and blisters.

After a midwinter evening of digging, Kane carried Alfie in a half-slumber from the trench. As he did, he felt the cotton of his shirt become heavy with Alfie's sweat, and when he looked down he saw it had also turned from white to ochre.

"Does it look finished?" Alfie asked. "My family can't afford the cement. My requests for supplies have been denied for months."

"It's complete without the cement," Kane said.

"You should use it sometime," Alfie said. "We're friends. I'm happy to share it."

"Are we friends now?" Kane asked.

"You helped in your own way," Alfie said dreamily. "You came with the aloe."

"Maybe this weekend," Kane said.

"I lied to you some. When I said the pool wasn't for you. It may have started just a bit with you in mind. A small amount."

"I'm grateful. I had a feeling."

"My days are free now. We can take that walk."

"A walk around the track. That will be nice."

"I should have agreed to do it sooner. Now I've wrecked my body."

"It's still a strong body, Alfie. It's lighter now."

"It's wrecked. You know what they say about the cow body. Once it has moved its mountain."

"You will have to remind me."

"You must have faith your cow can move you a mountain. But once your cow succeeds, it stops making your milk."

"Does it start to spin straw into gold instead?"

"A cow has only hooves where hands should be. How would it work a spinning wheel?"

"Right. That would be absurd."

"The mountain, it was underground. I moved it for you."

"You did."

"I'm the cow. The milk is my body."

"I know I didn't finish college, but I understand how a metaphor works."

"And now you will have to throw the cow in the trash," Alfie said. And then he began to sob a little.

"Why would I do that?" Kane asked.

"That's how the rest of it goes, I think. There's the mountain-moving part. The squirting pouch. What is it? It is like bagpipes but for milk. A pink one."

"The udder?"

"Oh, udder. It's all shriveled and black. That's the second thing. And then you put the cow in the trash container."

"It doesn't so much sound physically possible, Alfie. A cow is large for the trash."

"You have to stomp it down pretty good. Probably have to sit on the lid. Your poor, sad, crying cow."

"Alright. Well I guess if people say it. Then there is no other way around."

"That is what they say," Alfie said. "Everyone knows."

"That third part of the saying—I remember hearing an alternate version."

"What was that?"

"It comes after the cow moves a mountain. After it stops producing milk. Because it no longer gives milk, it decides to stop being a cow. And it transforms into something new."

"A maiden."

"Well almost. She becomes a sort of prince. She becomes somebody's husband."

"What is the word? That's a nice promotion. No! An improvement from trash."

"Right, well very powerful magic becomes possible when a cow moves an underground mountain."

"The cow only finished half her mission though," Alfie said. "It won't do much good. There isn't water to fill it."

"I had a dream last night it was filled. Tonight I'll have it again and I'll swim there."

Beside the Ota barrack, the aloe vera and its offsets had grown massive and luminous. A few stalks of late-blooming pendulous flowers emerged out of the swollen gray-green leaves. Kane laid Alfie beside it and kissed his cheek. Alfie raised his face and pressed it to Kane's. The moon fell upon them. Their clothes tangled in a constellation beside their bodies. Kane kissed all the instances of half-light pooling in Alfie's body. Then he kissed all the darkness. They made quiet, exhausted love. And then the sky above Gila began to crowd with violent black clouds. They slept even with the rain striking their bodies. Even with the lightning flashing across their faces. The common claim is even the thunder did not wake them.

a disappearance
beside the yatsushiro sea

Margaret Morri was the name Yoshikane Araki used when referring to an apparition who squeezed under doorway or window mesh or rose between barrack floorboards to haunt the hot desert air above his straw mattress. At the age of eighty-eight, Kane had never witnessed the slightest apparition before, not in Kumamoto Prefecture where it was said shiranui might erupt over calm seas, nor on the Central Coast of California where visitations by slain Chumash warriors were understood as commonplace. But the appearances of his apparition in Gila River occurred nightly, and she was massive and bright as a second moon. The one he called Margaret Morri emerged in the form of an enormous moth, a wingspan not less than two yards across, wings white as bleached linens, and with eyes bearing the same clarity and intelligence as any friend or relative.

The same pattern of events occurred at night. Kane awoke in otherworldly blackness. Feeling he was still in California, his body roused with the urge to pick from his family's orchards of black thundercloud plums while the morning was cool and damp. Then he would remember he was in Gila River and, feeling parched, would wrestle with the thought of rising and disturbing his wife's sleep for a drink. Just as Kane reconciled with returning to sleep thirsty, the mighty white moth descended upon him and situated itself upon his chest. The weight of the moth over him was at least that of a grown adult, and though he could have possibly thrashed himself free, he was oddly soothed by its presence. In the half-dark, Kane and Margaret Morri inspected each other's faces and bodies.

And then in the voice of an adult woman, Margaret Morri spoke, "I have come with a message for you, Kane Araki. You are not safe in this camp. You must return with me at once to the Yatsushiro Sea."

But Kane could not return to Kumamoto Prefecture. He had lived his entire manhood in California. His wife had carried and delivered three radiant children in California cities. His daughters had grown eating the oceanic flesh of black abalone and red abalone. They had filled their pails and pots for years with bent-nose clams and Pacific butterclams. They had labored in fields of strawberries, grapes, peppers, and green beans. His children had married California Nisei and the geography of all of their dreams was in the shadow-California. So it was for Kane's sisters and brothers. Canal Camp was crowded with Araki blood. Hardly any of Kane's dreams were located in Kumamoto. Unless his dreams were of his parents who were both in the next world over. The moth knew every bit of this, he felt certain.

"If you die here in this desert," Margaret Morri said, "your family may never return to Kumamoto. It is a disastrous curse to be taken as a prisoner in another nation. To perish as a prisoner between nations would be ruinous for your family's good blood and reputation."

But separation was never an option for Kane. Relocation and imprisonment were agonies far less to bear.

And then the moth extended a long black arm, and it appeared like the arm and hand of a woman. The moth extended a handful of white flowers toward Kane's face. Kane did not recognize the sorts of flowers held by the moth. Were they the blossoms of a horseradish tree? Pincushion flower? Flowering bell of the thorn apple? Desert chicory?

Then, as though anesthetized with a rag of ether, Kane became overwhelmed in a dreamless, starless loss of time.

In the hospital barracks of Canal Camp, Kane discussed the entire phenomenon with his doctor, Peter Yamamoto. Was this vision a symptom of senility? Was he going mad? Was this a malady of the desert? Were these dreams ruminating the anxieties of relocation?

"You assume the moth was a dream," Yamamoto said. "Not necessarily is she a dream. All month the great white moths have been visiting men and women in Canal Camp. They are described in precisely the same manner. They practice the same behaviors. They are in favor of a return to a city of origin or of rebellion. The moths are too common to be attributed to old age, dehydration, or madness."

Yamamoto asked Kane to remove his shirt so that he might inspect the sounds of his heart and lungs. How did the moths expect their internees to travel? Kane wondered. Would she have carried him through the air? What would he do in Kumamoto if he arrived? He had no means and his countries were at war.

"They are troublemakers," Peter Yamamoto said. "Why do you call yours Margaret Morri?"

Margaret Morri had been the name of a young neighbor Kane had known and loved. When he was a boy of eight and she was twelve, she took him to the seashore to collect fiddler crabs. These Margaret later sold as pets. On a few occasions, Margaret appeared during the night and slept in Kane's bed beside him. Had this practice been agreed upon by Kane's parents? He couldn't remember any intrusions. What had frightened Margaret from her bedroom? On these occasions Margaret wore a ghostly white dress.

Thinking of it, Kane realized this dress was the same color in his memory as the wings of the great moth.

"And what ever happened to this Margaret Morri?" Yamamoto asked. Kane felt the cool metal of Yamamoto's stethoscope against his back.

Margaret Morri had disappeared one day by the Yatsushiro Sea. Could this be correct? Had Margaret been swept away? Had she drowned? Or had an inexplicable crime occurred? Or had her parents simply moved away? As he probed deeply into his memories, he could only make out an afternoon where he observed the stiff and bewildered expressions upon the faces of his parents. It had been eighty years since he had discussed

Margaret Morri with anyone. His only impression was that all the Morris had disappeared at once.

a goshawk

From 1943 to 1945, the Japanese relocation camp constructed upon the Gila River Indian Reservation, being in possession of a perfect ratio of Sonoran heat to excruciating dryness, was the absolute finest location in America to dry one's laundry, the local saying was that you could steam ears of corn in the pockets of culottes and poach an egg in the cup of a bra, and pinning the family laundry among the groves of mesquite trees emerged as a social occasion and pastime, becoming the regular practice for cooks, typists, teachers, doctors, butchers, and mechanics to take an early leave on laundry day, to retreat home and pin and chew the fat of the afternoon with friends and neighbors, and it all later turning to sport, with Yoshikane Araki accepted as the fastest hanger and folder living in Canal and, by acclamation, Margaret Morri as Butte's supreme laundrywoman, and the pinning, retrieving, and folding competition between the two of them in the summer of 1944 attracted a crowd of ten thousand internees who bordered clotheslines erected just for that day, stretching a mile long, lines that could bear twelve or thirteen thousand damp socks, six thousand soggy undergarments, eleven hundred steamed bed linens, though pants it was announced that August morning as the contest's official clothing item, the small company of Kumamoto taiko drummers pounding their instruments in frenzied anticipation, the panel of judges pulling away a silky tarp to reveal the baskets of five thousand moist pairs of pants, pants! the word hurled into the air like a song, it's pants! rising over hundreds of ecstatic pumping fists, and then the fierce pop of Kane's and Margaret's muscles springing into a flurry of motion, quicker than combat, semi-soaked pants cast over the wire lines, Margaret suspending her pants in half and pinning at the crotch, Kane's more laborious method of pinning them at both knees for maximum spreading and drying, the sun blasting through the wet cloth, the white-hot wind slurping the vaguest dew, the pants strung and petrifying, fossilizing mid-kick, shining with sweat salts and minerals, the judges arriving to inspect for proper dehydration and folding configurations, poking their fingers into the stiffness of the pants, the judges recalling a dozen pairs of Margaret's already-folded pants, too damp! the proclamation passing from tongue to tongue throughout the crowd, a few of Kane's fans squealing and clapping and leaping into the sky, Margaret's mother pitching her sunhat into the dirt and stomping on it, Kane's fiancée applying another layer of flamboyant lipstick,

Margaret locking in and cranking her folding speed, lightning screaming down every fiber of her limbs, everywhere pants transforming into tight rectangles, Kane barking, jeering at his fellow competitor, wringing a fistful of perspiration from his shirt and flicking it in her direction, but then seconds later Kane dropping to his knees, his body contorted, compacted as if by otherworldly gravity, thighs, hamstrings, calves shot through with acute cramps, back squeezed by spasms, tears running down the agony of his face, the judges' whistles roaring, Margaret pulling the final pair of pants from her basket and flinging them into the crowd, fits of utter delight erupting from the Butte contingent, those crisp desert-dried pants wildly unfolding in the air, never in anyone's memory to fall upon the earth, the immense wingspan of a goshawk.

woods' rose, little hogweed,
orange flameflower

When Kane Araki hopped into the Canal mess hall bearing a puzzling wound upon his right ankle, the morning drew a meeting of Gila River's three premier working healers. This occurred in the second month following relocation from the Tulare Assembly Center, where Kane had been crowned The Fist of Tulare, a distinction meant to convey his prowess as a weightlifter and judoka.

The three who they called "crackpot healers" were Zee Okawa, Margaret Morri and Emiko Kadota, all of whom were loudmouthed and pretty and were looked upon warily by married women of the Gila River Relocation. For though they nursed the ailing to good health, they also commonly secured the attractions of men, pubescent or senior, bachelor or married, lecherous or the sanctified and self-denying, as if by supernatural control. Though they were assiduous practitioners, they were also victims of cruel rumors. To carry one of their names in your mouth to a social event would incite the cries of "crackpot," "Jezebel," or even "witch."

The three understood that to tend to The Fist, to become connected in some way to his recovery, would add significantly to their reputations and practices. Kane struck some as a reserved and private individual, but even those who knew him at a distance admired him as a noble hulk. The Araki family was also well-connected, and they were said to pride themselves on generosity and industriousness. From first light to dusk, Kane unloaded the day's fresh produce from delivery trucks to the mess hall pantries. Three evenings a week, upon the sweaty padding of the recreation barracks, he taught judo for youth girls and boys. Saturdays he spent with his mother chopping cabbages, cucumbers, radishes, and mixing brines for tsukemono. Sunday afternoons, he delivered bento lunches to the infirm or immobile Canal Internees. He was the first to carry your grandmother's heavy parcels to the foot of her barrack and the last in line to fill his plate at a church potluck.

Though the wound appeared minor, little greater than some shallow punctures thinly producing blood, the three healers asked Kane to lie upon a table at the center of the mess hall and to lower his leg below his heart.

"I never saw the snake if there was one," Kane said. "In the night I woke to a pinch in my right ankle. I kicked it free a few times. I thought perhaps it was a calf cramp. The pain didn't keep me from falling back to sleep. When I pulled my sock on this morning, it turned red and black with my blood."

Tomiye Moriguchi, the middle-aged manager of Canal's mess hall, sat beside Kane and patted him tenderly upon the hand.

"We should get you to the infirmary," she said. "Snake bites should be treated by doctors."

"This work was of no snake," Zee Okawa said, tipping a bottle of hydrogen peroxide, its contents splashing and buzzing where Kane's skin had broken.

"People have heard brown bats squealing in the evenings," Tomiye said. "They are roosting in the area."

"Not a bat either," Zee Okawa said. She retrieved a fork and gestured above the rim of the injury. "The teeth that made this were flat."

"A bat is a shrewd villain," Emiko Kadota said. "She makes a pair of incisions and laps secretly at the wound. This wound was hurried. Frantic. And its shape circular."

"What does it mean?" Kane asked.

"It was a man," Zee Okawa said.

"A man," Tomiye snorted.

"The White Flume," Emiko Kadota said. "The White Ghost. We have heard of a man who does this."

"Bring him chicken soup!" Tomiye shouted to the rear of the mess hall, wiping the sweat from her face with her apron, then rolling it and tucking it under Kane's neck for a cushion. "Kane should restore himself with broth before he goes into shock from all this nonsense."

"I have seen a thing like it before," Margaret Morri said. "In California."

"What do you remember?" Kane asked.

"There was a man in Los Angeles who attacked children while they slept," Margaret Morri said. "He came in the darkness and sucked the blood from their legs and feet. In one case it is said he devoured the feet."

"This is horseshit," Tomiye cried. "Little Billy or Scooter having his feet gnawed at the ankle. This is a tale meant to horrify unruly children."

"Who was this man?" Kane asked. "A vagrant?"

"Not at all," Margaret Morri said. "Those who discovered him in the act say if he did not retreat, he would offer immense sums of money in exchange for blood. He was a rich man. A rich hakujin."

"Why would a hakujin travel four hundred miles to camp?" Tomiye said. "It is not an easy road to find us."

"Who says he came by choice?" Margaret Morri asked. "Perhaps he is detained here."

"Camp would be tolerable for The Ghost," Emiko Kadota said. "There are abandoned bunkers on the outskirts of camp. No one much locks their barracks at night. Few of our windows have screens or interior locks."

"Why risk a beating from The Fist?" Zee Okawa asked. "This coward attacks who he can easily run from."

"It is daring behavior for The Flume," Margaret Morri said.

"We'll need to post word with the *Courier*," Emiko Kadota said. "People should be put on notice."

"Be suspicious of a hakujin lurking through your apartment," Zee Okawa said. "Though if money be tight, he may trade you a little to snack on some toes. People here will not be fast to believe this conjecture."

"We'll purchase a column inch asking to be on the lookout for peculiar bite marks," Emiko Kadota said.

"But what repels him?" Kane asked.

Margaret Morri had begun to wrap Kane's ankle with sterile gauze.

"Zee will fix you a salve for when you re-bandage your wound," she said to him. "You will keep it clean and dry for five days. Emiko will mix you a repellant that should be sprayed upon your sheets and your clothing. Borrow a baseball bat and keep it beside your cot. Let us hope The Flume did not like what he tasted from you."

Two mornings later, Kane appeared at the steps of Margaret Morri's barrack to reveal fresh bite marks upon his left ankle. This set had purchased deeper flesh, and a blue-black halo had appeared. Again, Kane had not witnessed any man, feral dog, or snake beside his bed. After waking with the injury, he had limped over to the clinic in Canal and the staff had treated him for swelling and pain. But there were no signs of venom in him. He was merely given an antibiotic and a tetanus shot to ward off infection.

"As I was leaving, my doctor slipped me a matchbook with your barrack's block and number," Kane said.

"Why would they do that?" Margaret Morri asked.

"She said you might help," Kane said. "She said you have helped her before."

"Who was your doctor?"

"Winnie Kamibayashi."

"Oh sure," Margaret Morri said. "Wild Winnie has been in to see me before. A dozen times."

"For curious bite marks?"

"No, no," Margaret Morri said. "Or maybe, yes. I can't say. Wild Kamibayashi. Do you know why they say Winnie is so wild?"

"I can't say."

"Are you positive?"

"Yes?"

"Darn," Margaret Morri said. "I was hoping you could tell me."

"Oh."

"Do you sleep alone, Kane?"

"Sorry?"

"Does your wife have the same bite marks?"

"I'm not married," Kane said. "I was engaged just before the war. My girlfriend lives with her family in Butte Camp."

"The separation must be difficult," Margaret Morri said.

"A few miles is nothing much."

"What is her name?"

"Why do you need her name?"

"Are you worried about what I will do with a name?"

"Julie Kajikawa."

"It's a pretty name," Margaret Morri said. "Honey Kajikawa. Is that her?"

"I've never heard a person call her that."

"You haven't? I thought it was because she was sweet as honey."

"I don't think so."

"No? She isn't sweet?"

"No. I mean, yes. Yeah, she is nice if that is what you mean."

"Why wouldn't that be what I mean?"

"I'm not sure."

"Is she sweet in another way?"

"She's nice. She is a nice girl."

"You know what? It was my mistake. I was thinking of Kajiwara. Honey Kajiwara on the far end of Butte Camp."

"I haven't met her."

"That's good," Margaret Morri said. "Because she's a real Goddamn shrew. All the Kajiwaras have a stick up their asses."

"My girlfriend is a different person."

"Or I suppose it is sticks," Margaret Morri said. "They each have their own stick. Up their plural asses."

"Okay."

"What do you call your fiancée?"

"She is just Julie."

"Julie? And her real name is Julie?"

"I like her the way she is."

"Do you know what some people call me?" Margaret Morri asked.

"No."

"Alright," Margaret Morri said. "Tell Julie I will need to observe you in your bed tonight while you sleep. Your sweetheart can come along if she likes."

"Why?"

"So she doesn't hear from a little bird that a seductress snuck into your apartment and spent the night. I'm not trying to get you into trouble."

That evening, in the quarter division that made up Kane Araki's private apartment, Margaret Morri sat in a chair at the foot of Kane's bed and smoked Lucky Strike cigarettes. In the blackness of the room, Kane watched the ember travel back and forth, presumably from Margaret's lips to the sardine tin of sand upon her lap.

"Trouble sleeping?" Margaret Morri asked.

"I'm not used to somebody watching," Kane said.

"A difference between men and women. A woman always has an unwanted set of eyes on her."

"I can't argue with you. I just don't expect I'll sleep much."

"I could give you a little something," Margaret said. "Knock you right out."

"What will you do if The Ghost appears?" Kane asked. "What if he attacks you after I've fallen asleep?"

"I have both a hammer and a ham sandwich in my purse," Margaret said. "He would experience a blow to the side of the head with one of them."

"You would try and kill him?" Kane asked.

"If I was lucky enough to reach for the hammer," Margaret said. "There is no lucky edge of a hammer coming to anybody."

"The man has only bitten me on the ankle."

"You asked what I would do if he attacked me," Margaret said. "If The Ghost comes to your barrack in the spirit of contrition, we can have a sit-down."

"What would you say to him?" Kane asked.

"I would say, please stop nibbling ankles. I have a ham sandwich. I know where you can get your hands on more ham."

"You don't have some sort of powder or a tonic you can throw into his face? Something to anesthetize him?"

"My favorite plans carry only a few moving parts."

185

"Why do you think The Ghost steals blood?" Kane asked. "Why would a man choose to do this?"

"I wouldn't call it a choice. He does this because he would die without it."

"How do you know?"

"It is a sickening crime," Margaret said. "It is a difficult and a risky crime. The man I knew who did this had been jailed several times. In the streets he was attacked and harassed. His family was ridiculed. If they had not been wealthy he would have been killed or run out of town. It would be foolish to assume he wanted his life. An insistent voice inhabits him. It tells him to find blood. It tells him if he does not search for blood, it will kill him."

"Why did he not leave the city after being found out?" Kane asked.

"He went into hiding," Margaret said.

Margaret Morri did not witness a disturbance that night. But in the morning, at the foot of the barrack, she discovered the hanging lock Kane used to secure his front door. It had been picked and cast aside. The wire mesh that framed his front window had also been sliced through.

"He was here, but he could not enter," Kane said.

"He certainly could have," Margaret said. "He chose not to visit."

Margaret Morri tended to Kane's wounds and then misted the barrack with a repellant.

"Talk to Julie this afternoon," Margaret said. "Tonight I am going to sleep in your cot with you. I will wear your pajamas, and you will wear my nightgown."

"If Julie hears of the lock, she will try to stay here with us," Kane said. "If The Ghost comes, I do not want her to be here. If this is your plan, we will keep it private."

In the evening, Kane and Margaret lay in Kane's cot. The cot was narrow and the two were pressed firmly against each other. Kane looked down into a nightgown of apricot rayon and cotton lace that strained against his body.

"I will ruin this," he said.

"Go ahead," Margaret Morri said. "It isn't one of my favorites anyway."

"You think he is attracted to the way I smell?" Kane asked.

"We are improvising," Margaret said. "Think of it as another coat of protection."

"Why does he only come after me?" Kane asked.

"Who says he is only coming for you?" Margaret said. "Three times he has come. Twice you have been an easy meal. But he is likely attacking others in camp."

"I thought he attacked children."

"He almost certainly is attacking children. And women and men. And the sick and elderly. And the MPs if they fall asleep. If we check in at the infirmary, they will have varied reports of people bitten by dogs and rats in their sleep. Few would expect this was the work of a man."

"Margaret," Kane said. "Please tell me the truth. Is all of this somehow an elaborate trick?"

"A trick with what purpose?" Margaret asked.

"Here we are," Kane said. "We are in bed together."

"Do you think I need to trick a man for him to get into bed with me?"

"I wouldn't think so," Kane said. "But then, is it stranger than a man who would break into my home? A man who would devour blood from my legs?"

"Do you know how The Flume was able to stay in Los Angeles after he had been identified?"

"I can't imagine it," Kane said.

"His family was very resourceful and influential," Margaret said. "The woman who discovered The Flume was an amateur healer. She made house calls. She also worked as a nanny. She cared for a young boy, Hiroki Takashima, the son of Gardena schoolteachers, living in a neighborhood where The Flume was active."

Margaret Morri rolled onto her side and retrieved a cigarette from Kane's nightstand.

"This is how he was apprehended. Hiroki had been attacked twice. So this nanny waited in his bed, posing as the child. She had shortened her hair and dressed in his socks and pajamas. One evening, when The Flume appeared, she sprang up and struck him in the side of the face with a hammer. He bled on the floor and she stood over him until the police arrived."

Margaret Morri pulled back the sheet covering Kane's right ankle. The moonlight from the barrack window fell upon it. She motioned toward his wound with her cigarette.

"This is why the halo of your wound is an incomplete circle. The Flume is missing two teeth."

Margaret Morri lit another cigarette from her own and offered it to Kane.

"The Flume had been caught breaking into the Takashimas' home and he was jailed. But after he was released, rumors began to circulate about this nanny. The rumors attacked her in a myriad of ways. Who was this Kumamoto immigrant to call herself a healer? More likely she was a superstitious crackpot. And didn't Mr. Takashima leave his wife following the incident? Did he replace his wife with this Jezebel? Had this been her scheme all along? Who had actually abused Hiroki Takashima? The hakujin of an erudite family? Or a witch who could find a thousand uses for the blood of a child?"

Margaret Morri played with a button at her neck. She stared down at her chest, covered in Kane's woolen pajamas.

"The Gardena residents who maintained the rumors were paid handsomely," Margaret said. "Some were Japanese. Some hakujin. Though after a while, the rumors evolved and maintained themselves. The best rumors propagate this way, like hydras. A lot of women with truth or power are also known as witches and tramps."

"And The Ghost went into hiding," Kane said. "Where did this woman go?"

"She was relocated to Tulare and then to Canal Camp in Gila River."

"Christ in a handbasket," Kane said. "I am sorry, Margaret. I am sorry this happened to you."

"Not me," Margaret said. "This is not my story. This is the story of my cousin. This is Zee's story. I was only her witness."

"Zee Okawa," Kane gasped.

"Does it excite you to wear my clothes?" Margaret asked. "Does it excite you to see me wear your clothes?"

"Not especially," Kane said.

"I am not here to bed you, Kane," Margaret Morri said.

"I am here to protect you. If The Flume appears I am here to strike him with a hammer. I am going to smash every tooth in his mouth if I get the opportunity. And I know you are handsome, but if you touch me and I don't ask for it, then I will be showing you the edge of my hammer."

The following morning, Margaret Morri said to Kane, "I believe my presence is keeping The Flume away. He badly wants your blood. But he smells a trap."

Then she treated Kane's wounds and said, "I will fix you a salve to rub on your legs at night. Some days we will have to ask Zee to fix the salve. She is more experienced than me. But she's finished fighting this villain directly. I will treat your bedroom with a repellent. And one night a month, I should occupy your cot with you. In this way, The Flume will know you are under protection."

It was in this way that Margaret Morri began her practice of occupying the bed of Kane Araki. This occurred even after the war and Gila River. After the West Coast was reopened to persons of Japanese ancestry. Even after Kane and Julie Kajikawa were wed in the Santa Maria Methodist Chapel and after Winnie Kamibayashi pulled three robust infants from between Julie's thighs. It wasn't solely her opposition against The Flume. Margaret Morri cured Julie's bouts of sleepwalking and insomnia. She saw Kane through stomach ulcers, slight obesity, unenthused erections. The Araki-Kajikawa children she treated for rashes, fevers, woolgathering, ill tempers, and broken hearts. Kane's marriage and family flourished while under the care of Margaret Morri, and this became an integral part of her reputation. Her practice as a healer blossomed.

The White Ghost never was apprehended in Gila River. Tales of a hakujin who peered into the windows of farming families migrated from Arizona back to California. Up and down the Central Coast of California, until just weeks before her death, Margaret Morri visited the homes of the Araki-Kajikawa sons and daughters, and the sons of those sons, and the daughters of those daughters. She rubbed the salves of sowthistle and horsenettle upon the legs of every generation descended from Kane Araki. She treated their bedrooms with repellents of woods' rose, little hogweed, orange flameflower. Once a month she visited in the night and guarded all the children in their beds.

one thousand remedies
for extraordinary sneezes

It was said between the years of 1942 to 1945 that Kane Araki attempted one thousand interventions for his monstrous sneezes. Kane's sneezes had always been deafening. Unsurprising since even as a child he had snored like a barbarian. But it wasn't until his lungs, throat, mouth, and nose met the extreme dry heat and desert irritants of Gila River that his expulsions became regular and intensified in force and volume.

It was said that a Kane Araki sneeze was violent enough to rock the Bible off your bedside and rattle a tower guard in his watchtower. His sneezes were said to shake caterpillars from sugar hackberry leaves and knock the bean pods from the limbs of a mesquite tree. They could burst the eardrums of a locust sitting upon a nearby spine of aloe or cause a nearby songbird to faint off its perch.

Every person living in the vicinity of the Araki-Morri family barrack wore a protective shell of some variety. Kashi and Yoshio Araki, Kane's mother and father, wore vests of foam rubber padding, as a sneeze once sent a bookshelf toppling, and they were clobbered by multi-volume encyclopedias. Kane's wife, Margaret Morri, wore a helmet, since once, when she went to retrieve a plum that had rolled beneath their table, a whopping sneeze startled her and she slammed her head, knocking herself flat and unconscious. Araki kin were not the only affected. Neighboring children were required to fasten cushions to the tops of their little heads with chinstraps. This was because young Wataru Miyake had been climbing a pinyon pine when Kane let loose a Herculean sneeze, snapping the branch where Wataru was dangling. Wataru bumped into eight other branches on his journey down, breaking both legs and smashing his only adult teeth.

Terue Yoshihara, the block manager overseeing the Araki-Morri family, considered relocating Kane to an encampment on the very southwestern tip of Canal Camp across Indian Route 9 and beside the sewage disposal. It wasn't a desirable resolution, but Yoshihara couldn't justify making an entire block miserable based on the ailment of one young man. Though the entire family felt embarrassed by their dilemma, they pleaded with Yoshihara to let Kane stay. A bargain was struck. The Araki-Morri family was given one month to come up with a solution to Kane's emissions.

In October of 2014, two mystifying artifacts were discovered by Corinne Araki-Morri when she was cleaning a trunk in her father's garage. The first artifact was a fifty-five-pound copper diving helmet. The second was a scroll containing hundreds of remedies for extraordinary sneezes. The scroll was divided into three columns. The first column listed the names of detainees in Canal Camp. The second column listed the remedy suggested by their family. The third column noted the results and conclusions of the remedy.

Yasuko Koga:	*"Rub your tongue against the roof of your mouth"*	*—No success. Perhaps remedy requires the tongue muscles of a town gossip.*
Nobuko Kitajima:	*"Say the words 'pineapple pickles' and squint"*	*—No success. A surprisingly stupid suggestion for a doctor's wife!*
Kingo Furukawa:	*"Pinch your upper lip until your eyes water"*	*—A drunken half-witted idea from a drunken halfwit.*

In the month allotted, Kane Araki attempted a series of homeopathic cures including peppermint oils, chamomile teas, concoctions of ginger and fennel, garlic wine, and a tiny sack of oregano worn around his neck. Margaret Morri held cold compresses of black tea and apple juice to his forehead and smeared a puree of red onion and beefsteak tomatoes across his face. He paid an acupuncturist to work on his elbow joints and the base of his cheekbones.

When Reverend Jun Shozaburo consulted with Kane Araki, he told him that excessive sneezing was often connected with sexual and malicious thoughts.

"You need to try and keep your mind clean," Shozaburo said. "I know it must be difficult work for a healthy man in his twenties. But you should think of things that are not titillating. When you get the urge to sneeze, I want you to try and imagine something horrific happening to your privates. Imagine being waist-deep at Guadalupe Beach and then a sand shark comes along and tears your knob off."

"Good lord," Kane exclaimed.

"Exactly," Shozaburo said. "Just try sneezing with that in your head. The more detailed your vision, the better. Picture the green waters surrounding you turning pink from your injury. Really try and see the sand shark with your penis and maybe also scrotum between its fierce animal jaws. Dragging them away to its black oceanic purgatory. You are going to have to practice this even when you do not have the urge to sneeze. Practice a dozen or more times a day. Then the mental tool will be waiting for you when the situation arises."

"But what if these fantasies have unforeseen consequences?" Kane asked. "I'm a married man. I don't want to frighten myself every instant I have a desire. I might become terrified of my wife."

"The desires you have for your wife are beautiful and natural," Shozaburo said. "This should be an exercise for when your desires stray from your wife."

"What if I become terrified of swimming or of Guadalupe Beach?" Kane asked. "Men in the Araki family are fishermen. We eat sand sharks."

.

"It does not have to be a sand shark you imagine," Shozaburo said. "You can imagine walking through the woods and being gored through the testicles by a stag. Or having your manhood feasted upon by mountain lions. The predators can change as long as the trauma remains the same."

For the collective wisdom offered to Kane in Canal Camp, his nasal condition did not improve. To inflame matters, one of Kane's sneezes had sent a shock wave through Terue Yoshihara's barrack, toppling a lit candle directly into his lap. Arlene Yoshihara had used a blanket to smother her husband as he rolled around on their barrack floor. She had saved his life, but in years following the event, he was hairless on the left side of his body. At the end of the month, Kane began packing a suitcase for relocation to Seed Farm Road, where there was a stand-alone barrack on the wrong side of the sewage disposal. There it was called the "Street of Poisoned Wind," because the fragrance of excrement was so thick upon the air even a detainee's dreams became polluted with otherworldly stink. With luck, Kane could be transferred after a few months to a stand-alone barrack nearer to Butte Camp, perhaps between the chicken farm and the hog farm.

Had it not been for Margaret Morri, Kane would have spent the remainder of internment humiliated and alone. But Margaret was the lead typist for the *Gila News-Courier*, and her monthly salary had shot to sixteen dollars. Her habit was to save half her earnings in a tin can disguised as Crisco shortening, and at the end of 1943 eighty-two dollars occupied the can. This is what she offered in a column inch taken out in the *Courier*—eighty-two dollars in exchange for an engineer to fashion a mask that could contain the power of Kane Araki's sneezes.

A handful of failed designs preceded victory. Ikuye Dendo presented Kane with a pillowcase to be sewn over the head. The pillowcase was packed with wadded paper. Two slits were made in the pillowcase—one to hold a pipe for Kane to breathe, and the other for Kane to squint through. Junko Aoyama presented Kane with a string shopping sack to be slipped over the head. The sack was wound with more string netting, and then fresh cornhusk was crammed into the nooks and crannies. The pillowcase nearly suffocated Kane and the string sack depressed him.

"Is my head a heap of fish to be packed in all this netting?" Kane asked.

It was Tadanobu Gennosuke, an engineer and amateur diver from Turlock, who appeared with the copper diving hat. The interior of the helmet was padded using burlap and rubber for comfort, and portions of it outfitted with egg carton crating so Kane would not rupture his own eardrums from any tremendous discharge.

This was how Kane Araki came to be known in Gila River as the man in the copper diving helmet. Kane was required to don the helmet when he resided in a public setting—the mess hall, canteen, post office, latrine, and recreation barracks. Much of the time the face mask of his diving helmet remained open. But if stricken by the urge to sneeze, he secured the thick glass window and only a very tiny eruption could be detected.

When the copper diving helmet was discovered by Corinne Araki-Morri in 2014, she removed it from the trunk and placed it over her head. Then she wobbled into the living room wearing it. Her father was there upon a reclining sofa, throwing back a fistful of walnuts into his mouth and watching television.

"What do you think of this?" Corinne asked.

"It's slimming," Kane said.

"What was this helmet for?"

"From when I was a diver in Gila River."

"You mean in the Arizona desert?" she asked.

"That's right," Kane said.

"See a lot of fish there, did you?"

"Mostly sand sharks."

"Good lord, Dad," she said. "Lordy. Do you think it could be the start of it?"

"What is starting?"

"The dementia."

"If I had dementia, do you think I would be able to diagnose myself?"

"You diagnosed your gout. You knew when you needed hearing aids."

"That's because I could see your mouth moving, but no insults were coming out."

"You seem healthy. You're being wise. We can ask your doctor when we check up on your diabetes."

"I don't need to see a doctor. That helmet was for my allergies."

"What is that supposed to mean?"

"My allergies were worse when I was young. I had to sneeze a lot. Things were different then. You wouldn't get it. You never had to live in the desert."

"You wore this in camp?"

"Yes."

"Well didn't you get hot?"

"It was a metal diving helmet in a hundred-degree weather. What do you think?"

"Well did you sweat in here? Did you clean it?"

"I can't remember that. It was seventy years ago."

"Gross," Corinne said. She shed the helmet and placed it on the floor. "It has a weird smell. Why did you let me keep wearing it?"

a tiny murder

Margaret Morri was working a month for the *Gila News-Courier* when she knocked a tower of back editions to the floor and discovered her own face gaping up at her. In the photo she was wearing a modest dress and singing Ruth Lowe's "I'll Never Smile Again" as part of Gila River's camp talent show. The caption further revealed the performer's name to be Alice Aoki, eldest daughter of Stan and Michi Aoki, from Mendota, California. Their family was currently relocated to the northernmost block, where families tended to be larger, the barracks older, more prone to the infestations of pests, and the mess halls rationed less meat.

Alice's resemblance to Margaret was uncanny. Both she and Margaret possessed the highest of foreheads, the most slender jaws, the most prominent limbal rings cordoning their eyes, the loosest, darkest curls settling against their cheekbones. The pattern of Alice's dress was even reminiscent of something Margaret had worn to her first adolescent socials. Margaret couldn't help folding the pages and sliding them into her purse. In the evening she clipped the worn image and taped it into a journal for future inspection.

Over the next days Margaret probed the *Courier*'s office for any information about Alice Aoki. The photographer credited for the shot, Henri Kamitaki, recalled the performance instantly. Alice had arrested the audience with her beauty and uncommonly rich voice. Henry had been so stunned that he'd forgotten to raise his camera to his face. Only later did he realize his fingers had unconsciously snapped and wound a series of photos of Alice while his camera hung against his belly.

"It's why the angle is a little low," he said. "It's miraculous the lens stayed in focus."

Kenneth Yano, the reporter who had written up the story, also remembered Alice's beauty and charisma.

"She was the most talented singer that evening by a long shot," Kenneth said. Afterward, he had eaten dinner beside her family and discovered Alice was also accomplished in ikebana and as a seamstress.

The more Margaret uncovered of Alice, the more her resentment began to swell in the recesses of her lower gut, the pit of her throat, the tension gripping her hands. Hadn't it been just two years before when everyone was praising the strength and precision of her own singing voice? When the exquisite fragility of her own flower arrangements was sought after? Wasn't her own physical beauty commended on a weekly if not daily basis?

But perhaps people had been sparer with their admiration lately. And what compliments she received were too chaste and impassive. Mostly it was the dull, monotonous praise of her husband and his family. What garbage that all seemed to Margaret, held up beside Alice's widespread acclaim, Kamitaki's photograph of her pristine features.

The arrival of Alice Aoki in Margaret's life provoked the competitiveness she'd learned to feed as a young girl. Her older sister, Laurie, had continually plotted to keep Margaret in her shadow. In their youth, Laurie established herself as a dutiful daughter and caretaker. Laurie was responsible. Laurie was a skilled cook. She knew how to pickle vegetables. How to crush and reduce fruit over a low flame for preserves. She regularly prepared the family's meals since both their parents worked long, hot days in the lettuce fields. Laurie had a natural gift for painting and for watercolors. She was also kind and pretty and drew the attention of many boys in her class.

In order to carve out her own personhood, it had been necessary for Margaret to undercut Laurie at every campaign. As a child, Margaret refused to let Laurie dress her or to comb her hair. Even as they walked together to school, Margaret demanded Laurie keep three paces behind her.

"Paces," she remembered confirming forcefully. "Not steps, Laurie. There is a difference. If you get too close to me I'm going to throw my juice on you."

Margaret suggested that, out of respect, Laurie should produce paintings of their parents and family friends. Then, no matter its likeness, she would criticize the result for its unflattering or melancholic portrayal.

"Why would you paint Grandma's face so gray?" Margaret would exclaim. "Is she smelly? Decomposed? Why do you want our grandma to die? You think she will leave you money? Jewelry? Selfish cow. You could've at least painted her a decent bouquet. The flowers she is holding are wilted."

In later years, Margaret planted the notion in her mother that Laurie should marry as young as possible. Laurie was the sort to settle into a frivolous, spinster existence with her parents if allowed to get too comfortable. If she did not capitalize on her looks, which soon would tarnish, she'd surely forfeit any ability to produce heirs. Just prior to her high school graduation, Laurie was arranged to marry a local farm laborer. Her husband was an older man with hard features. Margaret said he looked the sort to keep Laurie honest and well fed.

Laurie hadn't been the only woman Margaret had been forced to outclass. There had also been her former friend, Lilly Shimabukuro, who had once been engaged to Margaret's husband, Yoshikane Araki. The three of them had been schoolmates and friends for years when Lilly conspired to steal Yoshi's affection for herself. Yoshi was both handsome and a local competitor at bodybuilding events. And it was well known that he would never have chosen a girl so plain as Lilly had Margaret not acted as a catalyst for their friendship. A lazier woman would've conceded the fight at Lilly and Yoshi's engagement. Disowned the pair as ingrates. But Margaret only burrowed further within their union. Planted seeds of anxiety and mistrust until the two lovers transfigured into enemies.

After Margaret's marriage to Yoshi, she discovered him to be an unlucky gambler and a sloppy drinker. And though he remained muscle-bound, she often thought him too short. There were moments over the years where she fantasized that Lilly had outsmarted her. Somehow tricked her into snatching a marriage she knew would swiftly stale. Though these grudges were difficult to hold against a girl simpleminded as Lilly.

Perhaps a lack of a rival had been the problem, Margaret thought.

Marriage had turned her soft, uninspired. When was the last time she had practiced her scales? When was the last time she'd presented a flower arrangement? Of course the options for flowers were greatly diminished in Gila River. But varieties of rocks and bark and succulents were abundant.

In the weeks that followed, Margaret underwent a conversion. She woke in the dark, and in the latrines practiced her singing. She studied her echoes for imperfections in her pitch and timbre. If she was interrupted, she walked to the Methodist church and sang to the empty pews. In order to strengthen her vocal cords, she relentlessly hummed during work and through meals. She drank concoctions of cider vinegar and honey. She wrapped her throat in hot towels. She held her face over steaming bowls of ginger-infused water. At night she no longer made love to her husband, because she sensed that regular orgasms made her too undisciplined during the day.

She asked the mess halls for their discarded mayonnaise canisters, and in them she accumulated petrified leaves, bones, pebbles, berries, seed pods, the scooped-out carapaces of beetles. Anything that might work as decoration. She picked every desert flower she came across and bundled them in Mason jars. Her shelves swelled with failed arrangements. Yoshi began complaining that the pollen was giving him hay fever. So Margaret began placing some of her handiwork on the desks of coworkers. Soon she was receiving compliments for her artistic expression and resourcefulness, her ability to suggest verdant hills and valleys using minimal items.

Through her regimen, Margaret felt as though she was regaining some of the ground she'd surrendered to Alice Aoki. She wondered if she outdid Alice on every level, might she perform a tiny version of murder? Wasn't this what Alice sought with all her accolades? To erase the virtues of others by installing herself as a minor deity?

Three months from when Margaret first set eyes on the photograph, she received word that Alice would be visiting the *Courier*'s office. Dennis Shimabukuro, Lilly's older brother, and Alice were placing their wedding announcement for the following week. Margaret was stunned when she heard the news. Dennis was without peer in his kindness, but he was also ugly. Margaret had only to hold his name against her tongue to remember the ghoulish face, the crooked teeth, the cheap, unfashionable shirts. As long as Margaret and Lilly had been friends, Dennis had worshipped Margaret like a beaten dog. Now he was subjecting her doppelganger to the same affections. It was mildly offensive a woman of Alice's talents would settle for a man in Dennis's condition. Of course, she wouldn't have counted on Lilly to intervene. Lilly did not understand what comprised an appropriate match for lovers. If Lilly had had it her way, Margaret would be trapped in the same predicament.

On the one hand, Margaret was compelled to rescue Alice. Any number of fibs could sour Dennis's reputation. She could say Dennis was aggressive with her. That he'd once slid his hand up her dress. She could say he was a liar or a private drunk. She could say he was cruel to animals. That he'd once struck her family's dog with his car and never confessed.

A dead dog anecdote could be difficult to weave into a casual conversation, Margaret thought. She also felt hesitant to make this sort of confrontation. Could Alice be receptive to it? Lilly would have slandered her to Alice by now. Implicating her as the cause of her failed romance with Yoshi.

Margaret let herself fantasize a violent confrontation. The two of them caught in one of the *Courier*'s empty offices. Alice yanking her by the shoulder, feeling the heat of Alice's face held uncomfortably close to her own.

"Lilly told me some things about you, you filthy cow," Alice would say. "If you ever come near my husband, I'll tear the vocal cords from your throat and sling them over the fence!"

But then Alice must've had a sound reason for agreeing to marriage. What could it be? Dennis's family had no money. Their farm and property were stripped before internment. Had the Shimabukuro family inherited a secret fortune? Was there property or a family connection Margaret had no knowledge of? Was Alice a whore for pity? Was there a ploy to make her own beauty more apparent by standing beside a man so beastly? Had she become accidentally pregnant? Was Alice attempting to strike jealousy in a former lover who refused to marry her?

That best course of action was to avoid meeting Alice. Whatever Alice's intentions for becoming a member of the

Shimabukuro family, an encounter with her at this juncture was risky. She would feign a stomachache and take a long walk around the racetrack before returning home. But as Margaret entered the offices of Columbus Okawa, the *Courier*'s chief editor, she found herself eye to eye with the woman whose reputation had tormented her the past months.

Margaret had expected a slightly more mature woman. But in the flesh, Alice looked at least five years her junior. Alice's features did not impress her in the way she'd anticipated. Alice could only be called nearly pretty and was far taller than her photograph implied. Margaret knew Alice's height alone made her inaccessible to most men. Margaret had discovered men despised tall women and that when men complimented these tall women, it was only a method of obscuring their jealousy. Alice was also thinner and less feminine than her photograph implied. At a glance she might appear refined, but if one inspected her closely, it was clear her clothes were outdated and had been altered by hand.

"I didn't realize you were busy," Margaret said to Okawa.

But just as she turned to leave, Henri Kamitaki entered the office and placed a hand on her shoulder.

"Margaret, this is the woman you were asking about," he said. "Alice Aoki."

Kamitaki stepped away from their eyeline as they nodded over to each other.

"It's incredible you haven't met," Kamitaki said. "I was only just saying the two of you have a number of common interests."

"Good lord," Okawa said. "The two of them even look a bit similar? Don't you think?"

"Yes," Kamitaki said. "Around the eyes. I think I see that."

As Alice stepped between Margaret and Kamitaki, Margaret had to steel herself from recoiling. She sensed the dread of two discrete realities being erased for the existence of a single, mongrel reality.

"I've wanted to meet you for some time," Alice said. "A number of people told me the two of us could be sisters."

Alice briefly reached out. Then she pulled her hand back and touched her own cheek.

"I think it was too kind a compliment," she said. "You have to be the most beautiful girl I've ever seen in camp."

As Alice brought her hand to rest on Margaret's shoulder, Margaret felt the color drain from her face.

"My sister-in-law Lilly told me some lovely things about you," Alice said. "I hope the three of us spend some time together soon."

Alice waved goodbye to Kamitaki and Okawa. And at the sight of her leaving, Margaret shuddered and nearly collapsed.

a conception in 1944

Margaret Morri was the love child of Shyogo Morri and Chiye Sahara, conceived in 1944 within the northwest barracks, also called "The Yoshihara Barracks" of Butte Camp after block manager Terue Yoshihara, the administrator known for using bear fat to slick back his hair and for allowing internees to run amok, teenagers to sneak into recreation barracks after curfew, packs of old bachelors to press desert blackberries, figs, and prickly pears into spirits, schoolgirls to breed deer mice for pets, and all variations of shadow economy, Terue's barrack itself a covert market for jewelry, lighters, pork pie hats, raisin wines, and most coveted of all forbidden commodities, the pornographic postcards rendered by famed artist Eve Shimabukuro, also known as "Lady Nightmare Shimabukuro," for it was told those lucky enough to steal a glance at her work, no matter how fleeting, would be haunted by filthy dreams rooted in the image until the day they fell to their ancestors or the day their cocks fell from their waists like handfuls of black petals knocked from a dead flower, whichever arrived sooner, The Yoshihara Barracks was also known as "The Screaming Wife Barracks," for it was the site many a husband lost their monthly camp pay, sixteen, seventeen dollars to gambling, chess or checkers perhaps, dice, three shells and a pea, bets upon unauthorized boxing matches, and where Chiye Sahara won Shyogo Morri's Christian soul at the card table, the only prize sufficient to match against a box of dried dates, a .22 pellet rifle, and a Nightmare Shimabukuro postcard, its rumored title "Julie Kajikawa of Gomorrah," and the exclamations which were reported to have arisen after Sahara unveiled her hand, a hand so devastating it could have blown a crater into the face of the Sonoran Desert, those whoops and yelps were said to have deafened all the locust in Gila River, feral dogs howling, bottles lobbed and crashing, Sahara's girlfriends pounding their fists against the walls, grown men sobbing into their hands, grandfathers whipping the wigs from their sweat-glistening domes and stamping them upon the barrack floorboards, Shyogo fainting and crumpling before Chiye's small, hard-sole moccasins.

Days later, once the smoke cleared, much debate was had over what it meant for a farm girl of just seventeen to possess the very soul of a forty-year-old bachelor. Was Chiye in ownership of all Shyogo's belongings? Could this mean merely the suitcase of sweatpants and woolen caps and dress socks he had carried with him to camp? Or could Chiye claim his plot of strawberry fields in California? Could she dictate all his labors? Was she allowed to humiliate him publicly? What sorts of humiliations might be inappropriate? What forms of public shaming might be in good taste?

Of these concerns, Shyogo remained in a state of suspense until August of 1944 when Chiye began cornering Shyogo in the storage closet of the Butte canteen. She visited him three minutes after closing, while Shyogo was retrieving the items for restocking—chewing tobacco, candy bars, candles, Dixie Peach pomade, mouthwash. Those items Chiye would slap out of Shyogo's hands, pull his face down into hers, order his pants off and his cock turgid, and then would ride Shyogo against the stiff wooden floorboards until the muscles of her pelvis, hips, thighs, and calves knotted and seized, until her knees wore down to gelatin, until their moans went hoarse, until penned-in by discarded undergarments, a tide pool of sweat submerged them both and Shyogo's balls were as dry as soda crackers. And then a late-afternoon visit on the cusp of September, Chiye, a burning cigarette between her fingers, without having yet dismounted her straddle, a starfish of sweat appearing on the boards beneath Shyogo's limp body, announced that they were pregnant with their first daughter. Shyogo would remember experiencing a cognitive flash of panic and joy and skepticism, though he did not have the moisture in his throat to respond, and it would take him weeks with the Butte Camp chiropractor until he might properly pump his fist into the sky in triumph and gratitude.

Following the Gila River Relocation, though Chiye and Shyogo were married over forty years, Shyogo claimed his

211

wife never did formally return his soul, so that he some days had to wonder where Shyogo actually *was*. Was Shyogo in this bed pressed against the body of his napping wife? Was Shyogo upon this wooden bench massaging the knots from the center of his wife's tiny foot? Was Shyogo at this frying pan staring into the hamburger-beans okazu? Was Shyogo in this pediatrician's office kissing the baby fat where Margaret Morri received her vaccinations? Or was Shyogo actually locked away in another place? Where had Chiye placed Shyogo's soul in Gila River all those years ago? Had she been careful to keep it intact despite all their migrations? The shared rooms in Chicago? Detroit? All the California railroad apartments? Throughout the Central Valley? The little home on West Church Street in Santa Maria? When had she ever shown particular attention to a moving box? What were the chances his soul had been abandoned or misplaced?

In their forty years together, Shyogo could not sleep before he knew Chiye had nodded off. At night, he stroked her hair until her jaw became slack and a gentle snoring emerged. He was anxious when Chiye returned home late from work or from a meeting with friends. He was frightened by the sounds of her coughs or sneezes. Was Shyogo worried Chiye would die swiftly, abruptly, before she could return his soul? What did it mean for the owner of a soul to depart and an executor to know nothing of an agreement made in 1944? Did Chiye ever daydream of Shyogo's death? Did she ever wonder what part of Shyogo could actually dissolve and leave her, should his heart stop or his lungs collapse before his soul was returned?

"Or is this simply the way old men are so poorly designed to love?" Shyogo once asked Chiye. "Is love always so full of longing and agitation?"

"Love is a weak explanation for what all this is," Chiye had told him. "I own everything you have that there is no language for. Your soul has a name, but what we have does not. Time will steal love and our bodies. But there is no separation for us. It is the best we can call what we have. Never separation."

oxlip and pearl

Michael Araki, the eldest child and only son of Margaret Morri and Yoshikane Araki, was conceived years before their legal marriage, in the southeastern block of Canal Camp in Gila River during the month of oxlip and pearl. Mud poured from the chutes of barracks and froze from the outer rafters in blackened stalactites. Behind neighborhood barracks, under threat of that violence, Margaret and Kane stripped nude as calves and engaged in night after night of doomed, clandestine, teenage fucking. The stalactites rocked, hummed above their moans, glinted as they collected the ghost-steam of their breath, and threatened to spear them through. Overhead the tower guards could be heard patting their rifles, mumbling to their bullets. Still, Kane and Margaret gladly returned. They lived with their families in partitioned barracks that were shared with two or three other families and were rarely granted time to be alone together.

Through her pregnancy, Margaret craved fried meat. Because red meat was tightly rationed in camp, Kane found a way to blue-plate diners in Casa Grande and other neighboring Arizona towns. In the mornings Kane hid behind racks in darkened trailers of bread and vegetable trucks. The freight trucks left camp, pulled into Casa Grande to load their cargo, and that was the moment Kane would slip away, locate a diner, purchase hamburgers or hotdogs or fried baloney sandwiches wrapped in crinkled, yellow paper, and then squeeze back into the trucks for the long, cramped ride back into camp.

Kane was secretly carted around in delivery trucks for six months. The evenings were reserved for singing. Kane's brothers Dennis and Shimmy played guitar and ukulele. Friends and family gathered in the southeast block's mess hall and projected song after song toward Margaret's pregnant belly. Kane and Margaret were the first newly pregnant couple in Gila. The excitement of the Araki-Morri child vibrated through the teenage generation like radio current.

The morning of the snake was two weeks before Margaret's due date. Kane and Margaret were walking in the camp gardens amid desert trees and high grass when Kane saw Margaret go under like a stalk of wheat cut at the ground. Margaret made no sound. Kane opened his mouth but all his voice rushed beyond his teeth and lips. He choked on his silence and ran. Kane never found the snake, merely two holes at Margaret's ankle running with blood.

The venom did not kill Margaret. She spent two weeks in the infirmary, during which time she miscarried. Kane recovered the small, stillborn body of Michael Araki and carried him out of camp. On a pyre of mesquite and desert willow, Kane burned the tiny body and buried what the wind would not take. After Gila River, in the decades that followed their move back to California, Margaret and Kane Morri had three daughters. All three claimed to share recurring dreams in which they could hear singing and smell hot desert wind.

all your sweet babes

Before Gila River, the Araki-Morri family lived just outside Santa Maria on a property nearest where West Main Street turned from a paved thoroughfare and into unending strawberry fields. The intersection of Blosser Road and West Main was called *the corner of crying dogs* by locals, because owners who would no longer keep their pet for any reason—acquiring an allergy to their coat, a baby on the way, migration at the end of a picking season—found it a convenient spot to abandon them. It was a common sight when passing to find dogs of multiple owners tied to the final street sign. If they were of an anxious or aggressive nature, the sand would be marked with blood and bottle flies.

If a pup merely was left on the road and not tied to a street sign, then usually she or he wandered into the yard of the Araki-

Morris. Kane Araki, Margaret Morri, and the three adolescent Araki-Morri daughters doled out bowls of table scraps and hotdog meat, deflead, scrubbed, stitched the wounds, and showed inexhaustible love for the succession of unwanted pets. That transient pack usually hovered at around eight dogs. It was a good number with plenty of benefit to the Araki-Morris. The populations of voles, brown rats, and pocket gophers were kept to a minimum. Raccoons and possums did not rattle their metal trash bins in the night. And as a pack, they were impenetrable even for the most fearsome intruders. Twice the Araki-Morris discovered their dogs at the edge of their strawberry fields feasting upon the half-carcass of a slain mountain lion.

Because the dogs came to the girls without collars, they were bestowed one of two names. No matter their age or sex, they became either *Ouji* or *Ojiichan*, the first meaning *prince* and the second meaning *grandpa*. If the girls had been able to keep them all it would've meant dozens of Ouji, of Ojiichan, dozens of fur coats rippling like countershaded lightning through the rear orchard and around the rows of squash, heads of lettuce, artichokes, pumpkins, flowers. But every dog had their time when they would make their break and attempt to walk the twelve miles into town, back to their original owner. The Araki-Morris rarely recovered any dogs after that. They imagined either they were run down by a car. Or were overtaken by coyotes. Or it would be the familiar sickening crack of a neighbor's rifle.

When 9066 called for Kane and Margaret to board their windows and pack a suitcase each in preparation for evacuation, the girls worked diligently to place their eight

Ouji and Ojiichan with schoolmates. These were children of white, Mexican, and Filipino families who were covered with the promises that the Araki-Morris would reclaim them the moment they were allowed back in California.

And then on the April morning before relocation, the family awoke to discover no fewer than a hundred dogs rambling through their property as though in a daze.

The family recognized a number of them. Some were the dogs of friends and relatives. Though all of them were without collars, they approached excitedly, affectionately, to the sound of their names being called.

Pete Yamamoto, Kane's schoolmate and Santa Maria's dogcatcher, was sent for. But when he arrived at the Araki-Morri farm, he was out of uniform and explained that he had been forced to turn his job over to another. Even his own mutts he'd had to surrender over to his landlord.

"We have to think up a way to bring them with us," the girls said to Pete Yamamoto. "Don't you think every family will want one? They will want something to make them feel like they're back at home."

"If families thought they could manage to relocate with their pets, then we'd see more of them try," Pete Yamamoto said. "You have them here because of desperation. Plus, I don't see how soldiers are going to let one family board a train with a hundred dogs."

"We'll disguise them," the girls said. "We'll swaddle them in blankets. They'll look just like newborns."

"And who will carry in all your sweet babes?" Pete Yamamoto asked.

"We'll split them up between us. We're strong. We can punch air holes in our luggage and switch them in place of our clothes."

"And what clothes will you wear in Tulare? In Gila River?"

"We'll wear our extra outfits in layers," the girls said.

"And you'll faint from heat exhaustion," Pete Yamamoto said. "Dressed in layers of winter coats and carrying around thirty dogs apiece. It does not sound an easy job for young girls."

"They can follow us alongside the train then," the girls said. "We'll buy twenty or thirty pounds of weenies from The Aloha Market and chop them up. We'll tie some to sticks and lure them to the station. Once the train begins moving we'll start dropping chopped weenies from the windows every few seconds."

"It all sounds very clever," Pete Yamamoto said. "Very Hansel and very Gretel. And what will happen to these pooches if birds swoop down and take up their trail of hotdogs?"

"They can follow the tracks. The vibrations. Their ears are more sensitive than ours. We'll teach them a song. And we'll sing it the entire trip."

"It's more than a hundred and fifty miles to Tulare. The older dogs here won't make it. Even if you manage to gather them all, who will feed them?"

"Soldiers in Tulare will want dogs. Especially soldiers away from home for the first time. They'll keep them from getting lonely. A soldier can find a way to feed a dog."

"It's a compassionate plan," Pete Yamamoto said. "But it might be foolish to rely on military police to respond kindly to requests like these."

The Araki-Morri daughters looked on despondently. A kind of Border Collie mongrel appeared beneath their hands, entreating them. They ran their tiny fingers through his coat and called him Ouji.

"Let's not get ourselves down," Pete Yamamoto said. "There's something we can do while we think of better solutions. We'll nail signs all over town and in Guadalupe. I'll put some calls in to our friends in Arroyo Grande and Santa Barbara and Oxnard. The signs will ask for families to come and collect any dog they like. Whatever dogs are left the pound will have to take in. I don't like their chances there. But with luck, the people here will rally to help them."

The entire day was spent posting dozens of handwritten signs in pharmacies, schools, mortuaries, feed stores, theaters, butcher shops, department stores, bars, and diners. The signs gave a brief explanation of the hundred-dog situation and listed the Araki-Morris address. At the bottom of the signs it also read, *With thanks, pick all the avocadoes, asparagus, artichokes, snow peas, and sugar snaps you can carry away.* A couple of column inches were purchased in *The Santa Maria Times* to run the same information over the following days.

All day, the girls suggested further solutions. The dogs could be taken up by the Marine Corps to become war dogs for the Pacific. The dogs could be shipped to the Midwest to be used for herding livestock. The dogs could be sent to Nashville, Tennessee, to be trained as guide dogs. The dogs could be delivered to every firehouse and junkyard in California. In the late afternoon the girls set up a tent in the orchard surrounded by the heat of dozens of dozing canines. The girls slept not having any vision for the following days.

On the morning the Araki-Morris left, the hundred deserted dogs were still there. Black Labradors, Retrievers, cattle dogs, pit bulls, spaniels, Border Collies and other sheepdogs, German Shepherds, terriers, Huskies, Whippets, Rottweilers all drifting silently through the property in a stupor. The girls wandered beside them, attempting to sneak them slices of white bread they had hidden in their dress pockets. Before a commotion could be had, Margaret and Kane stopped them.

"They're all so hungry," the girls said.

"We don't have enough to feed them all," Margaret said. "They'll begin to fight if you feed only a few of them."

"There's something strange about the dogs who came here," the girls said. "They're like ghosts. What do you think they're waiting here for? Why do you think they haven't tried to walk back into town?"

The image of those animals would be the way the Araki-Morri family remembered their home during their years of relocation, first to the Tulare Assembly Center, and then to Butte Camp in Gila River. In 1946, the Araki-Morris returned to Santa Maria to find their home ransacked. The storage shed that'd kept much of their furniture and clothing had been burned to the ground. In their orchard and in the cut rows overtaken by foxtail and sow thistle and white clover were also the desiccated bodies of dozens of dogs. At the end of the year, the city issued an invoice to the Araki-Morris for seven dollars and sixteen cents. It was the price of the ammunition that had been used to shoot the dogs down.

a lesson

Yoshikane Araki and Margaret Morri once complained they lived in a barrack possessing the thinnest partitions in all of the Gila River Relocation. Though they had not performed a legitimate study of this, they were absolutely correct in their assumption. Extreme shifts in weather, cheap building materials, and the nesting of desert insects assured the Araki-Morri dividing wall was Gila's record-holding most slender wafer of wood paneling indeed by a margin of six and a quarter millimeters. Furthermore, Kane and Margaret's quarters were lodged in the noisiest, most overcrowded block at the southernmost, easternmost corner of all the Gila River neighborhoods. It was also the youngest, hippest neighborhood, host to dozens of interned artists, though this came as little comfort. If a military police board had bothered to perform a census, had taken down the combined ages of every married couple in the southeast block, they would've discovered Kane and Margaret, at their combined, respective ages of eighty-two and eighty-five, were the oldest pair by more than a century above the mean.

Although this statistic could never be discussed outright, those who observed Kane and Margaret couldn't help but speculate how uncomfortable the age disparity made them on a daily basis. Did being around such young couples fill them with nostalgia? Regret? Longing? Despair? Did it make them feel wise and superior? What did human senility actually feel like anatomically? Could they feel it against their bodies, rubbing against them along with the day's grime? Did they smell it on mornings they squeezed and lathered their dirty laundry? Did they hear it clinking around in their language when they exchanged greetings with the neighbors?

At the Methodist church, Kane and Margaret were the only couple who dared claim a front pew, an arrangement made more noticeable when they inevitably dozed during the sermon. In the showers, Margaret couldn't help compare the relaxed, discolored properties of her own skin to the seamless, almost pubescent bodies of the other women. And then there was the barber who slapped Kane upon the shoulder and announced enthusiastically that Jiichan Araki was his favorite patron, since he regularly asked for his nostril hairs to be pruned back. But the only aspect of the southeast block egregious enough to turn Kane and Margaret into sour, old goat curmudgeons occurred between the hours of 11 P.M. and 2 A.M. every night, when the two were awoken by the distinct noises of newly married couples fiercely, hysterically fucking each other.

Kane and Margaret's barrack was divided into sleeping quarters for three couples. Their dividing wall was shared with Joy and Shimmy Nakamura, who had been touring folk singers as well as peach and almond farmers from Stockton, California. And on the opposite side of the Nakamuras lived Randy and Mina Ota of Turlock, an aeronautics engineer and a painter. The Ota couple were the worst offenders, as they'd met and married in camp and made love with the doom and desperation of two people who imagined their bodies would dissolve if and when they slept. And this desperation was always punctuated by Randy's orgasmic squeals and his frantic, uncontrollable sobs.

"Why would a man feel the need to cry during sex?" Margaret asked Kane. "Is he not getting it exactly the way he wants?"

"Maybe he cries because sex is so beautiful at their age," Kane said. "And he can't take it how very much complete he feels. As he's down there sticking her with it."

"Of course there's that, the beauty thing," Margaret said. "Though it doesn't entirely sound beautiful and transcendent. It sounds as if he's starving to death and can't undo a lid from a jar of pickles."

"Anyhow, it isn't our business," Kane said. "I shouldn't have joked. We need to try and ignore them."

"I could understand if there was something painful about it," Margaret said. "If he had a medical condition. If his little weenie fell off every time, at the exact moment he finished. And he had to sew it back between his legs by candlelight. Then all this sobbing would make plenty of sense."

"You would like that to be the reason, wouldn't you? I can hear the excitement in your voice. You wish you were a doctor of that condition."

"Mina should be the one crying. She doesn't sound as if she is enjoying herself."

"How would you know that? We can hardly imagine what they might be doing."

"Listen to Joy when she and Shimmy are going at it," Margaret said. "That is the timbre of a lady who is enjoying herself."

"I've heard of some men who cry after," Kane said. "I've heard there are women who cry too."

"Who have you heard that from? About the crying after. Who does an old man like you talk to about those things?"

"Oh, I don't know. You want me to give you a name? The name of a specific person who told me that?"

"We're too old to keep secrets from each other," Margaret said.

"Aiko," Kane said. "Well, she used to cry occasionally. Afterward."

"Your other wife," Margaret said. "Jesus. Yuck."

"You wanted to know," Kane said. "It didn't happen all the time."

"Christ, your wife though. I wish you hadn't told me that. Now I'm imagining it."

"She's been dead over forty years. I didn't think it would mean anything to you."

"Why did she cry though? I mean, didn't you ever ask her why she did it?"

"There are situations you aren't supposed to ask questions."

"But, you never took it personally?"

"No, she told me not to. She told me it was just the way she was. She couldn't stop shivering either."

"I thought you said you never discussed it."

"We never did any more than that. It makes people uncomfortable to discuss it at length. I don't ask you why you cry when you get tanked."

"You don't ask me. But I can tell you precisely. When I drink I can't help but remember all the things I wanted to sing and write and paint and all the places I wanted to travel in my life. And I realize I'm only a drunk, ugly old woman who is trapped in this life and can't go anywhere."

"You aren't so very ugly," Kane said. "You're actually very pretty for a woman of your age."

"Jesus, they're at it again," Margaret said. "Listen to them,"

Kane and Margaret listened to Randy snorting. They could feel the Ota bed frame vibrating against the planks of the floor.

"I feel sorry for the Nakamuras," Kane said. "They must get it even louder than us."

"Those two pigs are always at it as well," Margaret said. "We should teach them all a lesson."

"What sort of lesson would we teach them?" Kane asked.

"I'm not sure," Margaret said. "Maybe I'll light this whole barrack on fire. They'll be so engrossed they won't even notice."

"This is how it should be when a couple is young," Kane said. "Like a pack of rabbits. Even our reverend would agree."

"To hell with the reverend then," Margaret said. "Our reverend doesn't have to share a room at night with these rabbits in heat."

Other nights, the sounds of the Nakamuras making love were slow and mournful, and Kane and Margaret were roused from their dreams gradually, painfully, as though being reeled back from the world over by tethers fixed about their ankles.

"I had my dream again," Margaret said. "I had my dream I was walking along Venice Beach, and I came upon an enormous whale dying gruesomely on the sand. It was crying through a massive, dripping eye like a black melon. And when the whale opened its mouth to speak to me, the disgusting sex groans of Joy Nakamura came out."

Kane pretended not to hear her and rolled onto his side. Margaret threw the covers back, crept toward the dividing wall, and pressed the side of her face against it.

"Margaret, get away from there," he said. "It isn't right to spy on them."

"I'll listen to what I want," Margaret said, waving Kane away. "They aren't hiding this from anyone."

As the Nakamuras' moans seemed to grow more urgent, more critical, Kane rose from bed and stood with his good ear near the partition.

"Oh boy," Margaret said. "How long are his strokes? I just don't understand it."

"Maybe he isn't inside her," Kane said. "Maybe he's using his mouth. They say he's a great master of the harmonica."

Margaret had to cover her mouth with both hands to smother her laughter.

"Quiet," Kane said. "They'll hear you and think we're perverts for listening to them."

Margaret climbed back into bed and pulled the blankets over her face. She continued to cackle. Kane moved beside her, and the groans continued to grow more troubled and insistent. Then abruptly they fell into silence.

"Sounds like he got it done," Kane said. "It didn't sound easy."

"I hope he brushes his teeth before he goes back to sleep," Margaret said.

From beyond the dividing wall they heard the wooden chamber of a guitar being knocked around, tuned, and then strummed. And then the muffled singing voices of the Nakamuras filled the barrack.

"Oh Jesus and Mary," Margaret said. "Now they have to write a Goddamn song about how great it was."

"They have nice voices," Kane said. "Sweet voices."

"Let them use their sweet voices when the sun is out and so am I."

"What does it matter? What urgent business have we got on our morning schedule?"

"That isn't the point. Discretion is the point. Respect for your neighbors is the point. And yes, by the way, all of us have jobs to go to in the morning. The mess hall doesn't take its own inventory. The *Courier* isn't going to write your stories for you."

"The mess hall and the *Courier* will run with or without us. The bread trucks will arrive in the docks. The meat will get rationed. When I kick the bucket they'll find a cheaper reporter to write on the JACL and the WRA and the people who leave camp."

"It isn't decent, neighborly behavior," Margaret said. "I tell you, I'm going to teach them a lesson. The Nakamuras and the Otas and the Goddamn couples we can hear from across the track too."

"A lesson," Kane said. "Who do you think you are to teach a grown person their manners?"

"We're just going to show them how it feels to have their sleep interrupted," Margaret said. "We're going to wait until we hear them snoring. And then we're going to let them hear the sounds of an old couple going at it."

"Don't be crazy. You want everyone in camp talking about us tomorrow?"

"Let them talk. We might die here in the southeast block. I haven't got anything at stake."

"We have children and grandchildren in the block over. You don't think they're going to be embarrassed?"

"You're telling me you won't do it? Fine. I don't need your help. I'll sit in a chair by their wall and do it myself."

"I didn't say I wouldn't do it," Kane said. "I just want to wait a moment and contemplate what you're dragging us into."

"If you're too scared of the consequences, I'll do it myself. I don't need a partner just to make dirty sounds."

"I very much doubt that," Kane said. "They'd know in a second it wasn't authentic. All I'm saying is we've got to have a plan. We may even have to write a script."

"A script, hell," Margaret said. "This is not an acting class. I know what sounds to make. They've been waking me up every Goddamn night."

"If it doesn't sound convincing, they're going to know we're doing this out of spite. And then it won't be a lesson. It'll only mean angry neighbors."

"Fine," Margaret said. "We'll have signals. When I point at the ceiling it means to groan louder. When I give you the thumbs-up it means to keep on at what you're doing. And when I slide my finger across my neck it means to gurgle and stop."

"Hold on a second," Kane said. "Just hold it one second. Now I'm feeling sort of nervous. You're making me nervous."

"What's there to make you nervous, you sissy? I'll do it without you."

"Well go ahead then," Kane said. "If you have to do it right this second, go on."

"I will," Margaret said.

She rose from bed and took a seat beside the dividing wall. The picking of the Nakamuras' guitar had broken off into the couple's harmonious snores. After a few moments Margaret got back into bed.

"Goddamn you," she said. "You've gotten me feeling nervous now. I had the momentum a second ago and now I've lost it."

"It isn't going to be easy to be loud on purpose," Kane said. "I think the easiest thing, for this first time, is we should do the thing for real."

"For real he says," Margaret said. She drew the covers to her chin and moved closer to Kane. "Do you even remember how? I wouldn't want you to injure yourself."

"I think I remember how to fake the part of a loving husband," he said.

"Good for you then. I also remember how to lie still and feign interest. Thank you for asking."

The two began removing their clothes from under the covers. Their undergarments slipped from the sides of the bed.

Kane kissed the side of Margaret's face.

"Clear aside the cobwebs then," he said.

Margaret felt momentarily shocked. It had been years since his lips had touched her body.

"Jesus," Margaret said. "Fine. We'll go through with it this way, this time, if you like. But I just want you to know the sounds I make aren't for you. They're out of hate for the Goddamn neighbors."

It was in this way that Kane Araki and Margaret Morri enjoyed a brief rejuvenation of their relationship, from the fall of 1943 until January of 1945. For several years prior to the war, the pair hadn't made any efforts to be intimate. If you'd found one of them in a candid mood, they would've admitted they hadn't seen much of each other during the last decade of their marriage. Kane had spent most of his mornings away from home, fishing along the pier for jack perch and drinking beer. And Margaret had spent most of her evenings by the radio, mending clothes or pickling vegetables and drinking sherry. It wasn't until they'd moved to the southeast block that the two began taking their meals and going to bed together.

Kane and Margaret put out their lights at six o'clock. Then at ten o'clock they revived to fuck each other with everything they assumed was the power and frenzy of a newly married couple. Some nights Kane wrote a script. Margaret insisted the Nakamuras and Otas hear them call out disturbing things to each other. She claimed she was out to spoil their libidos.

"You feel so tight," Kane yelled. "God, a woman of your age. Still tight as a baby kitten."

"Not so deep," Margaret exclaimed. "I'm getting raw. I'm raw as an open wound. You're making ground hamburger of me!"

"What is that smell? Something in here smells like tanning oil and bleach."

On nights Kane and Margaret felt too tired to make love, they lay beside each other and groaned loudly until they fell back asleep. Over time, as it felt a bit insincere to groan without touching, they held hands until their groans reverted back to snores. Shortly after the start of their routine, the two slept soundly enough so other couples never reawakened them.

Their children called their behavior shameful and in private asked them to stop. It had taken their children months, building the courage to broach the subject, but people were starting to talk openly about the elderly couple in the southeast block who woke others with the racket of their lovemaking. Their grandchildren cheered them forward.

"Don't listen to the disgusting things others say about you," their grandchildren said to them. "We're proud to have grandparents who still love each other after seventy years of marriage."

"I wasn't married when I was twelve," Kane said. "How old do you think I am?"

It was six months after the start of Kane and Margaret's endeavor that an announcement was made of Randy and Mina Ota's divorce. It was all a terrible scandal, and occasionally the Araki name was slipped into conversation with the Otas' troubles. Randy lived by himself in the last segment of the barrack, and Mina went to live with her family in the northwest block of camp.

"Do you think we had something to do with it?" Kane asked Margaret.

"Jesus, I hope so," Margaret said.

"I'm being serious," Kane said. "Should we stop?"

"God no," Margaret said. "You actually think we did that? Gladly I'd trade the marriages of the Otas and the Nakamuras to know our sex life has that power."

It was another six months before the sting of the Otas' divorce had faded from camp and the topic of Kane and Margaret's love life could be publicly addressed. Newly married couples began making visits to Kane and Margaret for their advice on healthy relationships. What were their secrets to resolving arguments? How soon after a fight was it appropriate to become physical again? How had they maintained their affection and vigor into their old age? What aphrodisiacs did they consume and what supply did they keep stashed away in the Gila desert?

As the barber tilted Kane's head to prune his nose hairs he asked him, "Jiichan, what is the secret to your long and healthy marriage?"

Kane found himself imitating a voice for what he imagined a wise old man would sound like.

"You must strive to understand each other completely without asking anything directly. You must make note of all the things she wants that you do not want to give her. And then you must make it your great passion in life to give her those things."

"Right, Jiichan, passion," the barber said. "But what about your positions? Do you drink snake wine? Do you eat cactus pears? Honeycomb?"

On the January evening Kane died, he huddled beside Margaret and made the low moan of a man in pleasure. It wasn't until morning she realized he'd passed. Margaret Morri continued to live in their barrack by herself until she too passed, just weeks before the end of the war. During those last days, her neighbors bought treats for her from the canteen and made visits to ask her. They asked her secrets about her long, happy life.

"Being around so many young people made us feel we were young again," she told them.

During her last nights she often woke and turned to rouse Kane so she could make love to him. Her eyes closed, her hands traced along the side of the cold mattress until she fell back to sleep. Other nights she dreamed of the tremendous whale on the beach. The black eye wept, but the sounds that came from the whale's mouth weren't Joy Nakamura. They were from the ghost of her husband.

Kane Araki and Margaret Morri were the only two people from the southeast block who did not survive the Gila relocation. As per their instructions, their ashes were transported back to California, to a shared plot in the Santa Maria cemetery, just blocks from their property.

a suitcase

When it came for Kane Araki to pack his suitcase for Gila River, he knew he could not survive the desert without his eight pairs of cowboy boots. For them to fit, he crammed one boot into another, then those boots he packed into another like Russian nesting dolls. Finally he was left with a single, densely packed shaft of cowhide and lizard skin he wedged into a crook at the base of his case.

Kane also felt his mother would be lost without her shell walkway. Three years prior, embers from a brushfire had floated up and purchased most of Youko Araki's vision. In response, Kane walked into the ocean, took a mighty breath, and dove through a thicket of kelp toward the deepwater crevices. When he emerged he hauled with him thirty massive red abalone. On Youko's porch he shattered the shells and laid down an iridescent walkway for her to follow. Before leaving for Gila River, Kane pried every shell fragment from the ground, stacked them like dinnerware, folded them into a sheet, and lodged them in his suitcase

Kane owned seventeen birds and a horse. For his birds he lined a picnic basket with a tablecloth and placed them in it, side by side. He gave them a tin of water and a tin of strawberry jam. Then he anchored the basket into the center of his toiletries, his hairbrush, bottled aftershave, toothpaste squeezing the basket at every side so it could not move during travel. Finally his horse he made step down into his suitcase where he'd made a bed of his shirts and long underwear. He combed away the mosquitoes from her back and hips and held a punch bowl of ice water before her to drink, then fastened her halter to a wood crate of contraband whisky.

Behind the Araki toolshed, a miraculous patch of wild strawberries burst through the soil every year. Their arrival became a minor celebration with the Arakis, who chopped the berries at an outdoor table and tossed them with bowls of milk and brown sugar. And though the Arakis could never help but ravage the plants, though they never saved seed or runners, the massive berries managed to reappear. Kane was cautious not to damage the root structures of the plants as he dug them from the ground and placed them in paper sacks, anchoring them with aerated soil and loose gravel. He understood the plants could only survive under the cool Pacific fog. With a funnel he sucked lungfuls of mist at the edge of Guadalupe Beach, then he exhaled them into the paper sacks before winding down the tops of them. That plot of fifty or sixty plants was the last possession he folded into his suitcase.

Kane wound his belt around one end of his suitcase and several feet of rope at the other, so that with a sudden bump, it could not spring open and release his birds into the train cabin.

the season of hair

At the age of ninety-two, Margaret Morri, who lived in a barrack on the periphery of Canal Camp, was said to have grown the longest, thickest, most supple, and most lustrous head of hair to ever fall upon the alluvial fans and flood plains of Gila's desert. Before relocation, it was rumored that if Margaret took a swim along the California coastline, it would mean three or four days, and the assistance of three or four family members, to remove all the sea grass, moon jellies, and blue mussels tangled up in that astounding mane.

For seventy years it had been a ritual of Kane Araki's, Margaret's second husband, to spend his after-dinner hours combing a portion of his wife's hair. Kane's instrument was either an immense comb with spines of apple juice Bakelite, or sometimes Margaret's hair would overflow and be gathered between his fingers, often until he was carried into dreaming, sitting in a chair at their bedside. This practice, held alongside those unbreakable tresses, lasted from Kumamoto, through California, and ended in Canal Camp where Kane fell asleep that final evening at the age of ninety. It was told the cycle of time necessary for Kane to finish combing the knots from Margaret's hair in its entirety, and to begin anew at the crown of her head, took two years. On the midwinter evening of Kane's passing, he'd been precisely halfway complete, his favorite season of hair, since much had to be pulled into his lap and over his belly like a heavy blanket.

Understanding time was stealing her vision, Margaret spirited away a knife from one of Canal's kitchens, and after taking three days to sharpen it upon a whetstone, she pulled her hair taught at the base of her scalp and severed ninety-two years' growth of hair. The strands, so lusty and thick, produced a bewildering sound when they snapped, like a pedal harp raised and shattered against a bed of rocks. Then knotting her hair around the leg of their bed, Margaret staggered, holding, spilling its astonishing weight through the doorway, covering her path past the WRA buildings, past the mess hall, the canteen, maneuvering around the military police post, until she reached Kane's burial stone, where she wound and tied all that remained around its base. Immediately following its separation from her body, Margaret's hair became knotted, its light dulled. The strands though only seemed to intensify in strength.

"It has always been this way with our women," Margaret told her daughters, Kazue and Shizue. "When these eyes fail, you must prepare your second set of eyes."

241

Grasping this cord was the method Margaret found to journey from her barrack to the Canal Camp cemetery for over two years until September of 1945.

every arizona night

From 1942 to 1945, Tokio Onitsuka was caretaker to the most famous Arizona unicorn mantis in all of Butte Camp. The mantis was striking in size and color. He stood at nearly eight inches high and bore alternating stripes, some bark-colored, some pale white like the blooms atop saguaros in early summer.

But the most remarkable characteristic of the Onitsuka mantis was his sonorous voice. Few mantises in Gila River were endowed with the gift of speech. And those who spoke did so in a half-whine, half-mewl no more pleasant than the utterances of a young child. The Onitsuka mantis possessed a tongue that was clear and low and resolute. It was as though the mantis had swallowed the voice of an aging gentleman, and his words echoed from inside the long, insect foregut, those words becoming loud and swollen, thunder firing from the thoracic tunnel.

Detainees from blocks three or four miles away made the journey for a ten- or twenty-minute long meeting with the Onitsuka mantis. Payment to Tokio ran from a quarter to fifty cents. In circumstances of financial difficulty, barter could be arranged for rare or unique items. These included boxes of dried dates, pellet rifles, or bottles of bathtub gin. Those arriving at the Onitsuka barrack bearing money or gifts were detainees at the height of a crisis and seeking guidance. Though doctors, ministers, and teachers were abundant in Butte Camp, many detainees felt the problems encountered in Gila River required counsel of an otherworldly variety.

The renowned seamstress Hamako Araki traveled from the southeastern tip of Canal Camp to ask the Onitsuka mantis why she was being haunted by the phantom of her late older brother. Tetsuo Araki had been playing with his grandson during transport from Tulare Assembly Center to Gila River when he suffered a sudden chest pain, lost consciousness, and perished. In the dead of every Arizona night, Hamako awoke to hear him calling her name and sobbing at the foot of her bed. What restitution might satisfy his spirit? What restitutions were available in this desert?

Canal High School teacher Isao Hirata offered Tokio Onitsuka his family's shortwave radio in exchange for what might cure a number of odd desert ailments. For Hirata, there were rashes, allergies, and head colds. Though he was a man in his thirties, his hair and muscles withered like a man twice his age. And on a few evenings, he horrified dinner companions when they witnessed him hack and vomit the mangy silk strands of a spider's web. Usually a man of good health, Hirata's students razzed him for his turn in appearance. Periodically he was forced to cancel his classes on days of cramps or excessive flatulence. Hirata experienced sleep patterns so tangled, he found himself nodding off in unfortunate settings—while eating a bowl of powdered eggs in the mess hall, while carrying a heavy crate of ripened fruit through the tomato fields, while mumbling from his hymn book during Sunday service. Most troubling, Hirata's sleepwalking became severe. On three occasions, Hirata walked in an unconscious stupor to the foot of a MP guard tower, pulled down his shorts, and delivered a pyramid of pebbled turds. The tower guard threatened that the fourth offense would earn Hirata a bullet. Why was he losing all his faculties in this way? Was this body inhabited by a demon?

In Gila River, few detainees had thought to question why the counsel of the Onitsuka mantis was in high demand. Camp life was unearthly and disorienting to those who had lived most of their lives in coastal cities. The mantis had a commanding voice. He had an elderly face and a bent posture that made him appear thoughtful. The popularity of his services was widespread. A common expression used to rib a detainee in distress was to tell them, "Tokio's coin purse will sag like your eyelids." A meeting with the Onitsuka mantis took place in Tokio's living quarters where the mantis rested on a majestic pillow placed atop a charcoal kotatsu. A guest sat slightly lower than the mantis's eyeline on a thin, plain cushion. These things added up perhaps to distract a detainee from recognizing the peculiarity of the whole practice.

Years later, after Butte and Canal residents had gained some distance from the war, many followers of the Onitsuka mantis found themselves mystified that they had ever put so much stock into the wisdom of an insect. Why had they not thought to debrief his reasoning with another person? Why had they never questioned that a wristwatch or an expensive bottle of perfume was standard payment for their visit? Why had they never questioned the mantis's ability to keep their problems confidential? And where had that mantis pillow originated? It was not as though a pillow had always existed to accentuate the majesty of this mantis. And why, after hearing the rumors that the counsel of the Onitsuka mantis often led to deeper troubles and suffering, did internees continue to clamor for his company?

When Shoji Aoyama called upon the Onitsuka barrack to deliberate the quarrelsome nature of his marriage, the great mantis suggested to him a series of dubious repairs.

"Shizue complains that I am not ambitious," Aoyama explained. "I don't work enough. I don't make enough money. But what money is there to be made in camp? What is there to buy? Should we want to own these barracks?"

"A wife who fixates on her husband's ambition is saying she requires more time to herself," the Onitsuka mantis said. "How many hours in a day do you lock up your wife in the closet?"

"Our closet?" Aoyama asked. "What do you mean? Why would I lock away my wife? She might suffocate."

"You need to put holes," the Onitsuka mantis said. "Have you considered that if you stuck your wife in your closet in the morning before work, she would want you to work fewer hours?"

"Is that a metaphor?" Aoyama asked. "Does a closet have another meaning?"

"If you don't have a closet, you can tie a pillowcase over her head," the Onitsuka mantis said. "Tell her she is not to remove the pillowcase until you return home from your shift at the dehydration plant."

"You are saying I should teach Shizue what it feels like to be alone for hours on end. Then she will demand more time together."

"Is your goal to spend more time with your wife? Or do you need time to pursue your second wife?"

"A second wife? Perhaps I've given a distorted account. I love only Shizue. I simply don't like to argue with her."

"That is the joy of a second wife. The moment your wife begins to squabble, you walk out the door to visit your second wife. And she has been walking around so long with that pillowcase on her head, she will be overjoyed to see you."

Kayo Hyosaka, the head nurse of the Butte Camp hospital barracks, received no better direction in coping with the behavior of her father-in-law, the retired minister Toshi Hiramatsu.

"My father-in-law humiliates me," Hyosaka said. "He says I am small and ugly and simpleminded."

"A man who fixates on his son's wife is plagued by his own regrets," the Onitsuka mantis said. "Have you pointed out to Hiramatsu that his accomplishments are utterly small and mediocre? That he is not a warrior, scientist, teacher, or artist of any reputation? Why would he expect a rare person to marry his son when his own blood is so unremarkable?"

"But won't recounting this only provoke him?" Hyosaka asked.

"Perhaps if you confront him personally," the Onitsuka mantis said. "But a man who humiliates others is shattered when his inadequacies are recognized and given a voice louder than his own. No doubt your father-in-law is aged and impotent. His hearing fades. His teeth grow black. A measly thatch of crusted hair clings to his scalp. Have you thought of taking out a column inch in the *News-Courier*?"

"The paper? For what purpose?"

"So that you might broadcast all the qualities I mentioned," the Onitsuka mantis said. "Why are you not writing what I say down? Every bit of this is gold to you."

"Our newspaper is for announcing talent shows and the elections of community councilmen. It has never been used for slander."

"The sooner his impotence is on the lips of others, the sooner your shortcomings are robbed from his mouth. Do this the right way and he will never speak ill of you again. If he is as fragile as I believe, he may never regain speech. He will become bedridden."

"I don't want to injure him. I want him to accept and tolerate me."

"See if you can unearth the identities of Hiramatsu's competitors. The classmates who bested him in sports. The uncles who beat or shamed him. The ex-lovers of his wife. Any man who cheated him in cards. When you have your children, give them the names of these men. Surround your husband with the names of this father's rivals. And then, how often will he come around to criticize you? And if you are exceptionally lucky, your father-in-law may become so distraught he will kill himself."

So went the consultations for Hisako Furukawa, Yuki Funatsu, Emiko Inouye, Nobuko Kunishige, Michi Furuya, Edward Kawaguchi. Heather Osaka, who asked how she might inspire her boyfriend to propose marriage, was told to greet all of his male friends by kissing them on the lips. Yukio Moriguchi, who asked how he might thwart the high school bully, Shyogo Ishimoto, was told to break into the Ishimoto barrack at night with scissors and snip every hair from Shyogo's scalp. Shiori Fujinami, who asked how she might defeat an infestation of Arizona deer mice, was told to sprinkle HiHo crackers onto the barrack steps of all her neighbors. In retrospect, detainees agreed it was merely a matter of time before the leeway lent to the great mantis wore thin. Every week, blows were exchanged between family members, community leaders were insulted, property was stolen or destroyed, and bridges were burned on account of the advice of the Onitsuka mantis. And then the reign of that pterygotic trickster, that mantodean devil, came to a savage end.

In January 1945, Tokio Onitsuka awoke to find the door to her barrack forced open and the great mantis missing. The next day she discovered the raptorial forelegs of her mantis at the center of the ornate pillow. Days later, the slender abdomen was found resting like an extinguished cigar on the mat of the Onitsuka doorstep. The jointed hind legs were received by

Tokio in a sealed envelope in the Butte postal barracks. The mantis's prothorax turned up in one of Tokio's rain boots. The face of the Onitsuka mantis was found nailed to the door of the Methodist chapel. The carpenter's nail pinned the head directly through the center ocellus.

Though Tokio Onitsuka pleaded for a formal investigation, military police were ambivalent about digging into the murder of a desert insect. Understandably the mantis had been a significant presence in the community. His gift had entertained a surprising quantity of detainees. But were there not ten thousand more unicorn mantises roaming the tomato vines and castor bean shrubs of Gila River? Was there not a block manager or a neighborhood watchman who might poke around the matter? Was the influence of the mantis not highly contentious? After months of petitions, Tokio's skin became warty and her hair transformed as white as Mojave buckwheat. She developed hollows between her brow and eyelids. During the day, she became an embittered recluse. In the evenings, it was told, Tokio could be seen stalking the Butte community gardens, kidnapping unicorn mantises with a butterfly net. Neighbors claimed they could hear Tokio through their barrack partitions instructing a second mantis in the occupation of the first. But the insect voice heard in tandem with her own was shrill and unpleasant. No further notoriety would touch the Onitsuka barrack in Gila River.

In the recollections of the parties most intimately involved, the likeliest culprit in the murder of the Onitsuka mantis was Margaret Morri of Butte Camp. Morri was a community college dropout. She was known to run with a wild pack of troublemakers and was therefore supplied with all the eyes and fingers that would have been necessary to silence, abduct, dismember, and distribute the robust insect. Morri herself never denied the assertion. It was rumored that Margaret Morri had surrendered her boyfriend, Leo Minami, on account of some grisly advice provided by the late mantis. A noteworthy loss, given that Leo Minami, by acclamation of women and men of every generation, was the most handsome man ever to live in Gila River.

"How can I make a hunk somehow undesirable?" Margaret Morri supposedly asked the Onitsuka mantis. "Undesirable to all but myself, of course."

"There is but a lone solution to your request," came the Onitsuka mantis's supposed reply. "Circulate a rumor that Leo Minami is obsessed with devouring human feces. Spread word far and wide from Butte to Canal to Heart Mountain to Manzanar to Minidoka. From Jerome to Topaz to Tule Lake. Leave no ear or mind unburdened. Be ready to defend the rumor vehemently. Claim you watched him do this. He begged you, in fact, for a tiny ration of your own leavings. Not even a saint recovers from an accusation as this. Only God and the person who hatched the lie will have the strength to love this man."

A decade after the war, Leo Minami relocated from Chicago back to California and married his grade school sweetheart, Sugar Sugai. The couple raised three exquisite daughters. Margaret Morri never married. She never returned to the Central Coast. She lived the rest of her life in Michigan, in a house she shared with her siblings.

The wings of the Onitsuka mantis were never discovered, but a handful of people claimed to have witnessed them in Margaret Morri's possession. The common report was that the green-and-brown wings were pinned to the elegant uchiwa that Margaret Morri used to fan herself on hot evenings.

an october

Yoshikane Araki passed away in October 1944, stretched upon a military cot, at the age of sixty-four, and in the presence of his wife, Margaret, his three exquisite daughters, their husbands, and with the sounds of his grandchildren laughing and chasing one another just outside the wooden frame of the Araki family barracks.

Kane's final perplexing words to his family were, "I don't want you to worry. You take it off when you need to take it off."

Then Kane smiled and used the last of his strength to push himself onto his side. And when he was facing the western wall, he went free.

At the instant of his death, his youngest, prettiest daughter, Hanna Kawafuchi, pulled the wedding ring from her finger and gripped it against her palm. Only weeks prior, Hanna had come to Kane to discuss the possibilities of her divorce. Hanna was married to Edward Kawafuchi, a serious but loving man, and though she recognized in him all the qualities she wanted in a father for her children, relocation to Gila River had given Hanna the opportunity to reconcile with her high school lover, Ken Fukuhara.

Kane had always been very kind and generous with Edward. He'd taken him to a tailor to buy his first suit. He'd helped the Kawafuchi family to secure loans and farmland. He'd paid for and nailed together the planks that would become the Kawafuchi Farms fruit and vegetable stand.

Hanna felt certain her father would admonish her for reconnecting with Ken. The Fukuharas were known for being a loud and intemperate bunch. Back in Santa Maria, Ken's father and brothers were either banned or avoiding debts throughout most of Tiger Town, the small strip of Japanese-owned bars and restaurants. In high school, Hanna had often found Ken with his shirts torn away at the collar, his teeth stained red following a brawl, defending the reputation of his family.

"What I admire of Edward," Kane had said to Hanna, "is I know he sacrifices his time and strength to make you happy. You wanted to own your home instead of leasing one. You wanted a car and a radio. I watched him kneel in the dirt and work those extra hours on another family's farm to give those things to you. I watched him thin handfuls of carrots until he fell asleep into them. And when Edward sees you happy he has amnesia for those hours in the fields. He can just live in that moment. That is his gift. Lots of men can do the work, but very few can forget what they need to forget. They become resentful of their families. Edward's great joy in life is to make you and his children happy. You've made sacrifices for Edward too, obviously. Does seeing him happy give you any satisfaction?"

"I want Edward to be happy," Hanna had said. "But making him happy isn't my joy or my mission. When I see my children with their father, I feel happy. But after that, my happiness, his happiness, they never are aligned."

"Will Ken make sacrifices for your happiness?" Kane asked.

"I think he will," Hanna said.

"How does he prove to you that he will?"

"He promises me he will never be with another woman. He says he will just live to wait for me. And if I leave Edward, if I want him then, only at that time will he be allowed to love someone. Only then does he want his own children."

"Then there are a lot of lives at stake besides yours, Edward's, and Ken's," Kane said. "There is the happiness of the children you have. Then there are the children you may have if you remarry."

"Those children don't exist," Hanna said.

"It doesn't mean you shouldn't consider them," Kane said.

"If I divorced Edward, would you feel ashamed of me?" she asked.

"For the early years of my life I was a gambler and a thief. All the shame that touches our family is for me. There is nothing left for you."

"What do I need to do?"

"I won't give you an answer for that," Kane said. "The decision doesn't belong to me. Don't trust a person who says they will give that to you."

"Mom says I shouldn't even think of straying from Edward."

"She says it out of love for your children. She doesn't want to upset them."

"I feel afraid. I'm afraid of both choices."

"Of course," Kane said. "You can't ask for simple answers. Back and forth you are pushing around very complicated problems. You should struggle to find your way. Don't expect the right one to bring you any peace."

"He is going to hate me," Hanna said. "Edward is going to despise me so much. He may even try to kill me."

"You don't have to feel afraid," Kane said.

Kane cleared his throat. Then he said, "Of course you know, your mother was involved with another man when I met her."

"Yes," Hanna said.

"You understand I almost wasn't your father. If I had met your mother a month later—if she had never agreed to take a walk with me—do you understand?"

"She made the right decision."

"She chose me because she could hear you calling to her. It was very faint, but she told me when I was near, she could hear your voice. She could hear the voice of our daughters. Your mother loves me, and I'm so undeserving of it. She would've been happier with the man she loved before me. I wasn't good to her. I left her alone too often. I drank too much. But she dreamt of your voice. It was saying to choose me. When you dream, what can you hear?"

"I don't remember any of my dreams," Hanna said.

"There are ghost families near us. Ghost families that could never exist because your mother and I stayed together. We are all haunted because of it."

"I want children with Ken," Hanna said. "I believe it's the thing I want most."

"We loved you the best we could so you would know how to be loved," Kane said. "I can tell Edward loves you so much. If you say you know you will be loved again, I can trust you."

"How can I do this? This terrible thing."

"You'll do it soon," Kane said. "You'll do it after I'm gone. Edward will know he can't hurt you after that. And he won't try. And in a few months, you'll make plans to leave camp with your children. You'll go to Chicago or to Detroit. Your mother's sister is there. And Ken will follow you. Edward won't be able to leave his family in Gila River. His sister is as sick as me. Edward will stay in Gila until the war ends. He'll move back to California to run his family's farm. And by that time, you and Ken will be settled somewhere else."

Kane looked down at himself and said, "I've worn this shirt three days in a row now. Do I look nice in it? Your mother seems to like me better when I wear it. But when I ask her why all she tells me is that I sometimes miss a button."

Hanna checked his shirt and patted him on the chest.

"You look good, Dad," she said.

"Handsome? Good."

And then Kane said, "It really must be the fall. In my dreams I can see what is nearly ready in California. I'm starting to see figs, kabocha, and persimmons."

leave your drawings in this house

Jin Morri was the first dog laid to rest in the Butte Camp cemetery. Jin had been a sheepdog mutt, alert, oddly immaculate, a coat of thick, white-and-black fur that smartly reflected the oppressive desert sun. With the Morris, he had lived fourteen years along coastal and agricultural cities in California, six months within the Tulare Assembly Center, and his final eight months on the border between Butte Camp and Canal Camp in Gila River, Arizona. He had welcomed the births of two Morri children, and he had watched the oldest California Morri, Isaburo Beans Morri, collapse beneath an orchard of white prune blossoms and go free to his ancestors. Jin Morri's burial site was located beneath the shade of a blue palo verde, its ochre, seed-heavy pods collapsing onto his roof. All hours of the day were claimed by visitations from desert pollinators, wasps, bees, moths, flower beetles, the speckled forehead of the tree's yellow Sonoran flower seized and kissed a thousand times.

In the weeks after Jin Morri's death, Margaret Morri, the eight-year-old daughter of Tomiye and Tetsuo Morri, wept into every plate of food placed before her. Her tears fell upon the salted and scrambled egg, or in the bowl of raw egg whipped into hot rice, the bowls of miso soup and seaweed soup, the tightly rationed hamburger steaks, the plates of hamburger-beans okazu, the thick rectangles of cornbread and butter, the yellow cake served after Sunday service, the cup of brown sugar, hot oatmeal, and milk, the plate of chopped apples impaled with toothpicks.

"It is in the tradition of Morri women to learn to eat their tears," Sugar Morri, Margaret's grandmother, once said to her. "You eat your tears so your body might keep them for later. Tears are a powerful medicine, so we will waste none of them on the dust. We keep them and remember every pang, every unachievable desire, every defeat, and trespass against us."

In camp, it was Margaret's practice to draw for an hour in bed every morning before school. Jin Morri had occupied the foot of the military cot, snapping at moths or locusts who had found their way into the barrack. It was therefore no surprise that Jin populated hundreds of pages within Margaret's notebooks.

The illustrated world or Margaret Morri was in no way constrained to Gila River. There was the handful of drawings that documented the Morri barrack, the Butte community gardens, the canteen, the gymnasium, the watchtower. But what Margaret mostly imagined was the Pacific coastline.

There were scenes of crab empires emerging from underwater caves. Scenes of gulls spiriting clams into the sky, a scene of an otter raising a clam over its head like a prizefighter hoisting a trophy. There were scenes where the ocean bottom was an explosion of multicolored starfish, Jin bending down to inspect one of them like a spring blossom.

"Does Jin swim or does he float?" Tetsuo Morri once asked his daughter, looking over her shoulder at her artwork. "Some days Jin walks above the water. Some days he walks below the water."

"Jin needs to smell everything," Margaret Morri said. "When he is sniffing the bottom, he is walking the bottom. When he sniffs a bird, he walks in the air."

"It makes complete scientific sense," Tetsuo said. "You made a beautiful drawing. This gull has a baby clam friend. Why does he carry him into the air? Aren't clams afraid of heights?"

"Gulls don't have any friends," Margaret said. "They clobber the clams upon the pointy rocks and then peck out their faces. Then they feed the chewed-up faces to their chicks."

"Jesus," Tetsuo said. "Are otters and clams friends? This otter is hugging her clam."

"Otters hate clams. They put a clam on their belly and bash it on the head with a rock. Then they slurp everything out. Even their guts and butts."

"I didn't know clams had butts or heads."

"Oh sure," Margaret said. "Clams have everything we have. They have small butts and smaller farts."

"It's good since small farts don't have a bad smell."

"Their farts are really stinky though. Clams eat garbage all day."

"If clams have everything, do they wear clothes?"

"Clams don't wear clothes," Margaret said. "They like to walk around the house naked. But they have even songs and Gods."

"And clams go to church?" Tetsuo asked.

"When you look at a clam, their hands are like, practically always praying. They have angels. They have ghosts and they have pets."

"They have pets?"

"Yes. Sometimes they get a little fish to be their pet. And they play fetch with them throwing a fish bone. And they say, my last pet didn't play fetch, and now his job is being this fish bone."

"I think you are spending too much time in the camp library," Tetsuo said. "I want you to get outside and run around more."

In their years along the Central Coast, the Morri family had owned strawberry fields and operated a shack where they sold fruit, sodas, nuts, and popcorn. Although the land and stand had been handed to a competing farm amidst the Morris' relocation, Margaret drew dozens of remembrances of Jin jogging down the lines cut for berry plants.

"Do dogs gather and eat strawberries?" Tomiye asked her daughter.

"Dogs don't like strawberries," Margaret said. "Dogs only eat cats and bones."

"They eat cats?"

"They like quick meat. I mean, animals who run quickly. He gobbles up their speed."

"It looks like Jin has a nice little pile of ripe strawberries."

"He is setting a trap for a possum. When the possum tries to eat the strawberries, Jin is going to jump out from behind a bush and eat the possum's head off."

"It isn't sweet or gentle of gentle Jin."

"We don't know their story. The possum was like, being really mean."

"The possum said some pretty hurtful stuff, did he?"

"He tried to eat Jin's leg. Now Jin is getting revenge back at him."

"It doesn't seem like a leg is worth the same as a whole life."

"A leg is everything to a dog. If a dog can't run, he gets so terribly sad he wants to crawl under the house and starve himself to death."

"I think you have been spending too much time with Jin. I want you to play with more of your friends from school."

Months beyond his passing, Jin Morri appeared in Margaret Morri's illustrations, arising in more ways than just a sheepdog mutt. Sometimes he was a white-and-black goat with curving, ridged horns. Sometimes an enormous white-and-black flower rising through the floorboards of a room. Sometimes Jin emerged as a handsome young man, sometimes as a beautiful white-haired woman.

"I see him like this when I'm dreaming," Margaret told Sugar Morri. "He isn't always in his old body, but I know it is Jin."

Sugar Morri told her granddaughter to save a few portions from her dinner—a chicken drumstick, a quarter of her biscuit, a small lump of rice and gravy—all of it wept upon by Margaret. Sugar told her to carry it over to the Butte cemetery and to place it before Jin's burial mound.

"You should feed him a final time," Sugar said. "He owns no permanent body, but his soul still searches for the food from your hand."

"He wasn't a man," Tomiye said from across their table. "Do we believe all animals have souls?"

"Of course Jin has a soul," Sugar said.

"I've never heard our Reverend Nobuko Miyake say so," Tomiye said. "How can you be sure?"

"Margaret dreams of Jin," Sugar said. "Jin dreams of Margaret. We must have souls to dream of each other."

"Do you still dream of Jin?" Tomiye asked Margaret.

"I see him some nights," Margaret said. "Other nights I forget everything but a feeling."

"His soul is near," Sugar said. "It won't be this way forever. The food you've cried upon is powerful medicine. Feed him while you can."

As she had done for years, Margaret Morri wrapped portions of her dinner into a handkerchief for Jin Morri. Then she walked into the blue palo verde trees of the Butte cemetery and buried the food beside a little pyramid of rocks she used to mark Jin's gravesite.

That evening while she slept, Margaret asked Jin Morri, "One day when I die, will I stop dreaming of you?"

"What has death got to do with the two of us meeting here?" Jin Morri asked.

"It is my dream though, isn't it? When I die, won't this end?"

"Who says your body is the house where this dream is happening? Who says your dream is the only place we will ever meet?"

"I just figured," Margaret said.

"No one owns this house," Jin Morri said. "This is the house of my Gods. It was here before us. We will meet here long after our bodies have gone."

"Is it at all scary to go on without your body?" Margaret asked.

"When you leave your body, you leave behind the rules of the body. The way the body ages and hungers. The body has so much it uses to teach the soul. But to leave it behind is not scary."

"This is our house!" Margaret exclaimed. "Aren't we in Santa Maria? I just recognized my drawings are pinned to the walls."

"Leave your drawings in this house," Jin Morri said. "I will leave my drawings here too. They won't always hang here. The purpose was never permanence. Another Margaret and another Jin will live in this house. They will paint over what we have left them. It's possible something in their paintings remembers something about us. Or they won't. That is wonderful too. That is also a treasure."

"I don't like living here without you," Margaret said. "The moths and the grasshoppers land on my face all night now."

"Would you have me come back only to scare away some moths?"

"It's just that I am alone with the moths. What will I do if I am alone and I need to reach you?"

"What do you propose? I have no more ears to hear you, Margaret. No more paws to carry me."

"You are really gone then. It hurts. I hate it."

"There was a blanket I slept on that you left in storage back home. It was a yellow beach blanket."

"There were fish printed on it."

"That was the one. If you ever really need me, draw that blanket. Slide the picture beneath your pillow before you fall asleep. I will return and keep the moths and locusts away in the night."

At the close of the war, the Morris were gifted twenty-five dollars per family member and train tickets to any city east of Gila River. They spent time in Chicago and Detroit before boarding a train in 1947 back to California. When they returned to their home, they discovered it raided and vandalized.

In her old room, Margaret Morri found constellations of holes in the drawings pinned to her walls. They were small holes from where someone, likely a neighbor, had sat upon her bed and fired rounds of a .22 rifle into her artwork. With the help of Sugar Morri, Margaret repainted the walls of her room a new color. Rather than patch the holes, Margaret painted around them. A constellation of eight holes became the mottled plumage of a ring-billed gull. A constellation of four holes became the speckled wings of a moth. A constellation of six holes became the empty chambers of a pomegranate, its sweet and dark arils falling out from the waxy and astringent pith and before the pried-open bulb.

a visit

Margaret Morri gave birth to Corinne Araki-Morri on September 2, 1942, in Butte Camp hospital. In the record of Gila River, it was a morning of unparalleled heat, a punishing finale to summer.

While most internees languished in the desert, mother and daughter dozed soundly into Arizona history's most fiery month. The infant population in Butte Camp was afflicted with sunken soft spots, wails that could not produce tears, and diapers dry as freshly baked rolls emerging from the oven. But the Araki-Morri baby remained calm and attentive and wet more than her weight in diapers every day.

The first fever of the Araki-Morri baby occurred at precisely the age of eight months. The exact temperature of this fever could not be measured, since the thermometers constructed from wood, glass, alcohol, and acetic acid fractured when held against the baby's skin.

Lukewarm baths spat and steamed as baby Corinne was lowered into them as though she was a rosy alloy being quenched.

And a sponge immersed in chilled water and the advised remedies of crushed lavender blooms, marigold petals, and chamomile flowers held to the baby's forehead was instantly zapped into a scalding mass of herbal soup.

Margaret Morri had never heard of such severe manifestations before, but when she described the symptoms to her mother, Reverend Tokio Morri, she was told that Morri blood placed in extreme environments occasionally produced uncanny results.

"You were the same as a baby," Tokio Morri said. "Strange and small and powerful. Are you having any unusual dreams of late?

"Dreams?" Margaret Morri said. "It's impossible for me to remember. I had a dream where I was milking a very big goat teat."

"You milked our goat when you were a girl. You called her Miss Fusa. I think it was the name of your Sunday school teacher."

"Right, but I saw my pail was overflowing. And then as I turned to bring back another pail, the goat let out a cry. It was a terrifying human cry, and her udder erupted, and a flood of milk broke free and covered the farm and the valley. I was knocked over in the current. When I stood up, it was in a roiling white ocean. And I had to take the goat to see the doctor in a rowboat."

"It's strange because you don't have a rowboat."

"Right, that was the strange thing. Also I remember I was taking the goat to see Doctor Mikuni. But she is not a veterinarian. Is that what you mean by dreams?"

"Possibly," Tokio Morri said. "Any dreams where you meet a lost sister? Maybe even a twin?"

"No."

"Or dreams where you have more arms or legs than you know what to do with? Six or eight legs perhaps?"

"Yuck, Mom. No."

"Or a dream where your arm falls off and you watch it grow into a woman who appears to be your sister?"

"Nothing like that. Have you asked me this before? These sound like familiar questions."

Tokio Morri shrugged. "It's probably nothing. You can take Cori-chan to Butte's hospital, but the nurses there will tell you it is nothing."

Butte hospital's waiting room was crowded with crabby internees and the sharp, minty odor of mentholated ointment. Margaret Morri had to keep wrinkling her nose to keep from sneezing as she discussed the baby's condition with Sugar Sugai, Butte hospital's chief nurse.

"We noticed she was hot to the touch," Margaret Morri said, tucking the fine strands of baby hair behind her daughter's ear.

"How hot are we talking here, Mama?" Sugar Sugai asked. "Did her clothes catch fire?"

"Her clothes?" Margaret Morri asked. "They're damp, I guess. She is sweaty. But she has a burning fever. Her cheeks look very flushed."

"Alright, some flushy cheeks," Sugar Sugai said. "But her cheeks did not actually break out into flame?"

"Well, no."

"What about her forehead? It shoot any hellfire your way?"

"No."

"And you're saying she sweated? Here in the Arizona desert? The way I'm sweating right now?"

"Well, yeah. I mean, I don't know if she is as sweaty as you. I feel like you aren't taking me seriously. Look at how red her face is."

"That chubby face is a little on the pink side," Sugar Sugai admitted. "More snapper-like though. Not red like oxblood. Or a turkey neck."

"Her behavior has changed too," Margaret Morri said. "She hasn't smiled today. Usually I can make her smile."

"Did you tell her some jokes?"

"What? No. She usually smiles when I make faces and do freaky voices. Corinne is a smiley baby."

"What sorts of faces are we talking about here? Fish face? Bird face? Smooshy face?"

"Well, no. Just faces. You know, I open my eyes really wide and look from side to side."

"Sounds like frog face then."

"I guess you could call it a frog."

"And you do the same face every time? Or do you change it up? Maybe she is tired of this one-face routine."

"But that's my point. If I do my funny face it makes her laugh every time."

"Well this big cross-eye face doesn't sound all that funny. I mean look at me. I'm not even smiling."

"I don't claim to be a comedian. I just know what makes my baby laugh."

"Alright so Baby lost her sense of humor, Mama."

"She is so sleepy. When I hold her, she falls asleep in my arms."

"Does she stop breathing when she goes to sleep?"

"No, but she goes a bit limp."

"Is she a limp noodle? How limp are we talking about here? On a scale of noodle."

"I'm not sure. A chicken noodle? Do you mean a stiff or a cooked noodle?"

"You tell me, Mama. You brought it up."

"A chicken noodle, then, maybe?"

"Noodles aren't made of chicken," Sugar Sugai said. "They are made from flour and fat. It sounds like girl enjoys her nap time, Mama."

"Also, when her fever was very bad, she shivered."

"Was she shaking like a leaf?"

"Not really. Just for a moment, well, like she was cold. But she was feverish."

"But it wasn't as though she was an actual leaf, shaking in a stormy wind."

"No. She is an actual baby. She is skin. And other stuff. Hair. Skeleton."

"Sounds alright to me then. What else have you got for me, Mama?"

"That's all. Well, she was staring. She stares off into the distance."

"Was she looking at something out the window? Maybe there was a donkey or some poodles or something."

"I don't think so. She was in a trance."

"But now she is blinking. Or is she still hypnotized?"

"Now she is fine. It was just a couple of minutes this morning."

"So your baby looked at something for a minute. And she is hot and not smiling. Correct?"

"Yes."

"But she is not on fire, correct?"

"She isn't on fire," Margaret Morri said. "I am holding her, aren't I?"

"Maybe your skin is—what do you call it?" Sugar Sugai snapped her fingers in the air. "A retardant. Retardant? Flame retardant. That sounds weird."

"I have a regular woman's skin," Margaret Morri said.

"She looks fine," Sugar Sugai said. "It's probably roseola. She'll be back to her magnificent self in a few days. But the doctor can see her after he deals with about a dozen people who were attacked by scorpions and poisonous snakes."

Three hours later, the doctor Yuki Funatsu told Margaret Morri it was likely that baby Corinne was reacting to a mild viral infection. She was told to breastfeed normally and to let the baby rest.

That night, sleep did not come easily to mother or to daughter. The Araki-Morris lived in the northwestern block of the Yoshihara barracks, those stuffy, insect-gnawed habitations overseen by acclaimed kabuki actor Terue Yoshihara. A combination of roaring winds, shoddy windows, and loose barrack planks produced noises that startled baby Corinne awake long past midnight.

271

Margaret Morri swayed back and forth in the sturdiest corner of the barrack, the sweat from her daughter's neck and forehead a damp darkness upon her shirt. Margaret Morri considered that her daughter's condition might be worsening. A second visit to Butte's hospital could make her appear foolish, but how could she tell between a routine and an urgent ailment? Corinne Araki-Morri drifted in and out of sleep and moaned weakly and dryly through both states. Margaret Morri patted her back and vaguely chanted a nursery rhyme.

"The dragonfly and the damselfly—they're drunk on daydreams and lullabies."

Margaret Morri did not recall falling asleep. In fact, in her memory, the thing she recalled was seeing herself awake and holding her baby daughter. It was an odd memory, as though she had stumbled in front of a mirror.

Half of her attention was housed in her body. But being able to watch herself in this way, she realized that Margaret Morri was only her first body. And in the moment she realized this, she found that this second sight belonged to a second body that could move out of the mirror and down the barrack steps and into the dirt path that led to the Butte Camp watchtower.

The sensation was somewhat like the inversion of being startled out of a dream. Margaret Morri had experienced this many times. In the course of her childhood, she and her siblings had often been roused to complete their farm work while the sun was absent. And she recalled those moments where she experienced an intense loss of gravity, where her dream body, that had been acting autonomously, was being pulled down into another body, a body anchored beneath a set of heavy blankets.

The following morning, the Morri barrack awoke to commotion. In Margaret Morri's arms, baby Corinne slept peacefully. But raised voices and the slamming of neighboring barrack doors pulled Margaret Morri's husband, Kane Araki, to the window, where he saw a crowd gathering at the end of the block. He walked outside shirtless. Then he returned a moment later to retrieve an umbrella to shed the blinding morning sun. Kane Araki returned to Margaret Morri an hour later with a report that the most southwestern watchtower and much of the barbed-wire fencing surrounding the area were reduced to smoke and ash.

Rumors circulated of an attack. Military police speculated that factions of enemy Japs could be attempting to undermine the internment of domestic Japs. Other rumors accused saboteurs from within Butte Camp. Butte Camp internees were bewildered by both possibilities, as the burning of a single watchtower was unlikely to improve anyone's situation in any way.

The most peculiar rumor Kane reported was from Pete Yamamoto, their neighbor to the south, whom Kane overheard being questioned by a Butte MP.

Yamamoto claimed that he was aroused in the dead of night when the powerful light of the moon struck his eyelids. But when he rose to face his barrack window, he was shocked to see the light was not coming from above. He then watched a creature made entirely of fire walk down the dirt path leading from the Yoshihara barracks and toward the southwestern watchtower. The creature took the common shape of a man, and this man was not *on* fire but was *of* fire. This point he

273

repeated to be clear. The movement of the fire creature was deliberate and unhurried.

Yamamoto was so startled it took him longer than usual to scramble the darkness of his barrack and recover his glasses. When he stepped onto his porch, he still witnessed the body of fire in the distance, moving at the speed a person would walk. However when he moved to follow, he fell headlong from his porch and was knocked unconscious.

Later that afternoon, Margaret Morri relayed all of the information to Tokio Morri, who remained nonplussed.

"What does the tower guard say?" Tokio Morri asked.

"The watchtower was unmanned at the time," Margaret Morri said.

"MPs aren't going to find signs of explosives or gasoline near the watchtower," Tokio Morri said. "They aren't going to find a saboteur either."

"I had a funny dream," Margaret Morri said. "I could see myself holding Corinne in the mirror. I was watching myself. And then I walked out of the mirror, I suppose."

"I have the dreams too," Tokio Morri said. "My mother, too. She called them visits from her twin. Sometimes she called them a visit from the fire."

Tokio Morri took the baby Corinne in her arms and hummed.

"The dragonfly and the damselfly—will rise on wind like dandelions."

Tokio Morri said, "When the fire in this body is too much, the world creates a second body to contain the fire. Right dragonfly? Lion does not really rhyme perfectly with fly does it?"

Corinne Araki-Morri squealed with delight in her grandmother's arms. Tokio Morri kissed her neck.

"The MPs will get over the damage," Tokio Morri said. "What did the fence and watchtower protect? Who is going to walk into the desert? What welcome is on the other side of the desert for any of us?"

talking of the ocean with you

In Gila River the word for night was Margaret Morri. The name for the ten thousand visible stars was Margaret Morri. And for every visible star, there were ten thousand invisible stars, and those were called Margaret Morri. And the star-flesh that was cool and dark was also called Margaret Morri. And the interval of light that was the final record of a darkening star was called Margaret Morri. And the name given to the flesh of the human eye, equipped to collect day and night, that flesh was known as Margaret Morri.

The southern dike slicing through Gila River, its cold water brimming with damselflies, was known as Margaret Morri. And the damselflies with their black-yellow eyes and armor the color of lapis were called Margaret Morri. The word for the desert sand, when it burned hot enough to cook perfectly a chicken egg cracked over a little dune, was Margaret Morri. Also the bitterly cold months, where all internees wore two pairs of socks to bed, were called either Margaret Morri or "two-sock months."

Very little in Gila River was called Kane Araki. In the years between 1942 and 1945, the main thing people called Kane Araki was a little family of shrubs that grew beside the Butte Camp latrines. Sunbathing teenagers sometimes whacked sand from their towels, hanging them upon the Kane Araki shrubs. Some tied correspondences upon the Kane Araki petioles. At night, Kane Araki's branches vibrated with the songs of lustful cicadas.

There was also a weekday casserole served in the Butte Camp mess halls that contained powdered eggs, ranch beans, and turkey-eye peppers that residents referred to as Kane Araki casserole. And any man, woman, or child who experienced cramping, fever, or diarrhea after ingesting a helping of Kane Araki was said to have "the fire of Kane Araki lit under them."

Kane Araki was mostly the shrubs, the casserole, or the bodily condition. A lesser-known Kane Araki was a sow bug who lived under the barracks of Kashi Uchihama. This sow bug Kane ate alone, exercised alone, slept alone, and only came out from under the barracks to talk with the moon. Kane Araki was in love with every phase of the moon that appeared over the Gila River Relocation Camp. The moon was called Margaret Morri.

"What would I have to do," Kane Araki asked the Margaret moon, "to sleep beside you in the sky?"

"But you are a very small pebble," Margaret Morri said. "I am not sure you will fit in the sky. Likely you'll fall out of it."

"I am not a pebble," Kane Araki said. "I am an armadillo."

"Are you?" Margaret Morri asked, squinting. "Sorry. I thought you had tails and snouts. My eyesight isn't what it was. Still, an armadillo is not like a moth or a firefly. You do not have much practice living in the sky."

"Perhaps I could share a corner of your pillow," Kane Araki said. "I would not fall from there."

The following night, Margaret Morri asked Kane Araki, "Why do you want to sleep beside me anyhow? You hardly know what I'm like."

"I know you very well. I see you every evening."

"Seeing is not knowing. Seeing belongs only to you. I agreed to nothing."

"You know what I mean. We talk. We've talked of many things. Last week we talked of the birds you saw eating a rat out by the trash bin. It was smelly and hardened."

"It was not the most romantic conversation."

"I only mean we know each other well enough that we talk of the savage realities of existence. We talk of life and of death. In-between too."

"You did tell me your story of Susie Toyohara who pushed her friend into an organpipe cactus for insulting her granddaughter."

"Exactly. I tell you all the cactus drama that happens in my day."

"Well, I'm not sure," Margaret Morri said, tapping her chin. "Are armadillos very heroic?"

"I am incredibly heroic," Kane Araki said. "I sleep even in a suit of armor, in case I need to wake quickly and do something heroic, and have no time to dress."

"That's too bad," Margaret Morri said. "I don't like heroes. They only defend people who look and talk just like themselves and worship the same things they worship. They are often men who would assemble vast armies to attack petty criminals and women carrying stones in their aprons."

"Surely you don't mean all heroes," Kane Araki said.

"The famous ones," Margaret Morri said. "The ones running around up here."

"I have no armies," Kane Araki said. "I care very little if others look or feel or think the way I do."

A few nights later, Margaret Morri asked Kane Araki, "Do armadillos write songs? If I let you sleep beside me, would you sing to me?"

"I come from a family of proficient musicians," Kane Araki said. "If you let me sleep beside you, I will recruit every cicada and every katydid in Gila River. And we will write ten thousand songs and sing a different one to you every night. And all the songs will be called Margaret Morri."

"That sounds awful. Why would I want all the songs to be Margaret Morri? It sounds very boring."

"It would only be the titles. All the music that exists beneath the titles would be different."

"But that is very confusing. It seems to me, if you want to appreciate the personality of each song, you should start by accepting that their titles should be different."

"Perhaps we can call some songs 'The Morri Moon.' And some of them, 'Moony Margaret.'"

"No, this isn't going to work. I don't want to be around

another songwriter, because I am a songwriter. And I want someone who will listen to my songs."

"You are a songwriter? You never mentioned it before."

"Most people assume the songs should flow only in the one direction. Margaret's round Morri moon to be sung about. But why shouldn't I sing? I look at you as often as you look at me."

"What was the last song you wrote?"

"It was a tune called, 'Dead Rat's Last Dance.' It imagines the final night a little rat danced with his lover, before he had a heart attack beside a trash bin and his face meats were shredded by crows."

"The title is very provocative."

"Determining a title is one of my favorite stages of the songwriting process. When I say the right title for the first time, it tastes as though I've licked a thousand stamps for letters."

"Well, my ears have grown strong from listening out for you every night. And my voice is a little damaged from having to shout up toward you every night. So I would be much happier as a listener than as a singer."

A month later, on a particularly cool and clear evening, Margaret Morri said, "I forgot to put on my glasses tonight. So tell me, are you a very young and handsome armadillo pebble?"

"Most armadillos are very handsome," Kane Araki said. "But to be honest, I am old-looking, because I am quite old. And even my mother never told me I was handsome. She used to say, 'Kane, you must know by now you are very ugly. So life for you will be cruel and unforgiving. You will probably die alone, choking halfway through a meal that you cooked for yourself. And your funeral will be poorly attended if the town holds one at all. Probably they won't hold one for reasons of obscurity and also your face being too ugly to mourn losing. But the bright spot is no one will ever say you were raised by a liar.'"

"Your mother sounds like some sort of a ghoulish creature."

"No. She wasn't. She taught me why I should love music, and then she taught me how to create music. She taught me what it meant to be a good neighbor and a good citizen. She taught me how to value myself beyond what the rest of the world sees. She had a wonderful sense of humor. She was right about my life. I do eat alone, and I sleep alone. I wish that could change. But now that I'm ninety, I look more like a sow bug than a proper armadillo. I'm small and I'm gray and I'm wrinkled. And my snout and my tail have long fallen off."

"A sow bug. You mean like a roly-poly?"

"Yes. All armadillos begin to resemble sow bugs and wood bugs when they get old as me."

"Oh, well that is interesting," Margaret Morri said. "I had a crush on a roly-poly when I was younger. He was the one who showed me I didn't have to be a full-moon shape all the time. I could be more like the little hat a jellyfish wears. Or I could be a rind of bitter melon."

"Does a jellyfish have a hat? Or is the hat-part actually the fish? I thought a jellyfish was a hat-shaped face."

"Oh no. Jellyfish have beautiful faces beneath those swim caps and hairdos. I will let you borrow my glasses sometime. Then you can look carefully."

"You see everything I cannot, Margaret Morri. Just now, talking of the ocean with you, I feel as if I'm not living in camp under the barrack of Kashi Uchihama at all."

"I am all the oceans," Margaret Morri said. And she was right. In the years between 1942 and 1945, the oceans also were called Margaret Morri.

"Is that why you want to sleep beside me, Kane Araki?" she asked. "Is it because you don't want to live in camp any longer?"

"It's a part of it," Kane said. "But also, Margaret, you are the only one who never dies. And you are the only one who never stops talking to me. And also, well I guess, I'm attracted to you. I guess because we look a tiny bit like each other."

"Because you are attracted to yourself?"

"I like talking with someone who understands what it means to look like a pebble. But who knows they are so much greater than a pebble."

Margaret Morri reached down and brushed the tears from Kane Araki's face.

"Alright, Kane Araki. You've convinced me. Tonight you can sleep upon my pillow. But it isn't an invitation to sleep on my pillow every night. We will re-evaluate your pillow privileges tomorrow. And the next day."

"Of course," Kane Araki said, hurriedly combing the dirt from his antennae. "Of course, yes, thank you. Well shall I listen to your songs tonight?"

"Yes, you should listen. In fact, I am working on a new song called 'Kane Araki.'"

"Kane Araki!" he exclaimed.

"'Casserole,'" Margaret Morri said. "It is called 'Kane Araki Casserole.'"

"Oh, the casserole. Well that could still be good."

"I love spicy food. I love to sing about it."

"Yes," Kane Araki said. "Yes, I would like to hear that one."

And then Kane Araki walked into the sky, and he rested his head upon Margaret Morri's pillow. Kane Araki listened as Margaret Morri sang of her love.

acknowledgments

THANK YOU
Sumi Araki Kawaguchi, Tom Nguyen Kawaguchi, Janet
Kim, Amina Corinne Kim, Zadie Sumi Kim, Kyoko
Inouye, Mitsugi Kawaguchi, Emi Inouye, Big Uncle Katzuto
Kawaguchi, Mitzi Kawaguchi, Roger Batin, Mitch Suskin,
Dow K. Inouye, K. Wayne Yang, Christina Ree, Doller Family,
Kim Family, Lee Family, Gautam Rangan, Angela Eunsong
Kim, Aaron Fai, Jon Hoffer, Megan Cummins, Frank Cosgriff,
Masaki Matsuo, AK Mashhoon. Whelan Family, John Makar,
Evaly Long, Ben Ebert, Diem Tran, Usman Chaudhry,
Claudia Monpere McIsaac, Brian Thorstenson, John Hawley,
Rebecca Black, Ron Hansen, Juan Velasco, Julie Jigour, Sean
Reinhart, Philip Boo Riley, Nishikawa Family, Susette S. Min,
jesikah maria ross, Salvador Plascencia, Lucy Corin, Joe

Wenderoth, Alan Williamson, Greg Glazner, Pam Houston, Joshua Clover, Yiyun Li, John Lescroart, Lisa Sawyer, Manuel Munoz, Michael Davidson, Stephen-Paul Martin, Cristina Rivera Garza, Rae Armantrout, Lu Family, Elizabeth Losh, Alexandra Sartor, Amanda Solomon Amorao, Diane Forbes Berthoud, Keith McCleary, Hanna Tawater, Matt Lewis, Ben Segal, Julia Dixon Evans, Jim Ruland, Grant Leuning, Karen Stefano, Pepe Rojo, Paola Capo-Garcia, Baker Family, Lelio Lee, Maggie Thach Morshed, Leslie Carver, Izabel Caetano Francy, Shelley Streeby, Laura Martin, Ann VanderMeer, Jeff VanderMeer, Matthew Revert, Geoff Ryman, Gregory Frost, N.K. Jemisin, Catherynne M. Valente, Noah Keller, Amin Chehelnabi, Dash, Phong Nguyen, Brandon Taylor, Halimah Marcus, Jonathan Weisberg, Aimee Parkison, Joanna Ruocco, Dan Waterman

MUCH GRATITUDE TO THE SUPPORT AND WISDOM OF THE FOLKS AT THE FOLLOWING PUBLICATIONS WHERE CHAPTERS OF THIS NOVEL APPEARED:

Apogee Journal, Connotation Press, Covered with Fur, Crag, *The Doctor T.J. Eckleburg Review*, *Electric Literature*, Expanded Horizons, *Fairy Tale Review*, *Funhouse Magazine*, littletell, *The Masters Review*, *matchbook*, *Okey-Panky*, *Pleiades*, *Portland Review*, Recommended Reading, *The Southeast Review*, Spork Press, SpringGun Press, The Stoneslide Corrective, *Thin Noon*, Woven Tale Press